The Aussie The Irishman & Milady

Highland Mysteries

[A Vienna LaFontaine Novel]

JULIANA ANDREW

PROMINENT
BOOKS
EDGE

5830 E 2nd St, Ste 7000 #9983
Casper, WY 82609
USA

Contents

Also by Juliana Andrew
Vienna 2013, 2022
The Curse of the Infinity Bracelets 2014, 2022
Seventh Crossing 2015
The Ladies of Avanloch 2016, 2022
The Arcadia Project 2017
Beyond the Yellow Doors
{Mayria's Dragons} 2024
November Queen 2020/2024
Home Again/Home Again 2022

My Promise

Wait for me Roy, I'll catch up some day.
And then the always will be a forever
Like we promised each other.

Family Tree

Vienna LaFontaine Quinn

Parents: Lily Lane LaFontaine
Joe LaFontaine {Deceased}
Sisters: Sissy Lafontaine Jennings
Daughter Joanie
Husband: Jack Jennings
Son Jake
Sister Addy, daughter Sarah

Rainey Quinn

Parents: Paul and Patsy Quinn
Sister Claudia
Sons Morgan and Mason

Vienna and Rainey
Daughter Ava Lane Quinn Nash
Husband Colton Nash
Son Sammie, Daughter Calla

Daughter Lilliana Quinn
Partner Rusty {William} Thompson
Son JT Jeremiah Thompson

Twins: Daughter Novia, Son Zander

Adopted
Rosalyn McAllister Quinn Govern
Husband Evan Govern
Daughters: Colleen & Beth

Zoe Quinn
Tanny McCraken Quinn

London Family
Aunt & Uncle Jannie and John Tait
Sons Grey and Chandler
Sister-in-law Ash McAllister

Avanloch Family
Mary & Duffy McDuff
Amma and Johnny O'Shea
Butch

Characters of Interest

Meggie Magan
Jorja Elliot. Daughter Patricia Anne
Gracie Darling

Spirits of Avanloch
Lady Avaleena
Lady Maveryn

Chapter 1

Déjà Vous

Aunt Jannie welcomed me into her arms just as she had forty-two years ago. The circumstances were cannily similar, yet bizarrely different. I had left home in 1961 because I was pregnant with Rainey Quinn's child and I believed that he didn't love me. I wouldn't burden him or interfere with his career because I knew he would do what he thought was right and marry me. I didn't want him that way so I never told him of my pregnancy and my location was kept secret from him. Today I knew he loved me, but he was the one who had left home.

It was now two months and four days since he had mysteriously vanished in the middle of the night from our home in Hawthorne, British Columbia. All the evidence pointed to him being abducted, but why? It had taken ten days for a random note to surface. The puzzling thing was that it was sent to a partner of his from Quinn Enterprises in Vancouver. The ransom had been requested by Rainey himself. The supposed kidnapper was known to me and my family and they knew that we were wealthy so he could have asked for anything, and we would have paid it to have Rainey returned safely. I did assure that the ransom was paid, but it didn't bring him home.

My reasons for leaving our home in Hawthorne were two-fold. I'd had a life-like dream of him and Jorja, the woman he'd had a tainted relationship with before we were reunited after twenty years of being apart. She had abducted me and Rainey's and my son Zander many years ago, but I had won that battle and went on to see her imprisoned for life for the mentally insane. She had died in prison, but there she was in the dream riding off into the night on a black steed with my husband telling me she had won. In my grief-stricken mind I believed it was her twin sister who had died in the prison and that Jorja had somehow maneuvered to switch places with her. If I stayed here in the house that Rainey had built for me I believed I would relive the dream night after night and convince my tortured mind and heart that it was true and she had come back to claim Rainey again. I made the decision to go back to Scotland and Avanloch Castle where I had escaped to in 1961. It had been my home for over two decades and Jorja wasn't there and never had been. I could go crazy there again quite comfortably. The other reason was that I was becoming closer and more dependent on Jack, my sister's husband.

I had called my son-in-law Evan Govern who was married to my daughter Rosalyn after the dream and told him I was ready to come home. He had tried to get me to return to Avanloch with Rosy and him shortly after Rainey's disappearance. I wasn't ready then, but I was now. Evan had wanted to come and fly me home in the McAllister company plane, but I didn't want him making the long trip again so I opted to take a flight into London and spend some time with my aunt. Zander had chosen to come with me because he said that it was what his father would want.

My sister-in-law Ash, who was the sister of Lord Jeremy McAllister, Rosalyn's biological father and the man I had married in 1962, had picked Zander and me up from Heathrow Airport. I think back to the day that Jeremy had asked for my hand in marriage. He was not looking to replace his beloved wife Maveryn but wanted a mother for their daughter Rosalyn. She had already chosen me to be her new mother and had become very dear to me and considered my daughter Ava as her sister. I had weighed the surprise proposal over with my other options which were non-existent. How could I support Ava on my own and keep Rosalyn in my life as I had no occupation skills? Ava's father Rainey was not in the picture and probably never would be, so Jeremy's offer seemed to be the answer. We never shared the marriage bed as our hearts were with the ones we still loved. He was an absentee husband and father so I was pretty much in charge of Avanloch Castle. Marrying him had automatically escalated my statue to Lady. I was known as Vela in those days and so I had become Lady Vela McAllister, Mistress of Avanloch Castle. Those days were long behind me. I had become Vienna again when Rainy and I were reunited. We had left the castle to be overseen by Rosalyn and Evan and returned to Bridge Falls in Canada to raise our family in 1984. Rainey had built a house for us in his hometown of Hawthorne and we lived there for twenty-one years. We made many trips back to Avanloch over the years. Now he was gone from me again and I hoped to find refuge at the Castle once more. I was sure that it would be an unachievable plight.

Ash and her longtime fiancé Grey Tait, Uncle John's son, had bought and renovated a seventeen century Victorian mansion and had moved Jannie and John in with them. Jannie had many questions for me. Although she was happy that I was only 5 hours away by high-speed train and only 2 hours by plane if Evan was doing the flying because of his connections with the airport, she wasn't sure if Avanloch was the best place for me. She was overly curious as to why I had left Ava, Lili, baby JT and the rest of my family and friends and the house that Rainey had built for us to take up residence again in a remote castle in the highlands of northern Scotland. She thought that there was another reason behind my decision. I wasn't going to tell her about my dream and suspicion that Rainey was with Jorja. I didn't need her to believe that I had become unhinged, and maybe there was another reason which I also hadn't fully come to terms with, and that was Jack. He was my very best friend and I needed to keep it at that. He had been my rock since Rainey's disappearance just as he had been after I believed that I'd never see Rainey again back in 1961. Now it had happened again and my husband could very well be gone from me forever. A day had not gone by in the past two months that Jack hadn't been at my side. Sissy was with him most of the time, but lately he had come by himself in the late evenings. I spent the days hiding my desolation from my family as I needed to be strong for them, but I looked forward to Jack's arrival as I could be *me* with him. My daughter Lili, her partner Rusty and baby JT had moved in with me and I thought that perhaps I would move back to the Palace in Bridge Falls to have a little peace and quiet. I stopped myself in time because the real reason I wanted to go was because I would be closer to Jack. What was I thinking? He was my sister's husband, and he was her soul mate just as Rainey was mine. I had to let Jack go, but I didn't know how I could, and then I had the dream where I had seen Jorja with Rainey, and I knew it was time for me to "get out of Dodge" and return to the land of unicorns, fairies, folklore, and haunted castles. I needed to go home.

Zander and I spent another two days in London sight-seeing and visiting friends. It was not easy for me to see Rainey's long-time friend Stu and his wife Daisy. He was visually disturbed about Rainey's disappearance but he managed to keep his feelings in check. I promised there would be many more visits. Next was Roberge Farradan, the Duke of Shaughnessy. The title was bestowed on him by his wife Lauren, the Duchess of Cambria. Roberge's and my friendship went back to the sixties. It didn't start out that way as at the time his marriage was strictly for show, and every opportunity he got was to flirt with me. After Rainey and I were reunited, we became good friends. The tables were turned then as Lauren took a liking to my husband. Nothing became of it and Rainey and I ended up saving her life when Roberge was on a mission in the Brazilian Jungle to find his father. Throughout the many pages of Avaleena's diary that I had discovered in an underground room at the castle, the name Ferrani kept appearing. It was a Basque/Castilian name which translated into Farradan. It then became conjecture that Roberge and I were related. He believed his father had the information that would confirm it so he, along with Rosalyn and Evan set off to track Jacques Farradan/Feranni through the jungles of Brazil to a lost gold mine. Rosalyn felt that she may have ignored Lauren's illness and she needed to bring Roberge home. They had all returned safely without finding Jacques or the mine. He was still missing. The whole ordeal had solidified Roberge's and Lauren's relationship and shortly after Rainey and I had moved back to Canada they welcomed a son into their folds. I left them feeling a little bit sadder.

I made my first phone call home the next morning. Lili answered. I told her to hang up and that I would redial and she wasn't to pick the phone up until after her father had finished talking and then I would talk to her. She was still questioning me when I hung up. I redialed.

"Hi there; you've reached the home of Vienna and Rainey Quinn. We are unable to take your call at the moment so please leave your name and number and we'll get back to you just as soon as we can. Have a great day."

"Mommy, are you all right?"

"As all right as I can be without your father Lili. I will be calling home from time to time and you are to let the answering machine answer… do you understand? I might not always feel like talking so do not take it personally as I may just want to hear your father's voice. Will that, or hearing him talk upset you?"

"I won't let it. I miss his voice too and if it gives you comfort then I am comforted too."

"Thank-you Dear. Your sister doesn't need to know as she is still upset with me for leaving. I know you are too, but this is where I need to be right now. Zander and I are leaving for Avanloch this morning. Please don't bombard the castle with phone calls. I will call you tomorrow some time. Give JT a big kiss; love you all. Be Daddy's good little girl and know that he is thinking about us all wherever he is."

We arrived in Waverly at 6 P.M. It had been a long boring train ride for me. Because it was Zander's first trip overland I had opted to take the scenic train which was an all-day excursion. I tried my best to make it enjoyable for him by pointing out all the interesting landscapes and history along the way. The car I'd ordered was waiting for us at the terminal with the agent that I had booked the lease with. The transfer papers took all of five minutes. I drove to the McAllister suite at the hotel and called Rosalyn. We could have completed our journey to Avanloch, but night was upon us and I wanted Zander to have the full scenic drive in daylight, plus I was exhausted.

"Good, I'm glad you had a good trip and are spending the night in Waverly as the fog will be settling in soon. Evan will pick you up about ten in the morning then."

"I've rented a car so there is no need for him to come."

"You're driving yourself? You don't even like to drive… Evan is not going to be pleased that you've chosen to drive you know Mother?"

I laughed a little. "And, I am so looking forward to having that conversation with him. Have you forgotten that Zander is with me so he can do the driving? He has never driven on the wrong side of the road before so it will be interesting. See you tomorrow."

"Oh Mother; whatever am I going to do with you?"

*November 5*th

I drove to the outskirts of Waverly after I'd downed three cups of coffee the next morning. I pulled over at the junction sign. The north-western branch went to Durness which was between the most northerly village in Great Britain of Thurso and Ullapool. Thurso was situated on the North Sea and had a healthy population of 5,000. There were a few smaller villages in the area also. It was 100 miles from the crossroads that would take us to Avanloch which was 70 miles straight ahead. Because most of the lands that surrounded the estate were 30 to 50 miles or more from the sea, our temperatures were much warmer than those in Durness. I

had only been there once a long time ago on one of my excursions with Rosy and Ava when they were young. There was no road across country that connected any of these towns to Avanloch. Domne and Avanloch Castle occupied the last two names on the signpost. It read: PRIVATE RESIDENCE {Admission by invitation only}was inscribed under Avanloch Castle. Zander asked if that kept people out.

"No, the gate is never closed, but there is a gatehouse and is manned by the residents of the Village. There is no schedule as it is not a paid position. It is simply a volunteer position and periodically you might even see someone manning the post. If Haggard, the mill and Village steward, thinks anything is amiss he will act on it. Visitors were once frowned on but now there's a dairy and three or four little shops so they are welcomed but scrutinized. It's all rather amusing. I gave the wheel to Zander and prepared to give him a running contemporary of the Highlands.

He remarked that Scotland and England were much larger then they looked on the globe. He asked why there were two towns named Waverly. I explained that it was confusing as Waverley Edinburgh was called so because it was the principal train station in Scotland and that it was named as a tribute to Sir Walter Scott and his Waverely Novels, and that the spellings differed. Our Waverly is also spelled differently. Wow; look at me being a tour guide. One could not possibly take in all the diverse landscapes along the way from London to Avanloch on their first road trip whether it was by car or train. Evan would give Zander the full air view from the Heli around the estate I was sure. I would be the one to take him to my favorite place as soon as it was decent weather and the paths would be safe for the horses. Of course it was Widow's Hummock where the view was awe inspiring. The valleys were a rainbow of colors gently climbing to the towering peaks whose spires resembled stone castles. The river Tweed meandered its way through the valleys depositing pools of emerald-blue streams here and there. At a junction called The Bridge the river divided. The north-channel found its way to the North Sea. The south fork was Miller-Floss River and it flowed through the estate and points beyond. I honestly did not know where it ended up or if it joined up with another river. Then, in all its' glory was snow-capped Widow's Peak towering over Mount Wallace, Mt. Rob Roy, and Mt. Robbie. Three bewitching waterfalls cascaded from them. To my knowledge, no one knew for sure who Robbie was named for as there were so many famous Scottish Roberts. Zander asked me who Rob Roy was. All I knew about him was that he was an outlaw that had somehow become a folk hero. Zander said he liked that and would look him up.

He asked me if I knew anyone who lived in any of the small hamlets as we passed by them.

"I did, but remember that I have been gone for some twenty years now, so I doubt if any of those folks are around anymore. Evan is the steward of any lands that are under Avanloch's jurisdiction now, so I'm sure he keeps tract of anything pertinent."

"What does that mean Mom? Does Avanloch own all of these settlements, and are Evan and Rosy responsible for the maintenance of them?"

"No, but between the Village of Domne and Waverly there is no ordinance like a police force or administration so these settlements are home to people that we would call homesteaders in Canada. It was that way for hundreds of years. I believe the original consensus was that they were under Avanloch's auspices so the governing bodies looked the other way. I do recall Uncle John telling me that after World War 1, a Land Settlement was created to assist people, and especially servicemen to acquire land. I imagine that ancestors of these folks have inherited the properties and have to adhere to whatever legalities were agreed upon."

"I bet Avanloch's taxes are staggering."

"Actually, they aren't Zander. It is one of the Palatial Properties that was chosen years ago to be tax free."

"Wow, that's great. What about the village of Domne? Does it have a mayor and council like Bridge Falls, or is unincorporated like Hawthorne?"

"It is moving to become incorporated but is not as yet as far as I know. The towns people have always governed themselves by voting in supervisors every other year or so. They manage things like garbage disposal and street cleaning and everything else from A to Z. Johnny O'Shea is not only Avanloch's right hand man, but he is the overseer of the Mill and its employees. They and any equipment are deployed to the village as needed. They work hand and hand and could not function without this co-operation."

"I thought the mill was owned by Avanloch?"

"It was originally. I guess it still is, but it is nothing that I ever had to contend with. Evan and Johnny are the ones you need to talk to. When did you start taking an interest in such things?"

"I did a lot of reading when I was sick and learned such things about Hawthorne and Bridge, so am just wondering what laws are enacted here. That's all Mom; just curious. I do have another question though, and it is regarding the location of the castle. Most every picture I have ever seen of medieval fortresses shows them located on cliffs or on land that is surrounded by water so why did the first McAllister's not build along the North Sea? That would have been a natural fortification from invading countries like Norway wouldn't it?"

"It is not a proven fact, but the original castle which was called Kings Keep was not constructed by the McAllister clan. That is what I was led to believe by Rosalyn's father Jeremy. He told me that if I was interested I could find all the details regarding the McAllister lineage in the archives along with the original blueprints of the castle. I asked him where I could find these documents and he said that Uncle John had all that information. He did not, and as far as he knew nothing of the sort existed. I did pester Jeremy about it several more times over the years, and finally he admitted that all was lost in the great fire. There is no record of any fire, so that still remains a mystery today. I quit obsessing about it, but now in light of some of the things that we discovered last summer I believe Jeremy was keeping some very pertinent facts secret, but as to what or why, I do not know. Consensus is that there is a sacred artifact from the time of the Templar Knights concealed in the walls of Avanloch." I laughed a little. "Your father was the disbeliever in this theory because he had single handily explored every inch of the castle and he would have found the discontinuity if one existed."

"Do you believe him Mom?"

"The only thing I am sure of is that this magnificent structure called Avanloch which has been my home on and off for most of my life harbors many more secrets, and maybe you will be the one to discover one. Oh, we are almost there. That road we just passed is Thistle where Johnny O'Shea's uncle lived and died. Pull over at the top of the hill and you will get your first glimpse of the castle glimmering in all its glory. I'm sorry that the sun is hiding behind the clouds."

"It's beautiful even in this ashen mood. It kind of adds to the mystic of the castle. It's bigger than I remember though. Isn't there a courtyard on the roof? Oh, look Mom, those clouds look like dragons flying over the castle!"

I laughed. "You and Novia have always loved lying in the grass marvelling at the characters you discovered in the clouds. Your Dad did also and when we left here he said he was going to miss the Avanloch  skies. I reminded him that we had clouds in Canada. Yes, there is a courtyard. It is on the third floor along with the entrance to the tower rooms. You can't see it because it is near winter and so is behind the retractable doors, but you can still access it."

"Johnny's uncle was murdered wasn't he, and that was what Dad and you, and everyone else were investigating last summer isn't it? Has his assassin been apprehended yet?"

"Yes, his death did factor into our explorations, but our main objectives were on the documents regarding the history of the castle and was our main focus. As far as I know, Uncle Walt's killer has not been apprehended yet. That mess of trees to your left encloses the original cemetery of the village. It dates back to the fourteenth century so I have been told."

"Have you visited it? I bet it's scary."

"I haven't, but it is on my list of things to do. It is known as the "forbidden graveyard" and is apparently posted as such with signs that warn of danger and apprehension of trespassers."

"It doesn't sound like a place for you Mom."

"I guess I always knew about it, but it never interested me until last year when a tunnel in the castle came out under one of the gravestones there. I will fill you in on the whole story some day and why it is of interest to me. I wouldn't be trespassing as it is on the estate's land."

Zander started the car again. I prepared myself for the welcoming committee. It was as I expected.

Colleen and Beth were the first to throw their arms around me. They were young ladies now having had their sixteenth and fourteenth birthdays respectively last summer. Where had the time gone I wondered. I let them cry and carry on for a few minutes before I spoke.

"There are going to be many days for tears in the days to come, so how about if we leave a few for all the tomorrows before Pappy makes it back to us? Meanwhile, we can remember all the good times we had with him, especially last summer. We will pray that he is safe and is thinking about us the same way. I'm going to need you to be brave for me, but if I break down I will need you to understand and comfort me, okay?"

They promised they would. I sent them off to help Zander with the luggage and show him around. Amma tried her best not to cry, but of course she wasn't successful. Johnny was Johnny and hugged me and told me he loved me. Rosalyn didn't have to say a thing because her eyes said it all. Her heart was still in denial as to what had brought me here.

That left Evan. He stood waiting for me after everyone had gone into the house. He put his arm around me and said, "Whenever…" I knew he meant that whenever I was ready to let go he would be here. So, once again I was back where I had called home for so many years. It may as well be 1961 as I was without my love once more and the realization that he was gone to me forever was a distinct possibility *again*.

Rosalyn had wanted me close to her at night so suggested that I make LizBeth's rooms mine for a while. When I had been the one missing Rainey had taken up to sleeping in another room because it was too upsetting for him to be in the bed that we had shared. It was the opposite for me, and I couldn't imagine sleeping in any other room. He may be 'away,' but his essence wasn't, and I knew that I would be spending a great deal of time on the balcony that he'd had built for me even though winter was approaching. Zander was to have the rooms next to mine which had once been Rosy's and Ava's rooms, so that was comforting.

Nothing much had changed since Rainey and I had left two months ago except the weather. The problematic outside interference at McAllister Holdings had not been resolved, so Rosy was working three or four days a week. Evan would fly her back and forth to London. The commute took 2 hours whereas the train was a 10-to-12-hour trip. Rosy used to make this long trip once or twice a month before the purchase of Evan's helicopter. The original had been replaced by an Augusta 109 Grand Helicopter last month which held five passengers. It was Evan's pride and joy. Thanks to his connections to Land's End airport, the round trip was reduced to a 5-hour day for Evan instead of nine. He loved flying so it was just an ordinary day for him. Whenever the girls had time off from school they would accompany him and spend a few days at the suite that Rosy kept in London. Evan had trained in Australia to be an E.M.T. but had never taken a qualifying exam in the United Kingdom. He and his copter were called to assist with medical emergencies in the district. His qualifications had never come into question, but he had been contemplating taking a course in First Aid Emergency in Edinburgh, but it would mean that the girls would be on their own when he was away so he had decided against it. It looked like I had arrived just in time. Colleen, like others from the surrounding areas who were in grade nine to twelve had to travel to Waverly to attend school last year. Luckily, her father had the helicopter and could ferry her and other students back and forth. Things for the better had changed over the summer.

The population of Domne had welcomed ten new families into its realm. The Mill had seen three employees retire and had added a retail store in the dairy so employment was very much needed there. An addition to the elementary school which had been in progress for the last several years was finally completed and the older students no longer needed to travel to Waverly for their education except for special events.

A new housing development at the east end of the village had also been completed last spring and saw the arrival of the families over the summer. The Mill had new employees and the school had three new teachers.

Rosy, Evan, Johnny and Amma had been instrumental in an official welcome to all the newcomers at a party at the town hall in October. Many of the older residents of the Village were not happy that their quiet little hamlet had been invaded by strangers and boycotted the event. I understood how they felt and wondered if the new settlers would be detrimental or beneficial to the community. Time would tell. It would be sometime before I would be comfortable outside the caste walls, and maybe I'd never be.

I had resisted calling Jack while I was in London, but I couldn't any longer. It was half past ten which meant that it was six-thirty a.m. in Bridge Falls. Maybe Sissy would be up and would answer.

"Hello."

"Hi Jack."

"I've been waiting for your call. Are you at Avanloch?"

"Yes; Zander and I arrived this afternoon. Is Sissy up?"

"Probably, but she's in Hawthorne with Lili."

"Oh, what's wrong?"

"Nothing that I am aware of, so need to worry. I think Sissy just needed a break from me."

"I doubt that Jack." I laughed a little.

"I admit that I've been a grouch. Nothing is the same with you gone Vienna. I'm trying not to miss you, but it's not working."

"Coming here was best for the both of us Jack. We were getting way too close. It wasn't healthy for either of us. Someone was going to get hurt and I couldn't let it be my sister. You'll always be my very best friend just as you have been for all these years, but there has to be miles between us. Even though the dream was vividly real I still believe that Rainey is alive and maybe, just maybe he'll come back to me. Promise me that you'll mend any broken fences with Sissy. Tell her I love her, and she can call me anytime. I must go now Jack."

"Just a minute…what's this about a dream, and I'm not ready to say good-bye yet."

"It was just a silly little dream, but it made me see that I needed to be here. I think I would have gone crazy staying in Hawthorne. My home and heart have always been here. I will talk to you again soon. Be happy Jack."

"Vienna…"

I hung up reluctantly. Tears ran down my face. Did I make a mistake by coming here? Would I be happy anywhere without Rainey? I needed to hear his voice. Lili would understand and she wouldn't pick up. I dialed the number on the house phone and recorded his welcoming message on my modular. There, now I could listen to his voice whenever I wanted.

Unfortunately, Rosy had to return to London two days later. She apologised profusely. I told her I understood, but in fact I didn't. I had been aware that things were not as they should be at McAllister Enterprises, especially with the shipping end last summer, but Rosy had assured Rainey and me that the problems were almost over. Obviously, things had taken a turn for the worse, and the threats to a foreign take-over had multiplied. How this was even possible was a mystery to me.

Life was basically the same at Avanloch despite what was happening in London. The days were shorter now that winter was on its way. One never knew what the bleak month of November had in store for us weatherwise so I best make the most of everyday. My walks took me through the rose gardens, down to the ponds, over the bridge that led along the rocky steep path to Amma's and Johnny's at Brackenhurst Manor, and of course the McAllister crypt to talk to Rosalyn's mother, Lady Maveryn. Soon I would visit my dear friend Meggie Magan.

Chapter 2

Divination and Nightmares

November 7th

*I*t was Friday; one more day of school for the girls so I decided it was a good time to visit Meggie because in Rosy's absence I wanted to be available to them over the weekend. I found the key that unlocked my treasure chest. I wasn't here to reminisce. I was here for one thing and one thing only. I needed to know, and this, plus a Tarot reading from Meggie would answer all my questions I hoped. I didn't want anyone to see what I was taking to Meggie's besides treats, so I stashed it in one of my large colorful satchels. In the kitchen I loaded the bag with a tin of coffee, fresh fruit, bread, and biscuits.

"Need I ask where you are going with all that?"

"You know where I'm going Amma. I know you'll be busy with supervising the cleaning crew today, so I thought I'd get out of your hair."

"Or you could stay and overseer the undertaking yourself like you used to do."

"That was another lifetime ago, and I am no longer Mistress of the castle."

She laughed. "Try telling that to the castle and all of us who know better."

"I'm only here for the respite Amma. Do you know if the road is car worthy?"

"I do know that Johnny graded it last week, but he'll want to take you, so I'll call him."

"Let's not; it's more fun if he has to rescue me from a ditch don't you think?"

"Life has been so boring without you. Sorry that this cleaning was scheduled before we knew you were coming. Rosy was supposed to be here, but you know how that turned out … Say hello to Meggie and take this jar of soup to her."

I hugged her and told her that I had dinner all planned so not to worry.

Johnny had done an excellent job filling in the ruts on the hard packed dirt road. It was usually impassable after a storm so luckily for me and my car that it hadn't rained recently. More so for Johnny as he wouldn't have to pull me out of the mud or a ditch. Meggie waved to me from her rocker on the front stoop as I pulled up.

"Did you know I was coming?" I asked as I helped her up and embraced her affectionately.

"I had the feelin you be comin. You know they say I be a little bit psychic. What's you got for ole Meggie there? Come on in, the cauldron is bubbling along and the kettle be on."

"I brought coffee."

"Say no more, you make, I see what's in here. What's this; you know I don't like in the house!"

"I need answers."

"An old piece of silly wood will not have what you seek."

"I just have one question, and then you can read for me."

"Read first and then we will see. Give me nettles a stir while coffee perking. I'll prepare the table and dig out the cards."

A few minutes later I joined her in the front room. I set the coffee mugs and a bowl of cookies on the table. "These aren't your usual cards."

"I been helping Millie with her channelling, and she bring me these new cards. You like?"

"I didn't know that Millie was into Tarot."

"She be, and she reads for the Village. Give them a good many shuffles Milady. Good girl."

She reshuffled, cut the deck into threes, gave each a knock, rejoined them and knocked again. I had no idea if this was common practice for Tarot readers as only she and her grandmother had ever read for me.

"Let's see what Spirit has for you. This be you here with the Temprance card. You know you must have patience. Next, The Hangman; yes, you are waiting for a difficult situation to absolve itself, you know what it is, patience again. The energy of the 9 of Swords presents itself indicating a peaceful solution. Ah, the Queen of Wands sees that you are held in high regard and your intuition shows you are ready for anything. Here we have the 9 of Pentacles which is definitely you having a comfortable lifestyle. You have everything you want and need. The 10 of Water says you are happy, fulfilled and the 6 of Cups shows you are feeling nostalgic. The 9 of Cups, a lovely little card shows you are independent and passionate. Ah, the Queen of Fire, your card, and you are energetic and ready to take charge. The 7 of pentacles sees you are waiting for something and the 4 of Wands shows stability and excitement as your ship has come in. Two more…the Justice card; everything is in balance, you make the right decision to correct what's been wrong, and the 6 of Wands…a huge victory is in the wings. Here's two jumpers…the Ace of Swords, truth, and clarity and triumph. Ah, the Star card to end and brings a full recovery and new beginnings. Sit back now and we will clarify."

"I need no clarifying; the cards lied. I don't have all I need, and I am not happy. My ship may have arrived, but Rainey isn't on it, so I am not fulfilled. The Ouija will give me an answer."

"You already have the answer you want so there is no need of it."

I took the board out of its case and laid it on top the cards. Apparently, that was sacrilegious, and I was shamed for doing so. I removed it quickly and waited until Meggie rearranged the cards. Reluctantly, I sat back and let her ramble on explaining the cards in great detail. It seemed like an hour passed before she was finished and cleared the table. I thanked her and placed the board down. She had a little trouble settling her fingers on the placard due to her arthritis. I asked my question. It was answered with a "YES."

She removed her hand and pushed her chair back. "You have the answer you wanted, so are you happy now? You better put it away because Johnny is here."

"Damn it! I can't believe Amma sent him to check on me. They don't trust me you know?"

"What have you done to have them worry?"

"Nothing!"

"Put your temper in your pocket as Johnny is here per my request."

"Why didn't you say so?"

"I just did. Think I'll warm me up some of that soup."

I followed her into the kitchen and watched out the window as Johnny and Zander erected some new boards and installed a new latch on her fence. I asked her why she didn't have a crystal ball.

"What do you think that purple globe is in the garden?"

"I thought it was a globe to capture the sun and moon's beams."

"Same thing."

I took that to mean that she didn't believe in crystal balls.

The boys stopped in to say hello to Meggie and said they'd see me back home. She thanked them and ladled a vial filled with whatever was in her cauldron and passed it to me. I asked her what it was and what was I supposed to do with it.

"Just a little potion to poison your ugly mood."

I hugged her and apologized. I was worried about Rainey and that no amount of help from the psychic world could guarantee his safe return.

She said that only God could do that, and so I must have faith. I did not tell her about the dream.

I arrived back at the castle just before noon. Amma and the cleaning crew were upstairs. I said a quick hello and retreated to the kitchen. Zander and Johnny were lunching at the workshop with Butch and Shem, the only crew that remained for the winter months. Butch was a bachelor and lived on the property in a small cabin between the shop and Brackenshire Manor. He was a Jack of all trades, but from spring until mid October he was a full time cook when the estate employed a dozen or more hands. They resided in the bunkhouse. Shem lived in the Village with his wife.

I made myself a sandwich and sat down contemplating what I could concoct for dinner. I wanted to make something special for my granddaughters and son-in-law as they were so very special to me. I guess I succeeded as there wasn't a speck left. We played cards until eleven. The weekend was warmish and we went on a hike along the lakeside on Saturday. Sunday was spent with Johnny and Amma at Brackenshire playing various games and feasting on Johnny's barbecued ribs and Amma's baked beans. Then it was Monday and back to work and school.

November 11ᵗʰ

I had been on my best behavior and had avoided my nighttime ramblings because I didn't want to disturb the household which I might do if I opened a squeaky door or landed on a creaky stair. The porch outside my bedroom had allowed me to have some freedom so I had been retreating there and of course I could light up out there. It was 12:15 when I stuffed my feet into my dainty slippers. I opened the glass doors and was met with a wind that blew a chilly rain in my face. I shut them quickly, donned a robe and made my way to the foyer. I had opened my door as quietly as possible and waited a minute making sure I hadn't awakened Zander. I stood in front of the bookcase wondering if it could still open. It wouldn't do any good if it did because the stairs had been torn down last summer so there was no way to get down to Avaleena's rooms from here. I proceeded down the grand stairway. I scolded myself for being so paranoid that someone would hear me. I stopped abruptly on the step above the first landing. Was that smoke I smelled? No, it couldn't be. This was a non-smoking house and no one smoked besides Johnny and me, but why would he be here at midnight? Maybe it was an intruder. I retreated to the foyer, grabbed a large candelabra off the table and started back down the stairs. I stopped and went back to the top. I needed to count the steps. There was forty wasn't there…or was it forty- four? Just a minute, the dismantled stairs had a count of twenty- two. I knew that to be true, so why was there twice as many here? They both started on the second floor so it didn't make sense. Why had I never questioned the anomaly before? I started down the stairs again thankful that each step activated a recessed light. The aroma of the smoke increased as I rounded the second landing. A figure sat on the chaise that snugged up against the alcove behind the stairs. The glow from the tulip lamp illuminated the hand that held a pipe.

"This is a non-smoking establishment you know."

"I do, but people keep telling me that I am Laird of this monstrosity, so I am making a few new rules. You are most welcome to join me for a puff."

"I made the rule, so I won't be breaking it. What are you doing here Evan?"

"Waiting for you Milady."

"How did you know I would be coming here?"

"Simple; it's raining so I knew your balcony wasn't an option. Come and sit beside me and have a cup of hot chocolate and tell me all your troubles, and why you're carrying a candelabra?"

I walked over and sat opposite him in a highbacked Queen Ann chair. "I thought there was an intruder. I have only one trouble and you know what it is and there is no point in talking about it as there is no solution."

"Only one question then. Why did you choose to come here instead of staying in Hawthorne?"

"Do you not want me here?"

"Yeah, that's it." He chuckled. "So why did I try so hard to get you to come back with me and Rose right after Rain disappeared do you think?"

"That was then and this is now…maybe I'm a bother."

He laughed. "We need you more than you need us. I miss Rose more than anyone can imagine, except maybe you, but I can't do anything about it except give her all the support she needs. This bloody thing with

McAllister isn't going anywhere soon so she needs to be there fighting as best as she can and not worry about us back here. So, that is where you come in. Having her mother here during this crisis is a blessing to her, the girls are overjoyed to have their Ana here, and you are an immense help to Amma, and Johnny is happy to have his best friend back, so that just leaves me. Do you know what you mean to me Vienna?"

Tears were stinging my eyes. I nodded. "I do. For the briefest of seconds twenty-one years ago I locked eyes with the man who found me in a pool of blood on the path to the crypt. He was my savior then and again when he gave me the courage to forgive my husband, and now I need him again because I'm broken, and he is the only one that I can let into that emptiness. It's you Evan, and you already know that. I almost made a mistake and let someone else in…"

"It was Jack wasn't it?"

I nodded.

"Thank-you for your trust. I know we share something unexplainable. I'll never be able to explain it and that's because there is no explanation, so I have learned to accept it a divine intervention. I'm not a religious person, but I know God sent Maveryn to me that night. That moment when yours and my eyes became one I felt a peace that I had never experienced before and never have again, and probably never will and yet I was scared to death that you were dying. Here I was following a wisp of a being who just happened to be my wife's dead mother directing me to my wife's other mother who was barely breathing. If Johnny and I hadn't been able to save you…"

"Talk to me then. The three of us just exchange glimmers of that night now and then, but we don't talk about it. It's been over twenty years; don't you think it's time?"

"You're wrong because Johnny and I talk about it all the time."

"I know; Amma and Rosalyn told me. But, what about me? Maybe I need to know more."

"And, perhaps you do, but right now we need to talk about Rain."

"Okay, but first I want you to answer a few questions for me." I nodded towards the stairway. "How many steps are there? Forty I am sure, so why were there only twenty-two to the room downstairs? I know that you or Rainey did something to enable the bookcase from opening last summer, but can it be reinstated?"

"I have never counted the steps but will take your word for how many there are. The reason the count is different is probably because the steps are of different widths. Those that led into the cellar were much older and I mean centuries older, plus the woods are different materials. How about we leave the discussion of the bookcase for another day?"

"That makes sense, but there is something more I feel, and I also need answers to half a dozen other things which were never answered last summer, so you're not off the hook just yet. However, I will leave it there for now and answer your question of why I came here. Thanks to Liliana, my midnight excursions outside after Rainey's disappearance became known to everyone. I had asked her not to tell Ava, but of course she did. My wanderings didn't upset Lili as much as they did Ava even though she knew it was a common thing for me to do. Reminding her that I had been doing it for years didn't pacify her as I had never taken my walks outside before, at least not that she knew about. I told her that it was out of my control, and I was incapable of stopping so she just had to live with it or come up with a way for me to stop, but until her father came home, I was going to continue looking for him. Then I had the dream, and I knew I was never going to find him. I picked up the phone and called you." I put my cup down. "That's it."

He nodded ever so slightly. "I see. Are you going to keep me in limbo wondering how a dream could make you come to that conclusion?"

"*She* was sitting on a black cloud looking down at me. *She* was taunting me. "I told you he'd come back to me, didn't I? I told you he loved me, didn't I? I win, I win; you lose Vienna!" *She* looked away from me. I followed her gaze and I saw a black steed rising from a silver mist which suddenly turned dark and ominous. Rainey was upon the stallion's back. He was dressed all in black…you know he never wears black Evan, not even to funerals. I knew he had gone over to the dark side then. I watched in dismay as he reached down and pulled her up and rode away laughing. I closed my eyes, and when I opened them again the nightmare played over and over again. I knew not whether he was alive or dead, but that he was with *her*, and that my life as I had known it was gone and I needed to come home to Avanloch."

Evan reached across the table, took my hands, and asked me if I'd had the dream since I had been here. I said that I hadn't.

"You know that's all it was don't you … just a dream?"

"In my heart I want it to be, but I know that it's still there floating around in my head just waiting to erupt again when I least expect it."

"Squeeze my hands and together we are going to burst that dark cloud and send it and Jorja into oblivion where they can never materialise again."

I closed my eyes and squeezed as hard as I could. "Did I ever tell you that next to Nash you're my favorite son-in-law?"

He laughed. "Yeah, and next to Johnny, Jack's your best friend."

"I should have been able to cope in Hawthorne with Nash and Jack, but somehow I needed you and Johnny more and apparently, this damn castle!"

"And, we need you. John doesn't say much, but when I told him you were coming the smile on his face said it all. You know, Amma said something just before you arrived that I puzzled over, but now it is beginning to make sense."

"What was that Evan?"

"She said it was going to be a most interesting time as the three partners would be united again."

"Partners in what?"

"I guess we'll find out won't we?"

"Collect your smoking paraphernalia and let's hope there won't be any lingering aroma as we don't want Amma asking questions. I'll wash the cups and make sure the kitchen is as she left it."

"Correct me if I'm wrong, but I think it was your kitchen last night."

"I did the cooking, but that doesn't make it mine. Do you agree that she works too hard and so does Rosalyn when she's home."

"I do, but my suggestions of hiring more help has fallen on deaf ears."

"I didn't come here to do laundry, or dust, or wash floors, so I have put a stop to that and I need you to back me on my decisions. I have hired the two young ladies, Janet and Jane who were on the cleaning crew the other day as house maidens. They live outside of Waverly. I told them they could stay in the suite above the garage if that will be all right with you. They would have weekends off unless otherwise needed. Now, to find a cook…"

"You've discussed this with Rose and Amma I assume?"

"You would assume wrong."

"Rose was worried that you'd take a back seat to the going ones around here, which believe me, are pretty boring. She was afraid that you'd forget that this *is* and will forever be your home. You have been rather quiet so far, so I am delighted that you have taken this lack of help seriously and have taken the first step to right it, and Rose will be too. Do you have a plan to convince Amma that hiring a cook is a good idea?"

"She was never hired on as a cook, but as my assistant. After I left, Rosalyn was in charge, so for whatever reasons, it appears that Amma's duties were reduced, and she took to the kitchen assisting Mary. But now Rosy's obligations to McAllister holdings have become front and center so Amma is not only chief cook and bottle washer but is also doing x number of other things. We had many assistant cooks throughout the years. Mary objected at first but came to enjoy the help and I am sure Amma will too. My God, she is almost 60 Evan!"

"I'm sure she will. That just leaves you then…what are you going to do with your time?"

"One thing I won't be doing is laundry. I'll cook if I feel like it. I'm going to keep you and the girls company, do whatever I can to help Rosalyn, and I'm supposed to have some adventures, so be it, onward and upward."

"I never wanted to have to make any decisions on the running of the castle as that was Rose's domain. Mine was the rest of the estate, but the tides have turned and I have had to take on a new role, so thank you for solving the staffing problem as I was getting nowhere with convincing her that we needed help. I'm in agreement with you on the hiring of the two young ladies and yes, they may have the suite. Good luck with the cook thing. I only ask one thing of you Vienna…please don't disturb the sleeping spirits when you are looking for something to do."

"I will do my best, but you do know that it is them who seek me don't you, and I think you share my belief that the third floor is hiding something?"

"That was just a slip of the tongue during the elevator fiasco so pay no heed to it."

"Okay, but if you're going to be my partner in a caper…just sayin."

He laughed. We walked arm and arm up the back stairs. I took my leave from him at the top and said, "You know, you might just be my favorite son-in-law after all."

"As if there was even a competition. Good night Milady. Hopefully, we have dispelled your nightmare, and if Chandler is victorious over the adversaries who are vying for McAllister Enterprises then I'll have my Rose home again."

"Chandler…surely you don't mean Uncle John's son Chandler Tait?"

"I do. John and Grey convinced him to give up his position with Sweden International to return to his old job here with McAllister. Apparently, he is an expert at overthrowing hostile takeovers."

"He left the company angrily years ago, so I find it hard to believe that he's willing to help now."

"I know you have some tainted memories of his flirtations with you, but that was forty years ago. Rose says he's a new and caring man. He's already discerned that this attempted take-over attempt has its roots in Canada. Food for thought eh?"

"Three wives probably wouldn't agree with you. Personally, I don't care, but if he solves the problem then good on him. I will say that a possible Canadian connection does trouble me though."

"Not your problem, so put it in your pocket. Good night again."

I hugged him affectionately. I was going to be all right.

It was still raining the next night so I was stuck inside again. I didn't expect to meet up with Evan, but he was there in the same chair below the stairs smoking his pipe again. I asked him if it was another sleepless night. It was midnight. He said he hadn't even gone to bed yet. He had a glass in his hand and asked me if I would like a brandy. I declined and said I was on my way to the Harem room. He asked what I was going to do there in the room that spooked me.

"I need to pay my respects to the Grandfather clock."

"I shall accompany you then as I don't want you having nightmares later on. You know he hasn't been repaired yet don't you?"

"What's taking so long?"

"Well, all the clockmakers we have called in believe we are pulling their chain when we relate the clock's history. Several have offered to haul it into London and have "a go at it." Of course we won't let it leave the premises, so that's where we stand. We do believe that the initials of T.T 1677 engraved inside the clock may belong to noted clockmaker Thomas Tompion who was a noted British clockmaker in the late 17th century. The time frame fits, and the search goes on."

I ran my hands up and down Grandfather's exquisite wood frame and lifeless glass face. The dials still read 9:33; the time he had stopped ticking when he had come to an abrupt stop on the tracks that Rosalyn's great Grandfather had installed for his train collection, or so it was thought. It had become obvious to us last summer that the clock was all part of the mystery of Avanloch. The dilemma of the two keys that had been found twenty years ago was finally solved when we discovered that inserting them into two ornamental notches in the clock it would move and reveal a chasm that led to a tunnel that came out in the old graveyard. The mystery of the two keys had finally been solved almost as we still had no answer as how one the keys mysteriously appeared on a table that usually held a painting of Avanloch. The painting had never been found.

And so, the depressing month of November continued. The two new girls, Jane and Janet fit in very well in every aspect and were a delight to have around. I was pretty much in charge of their work week duties which included kitchen assistance, so the need for a cook was put on hold.

It had been a common practice for the castle to put together goodie baskets for the residents of the Village at Christmas. The population had almost tripled since I had last been the curator of this undertaking so now it would be a formidable task and only the elderly, impoverished and special needs citizens would be gifted the hampers. Amma and I spent half a day deciding on a list of eligible recipients and the contents of the hampers with the help of Reverend James and his wife Audrey. Turkeys, oranges, candy treats and other food staples were ordered. Along with Jane and Janet we made a trip into Waverly to shop for small gifts and the ingredients for the Christmas cakes. It was a busy day. We brought six large pizzas home for dinner. The next day we set in to making the cakes and assembling baskets.

Christmas dinner at Avanloch would see Amma's sister Emma and husband Finn, Millie, and Meggie, Amma and Johnny's daughter Alexa, husband Ed, and all their children, Reverend James, and Audrey, and all of Avanloch's staff. Aunt Jannie and Uncle John were always a maybe depending on the weather and their health. I was sure that Ash and Grey would come. I only hoped that Chandler would not be with them. The count would be somewhere between twenty-five and thirty I expected so we'd have to add another table as there was only room for twenty at the formal dining room table and yet I seemed to recall we had seated forty at an October party when I was married to Jeremy. Maybe the dinner was held in the grand drawing room or the grand entrance. I'd have to put my thinking cap on and have it all figured out when Rosy got home as she had left it in my hands. Hopefully, there would be room for a Christmas tree.

Chapter 3

The Hawk Has Landed

Christmas Eve found me alone in the family dining room wrapping last minute gifts. Two days ago the girls had asked me if I would object to them putting a tree up in the foyer across from my rooms. Of course I wouldn't, so they enlisted Zander to help them, and off they had gone searching for the perfect little tree. This "little" tree turned out to be an eight-foot pine. There were already five trimmed trees embellishing the castle. The largest was in the formal reception hall. It was a twelve-foot Spruce. The main dining room, both upstairs and downstairs media rooms, and the kitchen had smaller artificial trees. Christmas had always been a big celebration at Avanloch. The doors were open to not just family and friends, but neighbors from the Villages.

Rosy was against the kids choosing a real tree instead of a man-made one but agreed to it if the lights were only on under supervision and unplugged at night, and Evan, Zander or me, would make sure of that. Zander had dried the tree and wrapped it in burlap to prevent needles from escaping as it was dragged up the backstairs and down the hall to the foyer. I had declined the invite to help with the trimming and left the four of them upstairs sorting through the decorations. I had promised Evan that I would help him with the wrapping of his gifts. We were doing just that in the parlor when we heard the distinct roar of the tractor. I followed Evan to the window to see what was going on.

"How long have we been in here anyway?" He asked me as we both were astonished to see how much snow had fallen in an hour.

I followed him to the back door saying that all had been reasonably calm then. The weather forecast had predicted a light snowfall with intermittently strong wind gusts. We opened the door to a blast of frigid air to see Johnny slogging through 4 inches of the white stuff. He had a big grin on his face.

"Want to come out and play Boss?"

"It's just like you to order a blizzard for Christmas O'Shea isn't it, and I suppose you want me to help you clean up the mess?" Evan razzed. "Vienna and I were enjoying a hot toddy and relaxing to the quiet." He nodded upstairs.

Johnny laughed. "Yeah, I can hear the peaceful sound of Santa Claus is coming to town."

"We just shut the parlour door and ignore what's going on upstairs and apparently outside too." Evan put his arm around me. "Sorry Honey, but duty calls. Can you manage without me?"

"I think I can, but I'll be lonesome. I'll be cutting and making bows while the two of you are out having fun racing to determine who can plow the most snow. Get on with you now. It's a good thing that Alexa and family arrived yesterday Johnny. See you at lunch then."

I walked back to Jingle Bell Rock echoing down from upstairs. I closed the parlour door to drown out the noise and continued with Evan's gift wrapping without him. I don't think that even ten minutes had passed when I thought I heard the doorbell. It was hard to hear anything with the door closed. There it was again. I strained to hear above the carolling radiating from above and made my way to the front door. I was prepared to see my son-in-law standing there challenging me to a snowball fight.

A burst of Artic air greeted me as I opened the door and looked up and into the dark eyes of a snow- covered hulk of a man. Me, barely five feet tall, usually has to look up to everyone, so that was not unusual. Rainey always said that I was five foot nothing. He and Zander were both 5 feet 11. Nash and Johnny were a little taller as was Jack and Evan was 6 foot

3. This man at the door towered over me. Mind you, he was wearing a 4inch Cossack hat. It was covered in the white stuff as was the rest of him including his long black beard. Was this a Santa Claus of a different color I wondered as I saw he was carrying a large sack. His dark-brown eyes looked gentle so I backed up and told him to come in and leave as much of the storm outside as he could. He was wearing a long dark coat that looked as if it was made from some animal hide. I suggested that he remove it and hang it up on the coat rack. I had no idea who he was but my spiney senses told me he was a friend of the family.

"I'm sorry Ma'am to intrude on you and I apologise for the mess I am making on your floor. If I could trouble you to make a phone call to Johnny O'Shea and tell him that I have ditched the truck and only made it as far as the castle, I will be much obliged to you."

"He is on the snowplough at the moment, but I will try and get through to him. May I inquire as to your business with him?"

"Yes Ma'am…"

He never got to finish the sentence as Rosy was on the stairs expressing delight. "Edward, is that you? We were starting to worry about you wondering if you would make it through the snowstorm." She welcomed him with a hug. "I see you have met my mother."

"Your mother…" he said stammering a little, "am I talking to the Great Lady Vienna? I can't believe that we are finally to meet again."

He removed a glove and extended his hand. I took it. "There is nothing great about me Sir; I am just Vienna. You have me at a disadvantage though as I have no reckoning of meeting you before."

"You knew him as Edward Mom. Johnny's cousin Hawk and he was the ring bearer at his and Amma's wedding."

I laughed. "Forgive me for not recognizing you Sir; you haven't changed in forty years."

He laughed with me. "I suppose I am five feet taller and a hundred kilograms heavier and a little hairier, but you are exactly as I remember you."

"I think you were six weren't you Hawk?" Rosy asked.

"Could be, seems like a lifetime ago. But now here I am standing next to the two most beautiful ladies in the whole of Scotland, and may I say that I am honoured to be doing so."

"As Mom said, we are just ordinary people no matter what others may think. How about we get you warmed up with a hot cup of coffee, or tea?"

"Coffee is fine Rosalyn. Please don't let me interfere with your day as I am sure you are all very busy with plans for the big day tomorrow."

"I assure you that you aren't. I was supervising the kid's tree decorating upstairs and Mom was helping Evan with his last-minute wrappings. I'm assuming that he is out on one of the plows along with Johnny as he seems to have abandoned her. Let me try and contact them. I fear this storm is not done with us yet."

"It's almost noon Rosy so the boys will be in for lunch any minute. Why don't you finish upstairs and I'll join Hawk for coffee?"

"I didn't realise that it was so late. You're right Mom as they wouldn't be late for rumbldethumps." She laughed. "I'll be back in ten then."

"I'd be honoured to join you in a cup of coffee Lady Vienna. It has been a very long time since I have even heard the most delicious Scottish dish of rumbldethump mentioned."

"You are in for a treat then as Mary McDuff's version is on the luncheon menu. She said it was a special Christmas treat for us."

"If that is an invitation I accept whole heartily. I must ask though, is this the famous hieroglyphic staircase that I'm standing beside?"

"I don't know how famous it is, but you are welcome to take a stroll up it. I'm afraid most of the script is hidden under the Christmas bows and lights however,"

"Thankyou. Another time perhaps when I'm a little cleaner."

"I think the snowstorm bathed you sufficiently." I joshed. That was a mighty large sack you had flung over your shoulders. I take it you are the intended O'Shea Santa Clause ?"

"I'm feared my one stop buying spree will not only be a surprise for them but me also as I'm not even sure of what I've purchased."

"Perhaps I can help you straighten it out. The parlor is gift wrapping haven so what say we take our coffee and do some sorting and wrapping?"

"You are a Godsend My lady."

"Please do call me Vienna. I get enough of the milady business from Johnny and Evan."

It took half an hour to sort out his "grab bag" as he called it. He had gone on a one stop shopping blitz at Liberty London Department Store. He had an assortment of toys, games, CDs, jewelry and adult oriented gifts. He pocketed two before I had a chance to see them. I thought that they may be unmentionables for men. He was a good conversationalist and entertained me with many an anecdote of life in the arctic as an oceanographer/meteorologist at the research station of the south coast of Disko Island in west Greenland.

I had been told that a nephew of Johnny's may be coming for Christmas but I hadn't thought about it much except that there might be one more guest for dinner. The ploughers arrived in time for lunch of course. After a hearty welcome to Hawk Johnny put his arm around me. "I see my girlfriend has been entertaining you."

I shook my head smiling. Hawk actually looked a little stunned and asked if Amma knew about it and hadn't I been his boss once.

"Amma encourages it as it keeps me out of her hair." Johnny laughed. "And for all purposes, Vienna is still my boss."

I pushed him away and told him he was full of it.

"Yeah, but you love me right?"

Evan had taken the bottle of Scotch down and poured us all a shot. "The rest of us are always in the middle of their antics aren't we Mary?"

"Sures shootin Mr. Evan and you be right there by their sides now aren't you?"

He passed her a glass laughing.

I knew that Grey wouldn't take any chances with the weather so unfortunately he and Ash and Uncle John and Jannie wouldn't be coming for Christmas. I knew my aunt would be very disappointed so I located my phone and called her. It was 2 p.m. The boys had left with Hawk and his bag in tow.

Jannie answered on the third ring. "Hello Dear, we just checked in and I was going to call you after I had settled and had a cuppa."

"Checked in where?" I asked surprised.

"At the suite of course."

"Are you in Waverly? Did Grey drive? Isn't it snowing over there?"

"We ran into the storm just outside of town but it has calmed down now. We are spending the night here. Chandler has been in contact with the Department of Highways and the forecast for tomorrow is favorable and there will be gritters out all night and just to be safe we can follow behind one tomorrow morning so not to worry."

"I'll try not to. Rosey did not tell me that Chandler was coming with you." I said annoyingly."

"Don't get your feathers in a ruffle Dear. It was she invited him. He's a changed man and will charm you off your feet. Now go get some rest as it will be a busy day tomorrow. See you tenish, love you."

I returned the sentiment and went to find my daughter. She did not apologise but said he was gaining so much headway on finding conclusive evidence on the culprits attempting to take control of the company that she didn't think I would begrudge him the pleasure of spending Christmas with the family. She thought I had forgiven him for his innuendos a long time ago. "In fact Mom, I told him you were the one who sent the invitation."

"It's a good thing Rainey isn't here. They did not get on you know."

"I wish he was here Mama."

What could I do but hug her and say I wished so too, but I did say that Chandler better not irritate me with his eyes.

Christmas morning was a delight to the senses. The golden sun shone down from a bright azure sky and turned the icicles dangling from the birch trees into diamonds. The logs were crackling in the eighteenth-century hearth. The aroma of cinnamon and nutmeg from the rising muffins in the oven filled the kitchen. Evan's sparkling tart apple cider was ready for sampling. I stood at the window waiting for Aunt Jannie and family. I wondered what was happening back home at the ranch in Hawthorne. Lili would have our house decorated like a Christmas tree while Ava's home would be adorned with Avanloch memorabilia. It was JT's first Christmas and neither Rainey nor I would be there. I had talked to them all last night. Oh, I mustn't forget to call Jack, yes Jack, and Sissy of course. The honking of a car horn brought me out of my melancholy. "They're here!" I announced gleefully.

Evan and I held back while Rosalyn and the girls greeted Aunt Jannie and the rest of the family. We took our turn with hugs and kisses. Chandler was the last in line. Evan shook hands with him and gave my hand a squeeze as Chandler stepped forward to address me. As usual he curtsied. "My Lady."

I bowed to him. "Mr. Tait, welcome to our humble abode."

"It is my honor to be invited. I suppose it's too much to ask for an embrace?"

"Why not; it's Christmas and I am feeling generous, but you must promise that you won't think of it as an engagement."

His laughter was genuine. He promised with fingers crossed. I was always being hugged by my Avanloch family but this was the first time since Jack that it was someone outside the family and I thoroughly enjoyed it. I quickly stepped back after a minute and suggested we go down to brunch. "If you behave I might just consent to allow you to be my dinner escort."

"Surely you jest with me My Lady?"

"Surely I do, but strange things do take place here at this haunted mansion."

"So I have heard and I look forward to one of your stories if I be so blessed."

He held my chair for me as we took our places at the family dining room table. I was seated between Jannie and Mary. Evan was across the table. His eyes were questioning. I winked at him.

After brunch Janet and Jane arrived to do the cleanup. They'd had their Christmas the night before with their families and had asked to be on the kitchen staff with Millie and Emma who were in charge of catering to us and our guests. Of course they would all join us for the celebratory dinner.

They sent us on to the grand reception room where the giant Scots Pine and all its treasures lay waiting. Evan transferred Mary onto one of the sofas beside Duffy, Jannie and Uncle John. Duffy had shuffled down with help from John and Chandler. He would be good for an hour and then would need to rest until the dinner hour. I was afraid that this would be his last Christmas. I sat on the loveseat with Zander holding hands. Colleen and Beth had organised the gifts last night and they took charge handing them out. There was the usual discussion about the gift and thank you after each unwrapping. I certainly hadn't expected to receive anything from Chandler so when I opened an embossed golden envelope was surprised to find that it had an invitation to attend a presentation of Carmen at the Edinburgh Opera House with him. I thanked him and said that it would be my pleasure though I wasn't sure that I would go. My favorite gifts were from Evan which included a mid length black and rose silk dressing robe and a fuzzy pink pair of slippers, a boa and half-length white evening gloves. He said the slippers and gloves were Rose's idea. There was also a journal from the both of them. The inscription on the cover read: *The Midnight Wanderings of a Lady of Leisure.* I was very amused by that and said I would make good use of it. I had given Evan a dark green brocade smoking jacket and an antique ebony wood pipe and a logbook. Ash commented that it was funny that we had given each other similar gifts. I didn't comment but my daughter did.

"My mother and my husband have a unique friendship as everyone knows, but perhaps you don't know that these two meet up every now and then at midnight in this very room and discuss whatever. Mom has always been a wanderer, not just here but in Hawthorne and Bridge Falls too. Rainey was upset by it at first but soon found out that there was nothing he could do about it. Now Evan has picked up the idiosyncrasy. He says that I am to blame for it started when I was spending more and more time away. Then Mom came and they met up one night. Apparently they don't plan their encounters; they are just happenstance. According to Amma, Johnny has the same habit and I'm sure that it's just a matter of time before his walks lead him here at the midnight hour."

Evan and I had a twitter.

Mary and Jannie both begged off joining the rest of us in the Drawing Room for conversation and games of chance which was Ash's speciality. Rosy and I excused ourselves several times to check on the dinner preparations. Amma and Johnny and family arrived at two with a sack full of presents so we had another exchange with them. I knew all the wrapping paper that I had used to help with Hawk's gifts so was surprised once more when one of the packages was to me from him. It was a beautiful snow globe of a castle in a snowstorm. This had not been in his bag so wondered where it had come from. A hand-written Christmas card was affixed to it thanking me for my hospitality and hopes that we could meet again someday soon. Shortly after that Johnny caught my eye and I snuck off with him to the veranda outside the dining room. He handed me a small silvery box. It held a pearl handle cigarette holder. He said he couldn't believe that I didn't have one and that it featured a filter to remove harmful toxins. I did not tell him that Jack had given me one many years ago. I hugged him just as the door opened and Evan emerged with his new pipe asking if he could join us.

The London family stayed until Sunday the 28th. The snow was crisp and just right for daytime snowshoeing and cross-country skiing. Johnny treated us to two nights of merriment on sleigh rides through the Village and around the estate on the hay wagon. Even Mary joined us on one. Charades and stories around the fireplace were enjoyed by all. Evan and the girls and I hated to see them leave and were doubly saddened as Rosalyn had decided to journey back with them and save Evan a trip.

Chandler reminded me of our date in April. I hadn't considered the invitation as a date.

All in all it was a jolly ole Christmas even if the most important person in my life was absent.

January was its usual self with temperatures hovering between 1 and 8c. The nights were long and we spent many evenings telling stories, playing cards, and reading around the fireplace ignoring the howling winds outside. Days saw Amma, Mary and me cooking up hardy traditional Scottish and Iris food. Butch would join us for supper once or twice a week and he always brought some tantalizing dish or dessert. I'm sure I gained ten pounds that month.

Hawk called me at the end of January and said he was going to be in London on February the 14th through to the 18th and was there a possibility that I might join him for dinner and a show. I told him I would have to think about it.

Chapter 4

Vienna's Promise

February 13, 2004

Millie Magan had popped in yesterday to ask Mary if she would like to accompany her on a visit to Meggie's tomorrow. Mary had replied that she would dearly love to but she could not leave the Duff alone.

"You should go Mary." I had interjected. "Do you not trust that I can keep my eye on him?"

"He be better in your hands than mine, but you be the only one home and you be busy with the cakes for tomoree will you not Dearie?"

"Not that busy. Now thank Millie for the invite as Meggie would very much like to see you as she is laid up with that bothersome ankle again and is house bound for another week."

"I not be much help you know Millie."

"You will keep her company while I do the chores, so that is good."

"I thought Johnny be doing the chores?"

Millie laughed. "I gave the dear man the day off because he was still sore after that mule of Meggie's kicked him in the shins the other day."

So it was settled, and after a few words of instructions this morning to not let Duffy take advantage of me and what he could and couldn't eat as if I didn't know already that he'd ask for chocolate. I walked Mary to the back door and helped Millie to get her in the car. I had suggested that they take my car as it would be too difficult for Mary to climb into Millie's truck.

I had a quick peek through the open door into the McDuff's suite to see what Duffy was up to. His eyes were glued to the television. I loaded a cart with the cake ingredients from the pantry and found the heart shaped pans and retreated to the kitchen. I popped a cup of old coffee into the microwave for reheating and turned the radio on low to a music channel as it was much too quiet for me. Mary was right; I was all alone except for Duffy who was recliner bound. Rosalyn was at work in London, Evan was at his class in Edinburgh, and the girls were at school. Amma was with her mother at sister Emma's place in the Village making treats for Valentine's Day. And, of course Zander was in the stables or workshops with Johnny and the rest of the crew.

I sat down to have a few sips of coffee. Was that the front doorbell? Yes…there it was again. I went into the hall to make sure. By the time I reached the door, the non-stop ringing was accompanied by loud poundings. Without bothering to glance through the peephole I opened the door to a hysterical young woman begging me for help. She was definitely in a panic state. Her words were almost inaudible.

"She said you would help her she wouldn't let me take her to the hospital she said she had to see you because you would take Darlena she knew you would like you did the McCracken girl."

I held on to her because she was shaking so much I thought she was going to collapse. I shook her gently. "Who is she, and who is Darlena, and **where** are they?"

She pointed down the driveway. "There…the car just stopped…" She pulled away from me crying. "She's dying, she's dying…"

I reached up and pounded on the alarm bell, took the hand of this frenzied girl, and ran down the drive with her to the car. I had never had the need to activate the distress siren before so hearing the boisterous blaring that followed us was unsettling. Johnny, Zander, and Butch were already halfway across the yard. We reached the car two steps ahead of them. People from the village were arriving at the gate. I opened the door to find a blanket covering up what I assumed was the dying woman. A tiny pair of hands was holding onto the blanket as I flipped it off. Two big sky-blue eyes smiled up at me. I pulled the baby into my arms and backed off. Johnny reached in and felt for the comatose woman's pulse. He said it was very weak and asked Butch if he could get her up to the house. Butch pulled her into his arms and took off up the hill. Johnny managed to limp his way ahead of him, opened the door and shut the alarm off. I told Zander to bring the sedan to the front door as we were most assuredly going to be making a trip to Waverly. Amma caught up to me just before I reached the steps. I quickly explained what had happened, thrust the baby into her arms and told her to look after the little Pixie.

Butch had placed the woman on the settee in the grand reception hall. I knelt beside her and took her hands in mine. "What's her name and yours too?" I asked the sister knelling beside me. She said she was Ada and her sister was Marianne.

"Can you open your eyes for me Marianne? Ada told me that you wanted to see me because you had something to ask me. Can you tell me what it is?"

Her eyes flickered. "Lady Vienna?"

"Yes, I am Vienna. We need to get you to the hospital as quickly as possible so please tell me what it is you want of me."

Through parched lips she spoke pleadingly. "My baby, my baby… you must take her. I am dying… I need to know she will be looked after. Promise me… promise me Lady Vienna, please, please…"

She lapsed back into unconsciousness with my name echoing into the eerie silence of the room.

"Let's get her to the car then. Johnny, can you drive?"

Before he could answer Zander burst into the room shouting that Evan was home. I told him to run and tell Evan to prepare the heli for a patient. Butch stepped forward and picked Marianne up again. I took Ada's hand and we followed him and Johnny to the heli pad.

Evan was already ready for the transfer from Butch and in seconds he had Marianne all buckled down for the ride. He asked who the patient was and did anyone know her diagnosis. Ada did not volunteer any information so I told him her name was Marianne and that was all I knew except her sister said that she was dying. Ada then spoke and said that Mari had cervical cancer and that it was stage four.

"Okay then. I'll ride with her; Johnny, you're driving."

"I don't think so Boss. Thanks for your confidence in my piloting skills, but it's imperative that this flight and landing is smooth and that's where you excel. There is nothing that you can do for her that I can't, so get out and get us in the air!"

Evan growled and backed out because he knew Johnny was right. He told Butch to quiet the crowd and to get the wreck of a car out of the drive. Ada wanted to ride in the back with her sister, but he vetoed that and buckled her into the passenger seat in front of Marianne.

"You're with me Vienna." He said taking my hand and walking me to the co-pilot's door. "I can't leave you alone for one minute can I?"

I didn't answer him until we were in the air and he had radioed the hospital in Waverly relaying our eta and what little he knew about the patient. Ada said Mari's doctor was Shelia Henning, so he asked that she be made aware.

"When did you take on the role of my husband?" I asked him cattily.

He grinned. "Yeah, I heard what I said. I must be attuning into your senses because Rain was in my head and the words just came out." He reached over and squeezed my hand. "Sorry."

"No harm done; just don't do it again."

"You have my word Milady. Now will you tell me how it is that you know these two ladies?"

I related the story to him emphasizing that I had only met them ten minutes before he had. I shocked him a little when I told him that Marianne had begged me to take her baby in.

"There's a baby…where is it?"

"At the castle."

"Our castle?"

"Yes Evan, our castle."

"Hell. How's our patient John?"

"No change Boss."

Two attendants were at the ready when we touched down. Evan and Johnny helped with the transfer. Ada and I followed behind. Evan told Johnny to look after us while he secured the heli and to have his leg examined. I asked him if he thought that Evan was sounding more and more like Rainey. He laughed.

We left Marianne in the hands of the professionals and made our way into the waiting room. We met Dr. Shelia on her way into the ER. She gave Ada a quick hug and said to give her a few minutes. I could see the questions in her eyes as she nodded at me.

The result of her examination was one that I expected. Marianne would probably not make it through the night. Her cancer had drastically metastasized. It was then that I learned that she had not seen a health professional for six months. She would be made as comfortable as possible and Ada could sit with her as soon as she was settled. Shelia then asked me how I was involved. I relayed the scenario to her. She applauded me for acting so compassionately. I told her that there was nothing to thank me for as my reactions were instinctive and I was thankful that Evan had arrived home unexpectedly or we would have had to come by car. I then told her that I was going to join Ada to keep vigil at her sister's side. I hoped that Marianne would awaken to know that I was going to honor her request. Shelia asked me what that was. I told her. She was stunned at first but then said that she now knew why I was known as the Lady of Mercy.

"I am no different from anyone else Dr. Henning. Why I have been chosen to grant a dying woman's wish to care for her child I do not know, but it is not something I can deny. The whys are not mine to question. I trust you will be checking in on her now and then?"

She said she would be and walked us to a private family area. Marianne was awaiting us behind a closed door. Ada and I sat down on opposite sides of the bed and we each took one of her hands in ours. I was surprised that it was so warm. After a few minutes I asked Ada to tell me about their lives. They had lived in Melton all their lives. Their mother and father had a small acreage where they raised vegetables, chickens, and ducks which they sold in Waverly at markets. The egg market was not enough to see them through the winters so their dad supplemented the income by doing odd jobs. He passed away six years back. Mari and she were very close until five years ago. It was sometime in the spring when Mari just up and left two days before her eighteenth birthday, just a few months before graduation. Ada was fifteen. For the first two years they had received postcards from all over England. Marianne always said she was well and happy and looking for the perfect place to call home. Until then she would make her living waitressing or whatever. Ada said she guessed she had found it four years ago in a swanky hotel somewhere outside of Inverness that catered to the rich and famous. She had landed a job as a hostess. Ada had never visited her sister there, but they would meet up every other month or so in Waverly. Two years ago Mari arrived home in Melton. Darlena was born two months later with only her and her mother in attendance. Shortly after that their mother had become very confused. They took her to the hospital where she was diagnosed with dementia and transferred to a care facility in Sterling.

"Now I am losing Mari and will have no family left." Ada lamented.

I reached out to her. "You have Darlena, and seeing that she will be living with me, my family will also be yours if you will let us be."

"You're really going to take Darlena in?" Ada asked surprised, yet hopeful.

Before I could assure her that I was going to, Mari started to stir. Her eyelids fluttered. A minute or so later she squeezed my hand and murmured faintly through trembling lips.

"Lady Vienna…you're here…"

"Yes, I am Mari. I am here to tell you that I will honour your wishes. I will care for Darlena as if she was my own and I will also take Ada under my wing. You have nothing to fear so just breathe." I gently put my hand on her throbbing breast to try and soothe her. Rainey had told me that was the way he had calmed me when I had the panic attack in the hospital when I had found out that Jorja, the woman who had tried to kill me was in a cell in the hospital basement. I shuttered, but quickly stored the image away.

Another whisper. "Paper, paper…pen…hurry,"

"Ring for the nurse Ada, ask for Dr. Henning." I instructed as I pushed my chair back and opened the door. Thankfully, Johnny was on the other side. I asked him to get me paper and pen from the nursing station and then to join me in Mari's room.

It seemed like an eternity before he and Sheila arrived. I kept reassuring Mari that all was well as best I could though doubtful that she would hold on. I clipped the paper to her bedside chart, removed it, and held it close to her. She could not hold on to the pen. Sheila came to her side and held it with her while she wrote. Twenty minutes later she stopped writing.

"Just one more word Mari…yes, that's it…amazing job my sweet." I kissed her cheek as I stood up and passed the sheet of paper for all the witnesses to sign. I tore a shred of paper off and wrote a phone number on it and gave it to Johnny.

"I don't want to leave Mari and Ada, so will you please call Uncle John? I know he has a solicitor friend here so perhaps he could ask him if he could come by and see that all is legal."

"No need to call John as I know who the lawyer is as he is representing me in Uncle Walt's legal affairs. I'm sure he can be persuaded to pop over if there's a dollar in it."

I thanked Johnny with a hug. Shelia nodded at me and said she'd be back in a few minutes. I pulled the declaration off the clip- board and read it over.

I Maryanne elsie Gibson of sound mind but dying body----------
Mother of Darlena Justine Gibson--------
Release her to lady Vienna--------Quinn

Who will keep her as her own----------with my dying breath this is my word------------------------megibson

It had been an agonizing half hour watching her struggle. She would drop the pen after writing every few words and then lose her place. Shelia would encourage her to keep trying and remind her where she had left off. She did not know my last name so had a problem there. I spelled it for her. I had no idea if this would stand up in a court of law, but I was hopeful that Johnny could convince the lawyer to attend a dying woman's assertion. And maybe, just maybe, Mari would wake up long enough to utter her last wish to him. I hoped he was a compassionate man.

The process of adoption was not foreign to me because I had legally adopted Rosalyn and Rainey had adopted Ava even though he was her biological daughter. He had wanted his name on her birth certificate. He and I had adopted Zoe and Tanny. The circumstances were different for all, but none had been with a dying woman.

Johnny arrived with a middle-aged heavy-set man and introduced us to Levy McPhee. He had kind eyes. I guessed that Johnny had already given him all the particulars because he didn't ask many questions. He asked Shelia if she would witness the questions he would be asking Ms. Gibson. She said she would but was doubtful that Marianne could speak and may not even wake up.

"Let's give it the old college try shall we? I don't think I was summoned here if there wasn't a chance that Ms. Gibson would respond. Am I right Lady Vienna?"

"Yes, you are right Sir. Shall we begin?"

"We shall. You will be her encourager, and Doctor Shelia will make note of her responses, no matter what they are. May I trouble you Miss Ada to relinquish your chair so I may be close to your sister?" He whispered something to her as they passed.

Johnny nodded for Ada to come stand by him. I smiled my appreciation.

I leaned close to Mari and asked her if she could answer some questions that Mr. McPhee, who was a solicitor was going to ask her. There was a slight tug on my hand. Her eyelid fluttered.

He took over then talking soothingly to her asking her if she could answer yes or no to a few questions by blinking her eyes, one was for yes and two was for no. Her eyes flickered once. We were in business. She answered yes to all his questions except the ones that pertained to years. After two blinks of no, she answered yes to this years' date. It took a little longer to get Darlena's birth date confirmed. She agreed on February 19th, 2003. Darlena would be a year old in 6 days. She had no response whatsoever to any questions that related to her status regarding Darlena's parentage beside herself. He said he understood and would note it as "unidentified." He held her hand while she made an attempt to initial the declaration.

Mr. McPhee thanked her and told her that she had made a wise and perfect decision by choosing me to be her daughter's adoptive mother. He said, "God is with you child."

He had us all witness the official paper that Shelia had been documenting. He shook our hands and thanked us stating that I was now Darlena's guardian and that he and I would be meeting again soon. We, all in turn thanked him. Johnny walked him out. Shelia said she was going to have the kitchen send us up some lunch. I talked with Ada for a few minutes assuring her that it had all gone exceedingly well and the adoption would be finalised in no time explaining that until then I was Darlayna's legal guardian. I thought I'd give Ada a few minutes alone with her sister and told her that I'd be right out the door if she needed me. I found Evan on the other side standing at a window holding a cup of coffee. He came over to me and offered me the coffee saying I needed it more than he did.

"What have I done Evan; what have I done?" I cried.

He put his arms around me. "You did what you always do; you made things right."

"You know?"

"Yes, Johnny filled me in. Sorry I was so long, but it looked like the heli had an oil leak so I had to have that checked out. I knew John was with you so I didn't worry too much about you."

"Is the heli okay, and where is Johnny now?"

"Disaster averted so nothing to worry about. Shelia sent an intern to assess John and take him for an x-ray. How is our patient?"

"She is still holding on. Before I go back in there I need to ask you something Evan. I don't have any idea what Rosalyn will say when she hears that I have brought a baby home with me, but I hope that she and you too, will let us stay at Avanloch until the adoption has been finalised. I only have legal custody of her right now so I can't take her out of the country. I don't know how long that will be but …"

"Out of the country; what are you talking about?"

"Well, I do have two houses in Canada, so we'll be going back there."

"Oh, you will, will you? Just like that you're going to take your new daughter and abandon *us*?"

"Colleen and Beth are all grown up and will be going off to college before you know it, so you and Rosy will have time to yourselves to do what you want. Darlena is just a year old and will have a lot of needs throughout the years so we will just be interfering with your retirement and taking up room."

"Oh, is that right? We live in a bloody castle for Christ's sake Vienna! A castle that has rooms that haven't been happy since you and Rain and the girls went home last summer. It is yours forever and it will always be your home and you know that. Have you forgotten that you are the one who made it what it is today? Now I can only chalk this silliness up to emotional distress so go back in there and give Marianne comfort and know that I love you unconditionally as does Rose and the girls. I can hardly wait to meet this little munchkin. Sometimes that place seems more like a mausoleum, so to have childish laughter and the sound of little feet running in the hallways is something I am looking forward to again."

"What's happening?" Johnny questioned us as he limped over to us leaning on a crutch.

"It's that bad then?" Evan asked.

"No, it's just a contusion like I told you. Nothing to worry about, but somethings happened here…has Mari passed over?"

"No, she's still with us. Vienna was just voicing her apprehension about adopting a baby and that it would be best for all of us if she moved back to Hawthorne."

"Well, if me and Amma are included in that decision then the answer is no, we don't want you leaving us. I just talked to her and she said that she's in love with Pixie so I think you know what that means."

"But Johnny, I am almost sixty and I don't have a husband anymore so she won't have a father, and what will the kids say?"

"Then I guess Evan and me will have to be surrogate fathers until Rain gets home."

"Right you are John, and Rose is one of your "kids" and I know what she will say, the same as me, and that is that you are our family and anyone you bring into the family is a welcome addition. I thought her name was Darlena?"

"It is, but I called her Pixie when I thrust her into Amma's arms so I'm assuming she thought that was her name. I will straighten it out when I get home. Yes, home, and it is because of you two. Now I best be getting back to Ada." I started to walk away but turned back. "We could be here all night so you two need to go home. Ada and I will stay in the suite. Amma has been all alone with the baby all day and Johnny, you need to get off your feet."

He laughed. "If you were still my boss, I might do as I'm told, but you're not so I'll take my cue from Evan even though I know the answer. What do you say big guy?"

"Rain would kill us if we left her here to fend for herself, so I guess we're hanging around." Evan said winking at me. "Besides, we took an oath…"

"Yes, I know, we never leave a comrade behind." I blew them a kiss and told them I loved them.

I found Ada with hands still grasping Mari's and eyes reaching for the heavens. I walked over to her and embraced her. She smiled at me and said she was glad I was here because she felt that Mari's time was near. I retook my place beside Mari and said a silent prayer. It wasn't but ten minutes later that a hush came over the room. Ada shivered and asked me what that was.

I looked at the clock on the wall. It had stopped ticking at 1:20.

"The angels have come for her Ada. Mari is in their realm now and will be with her as she journeys into Heaven."

"It got so quiet…and then I heard something…"

"The sudden silence occurs because angels are singing and consciously or unconsciously, you heard their heavenly chorus. It can happen any time but is more powerful at twenty past the hour and some say at twenty before the hour."

Ada's eyes followed me to the clock and whispered. "That is the most beautiful thing I have ever heard."

Dr. Henning arrived with two nurses. She voiced her condolences and glanced at the clock. She nodded to me. I believed at that moment that she also accepted the belief to be true.

Mari had made all the arrangements for her funeral months ago. Shelia was aware of it and told us that she would be in touch after all was concluded. Mari was to be cremated and Ada would be in charge of overseeing her sister's final resting place. Ada shook her head and was visually upset by this disclosure. I intervened.

"She will come home with us. Avanloch is to be her daughter's home so it is only fitting that Mari's ashes rest close to her. There will be a special window for her in the family resting house." I decided not to use the word crypt or mausoleum as it might have been upsetting for Ada as they sounded rather harsh and cold.

There was nothing left to do, or so I thought.

"I'm afraid I need to impose on you even more Lady Vienna as I came away without my purse. It is back at the castle in the car and I will need to find my way to Stirling where my mother is so if you could just lend me the fare I will be ever grateful."

I laughed a little. "Well, I too came away without any funds so have to rely on Evan to see me home. I should say *us* as you are coming home with me. Your mother has no concept of time and so tomorrow or the next day will be time enough to inform her of Mari's passing and we will do that together. I thought I made it perfectly clear that I am Vienna, just Vienna?"

"You did, but sometimes it just doesn't feel right, and how can I go home with you?"

"The same way I am getting there, with Evan and Johnny and the magic helicopter."

"That's not what I meant…"

"I know it isn't, but Darlena is there and I think she'd like to see a familiar face, so how about we go and see how she's getting on."

"Have a look Ada; we're fling over Melton. Can you locate your house? Curious if I'll be able to touch down close to it." Evan requested.

"That's it right to the left. Why would you want to land Mr. Evan?"

"Not today, but another day you'll need to go home and collect your belongings and check things out won't you? Is there anything that needs immediate attention, like animals?"

"No, we had a cat but Mari didn't like the way it was acting around Darlena so we gave it to a neighbour, and the chickens found homes with others. There is nothing much there for me as most of my belongings are in Stirling in my dorm room."

"Ada is enrolled in a business course at the college there Evan." I explained.

"I do have a few clothes at the house, but I did pack a few things this morning because I knew Darlena and I would be staying somewhere for the night though I had no idea where at the time. I thought we were going straight to the hospital so when Mari told me to turn right instead of left at the main road I didn't understand and I questioned her as to why. It was then that she told me that she had to see you Vienna, and that you would help her find a new home for Darlena. I had no idea what she was going to ask you until we arrived at the castle, or that she…"

She couldn't finish the sentence. I reached forward and put my hand on her shoulder. "It's okay Luv, we know that the turn of events was a complete shock to you, but you don't have to go through all the consequences alone as we will be facing all the tomorrows together. You need to trust that fate intervened at the right time and brought you all to Avanloch. You can do that for me can't you?"

"Did she know that this was to be her last day? She just said this morning that she thought it best if she checked in with her doctor and that Darlena needed a checkup also. She asked me to pack a few things because we would probably be spending the night in Waverly but we had to make a stop first. She was in perfect control. When she told me were going to Avanloch Castle I thought that she was joking or had lost her mind. She said there was someone there she had to see and she told me to hurry. The last thing she said just before we reached the gate was that you, Lady Vienna, would take Darlena just as you had the McCracken girl. It is still not clear to me if she already had an arrangement with you?"

"She didn't, and as far as I know we had never met before. It is, as I said, fate intervened and thankfully you obeyed her wish and brought her and Darlena to me."

"We are all in agreement of that Ada and I can assure you that my wife Amma has already fallen in love with your little niece and is waiting to welcome you into her fold. I think I can speak for Rosalyn also who is Evan's lady and Vienna's daughter, right Boss?"

"You know it John. I'm just sorry that Rose isn't scheduled to come home for a few more days, but knowing her, she may just say "to hell with work" and ask me to come and get her. Now how is it Ada that you just happened to be in Melton today; the day you were needed?"

"I had a few days off and wanted to check on Mari and see my niece, Mr. Evan."

"I am just Evan; no mister required."

"He's actually Lord Evan." Johnny interjected.

Evan scoffed as Avanloch came into view. "So, Mari was living at home?"

"She came home just a month or so before Darlena was born so she's been living there with Mom for a year. We didn't know that she was pregnant at first."

Johnny asked where she had been living before that. Ada said some fancy resort where she had been working for three or four years. He asked her if it was in the vicinity.

"I think its The Blue Parrot Roadhouse or something like that. I'm not sure where that is."

A look passed between Johnny and Evan that I found odd.

Zander was waiting for us by the hangar with the sedan. I told him that Ada and I were going to walk as we needed to stretch a bit, but Johnny could use it. He frowned at me and said, "That'll be the day!" I reintroduced Ada to Zander. He gave her his condolences. Halfway up the drive we spotted Colleen and Beth coming down with Darlena between them.

"She walks!" I exclaimed.

"She walks, she runs, she talks and giggles a lot." Ada beamed as she opened her arms to her niece. "Come to Ada my sweet."

Darlena cooed as she reached out for Ada. I backed away to let them have a few minutes alone together and asked my granddaughters why they weren't in school. They laughed.

"When the alarm went off we all ran to the windows and saw all the people rushing down the road. We were all dismissed from school and of course we came right home. We had never heard that alarm before but were pretty sure where it was coming from. You were just leaving in the heli when we reached the gate. Of course we had no idea what had happened and were terrified. Zander was waiting at the hangar and told us. Can you imagine how surprised we were to find Pixie with Amma?

She said that she might be living with us for a while. Can we keep her Ana; we just love her." Colleen asked.

Before I could reply Ada turned and asked me if I would like to hold my new daughter. I held out my arms to her and she came willingly into them.

Ada said, "Say hello to your new Mama Darlena."

I couldn't believe I heard the words "Mamma."

The girls were crying. Beth managed to get out, "I thought her name was Pixie."

I explained the blunder and introduced them to Ada. They asked if they could hug her and poured out their sympathies over her loss. Tears came to Ada's and my eyes when Beth said that she had always wanted a baby sister and Colleen wanted an older sister so it looked as if both their wishes had come true. She added that Darlena was a lovely name.

"Yes, but Pixie suits her to a T, so your Grandmother got it right." Ada agreed.

"We call her Ana and Grampa is Pappy." Beth stated.

Ada looked confused. "Mr. Evan is your father isn't he, and Johnny is Amma's husband, but I heard the name Rainey…is he your Grandfather? Then he must be your husband Vienna…is he here?"

"Sadly, he isn't right now. I will explain later, but right now I could really use a cup of Amma's lavender and honey tea."

Beth put her hand on my forehead and laughed. "Oh, you must be really tired Ana."

Ada said she had already found out about my distaste for tea.

Pixie wanted down. The five of us made our way up the hill to a waiting Amma and the new chapter that was about to unfold at the castle.

The Gibson Sisters

Sure enough the kettle was bubbling away on the wood stove in the kitchen. Colleen and Beth said they'd take care of Pixie until I had my tea. I introduced Ada to Amma and Mary. They hugged Ada and expressed their sympathies as they welcomed her. Amma ushered Ada to a chair and said that tea was ready.

"I don't think that I could eat anything Amma as we had sandwiches at the hospital."

Amma laughed. "Oh, it's not that kind of "tea". The main meal is called supper here, and tea is just tea and a sweet if you like. We are of many nationalities here so we took a vote many years ago and decided that tea could be anytime of the day. Vienna, Johnny, and Evan like their tea to be coffee, but Mary, Rosy and I like our tea. The girls usually have milk or hot chocolate after school but do join us for tea and a biscuit. So, what's your preference Ada?"

I answered for Ada as I'm sure she was overwhelmed by all the attention. "We had our share of coffee at the hospital so I think we could use a cup of your sweet lavender tea Amma. I promise not to make a face, and how come I don't remember voting on the tea thing?"

Mary said she didn't either.

Zander arrived and asked Ada what she wanted him to do with the wooden box.

"It's for Vienna, so wherever she wants it."

"A box … for me? What's in it and where did it come from?" I asked curiously.

"I don't know what's in it because I never saw it before this morning. I noticed it sitting beside Mari's suitcase and she told me that it was going with us. She did not tell me anything about it until we were well on our way here. She said that I was to make sure that you got it. I asked her what was in it, but she closed her eyes and didn't say another word about it. That's all I know."

I had a few sips of tea, picked up the mysterious box and said I'd see what was in it in the parlour. I stopped at the media room and asked the girls if they would bring Pixie to me and if they could show Ada around and make her feel at home. Colleen said that Zander had changed bedrooms because he'd thought that she'd want to be close to me and Pixie. I smiled and said it was a wonderful idea.

I sat my new daughter on my lap in the loveseat that had replaced the big yellow chair that I had read to and cuddled all my children in. It had made the voyage with us to Bridge Falls some twenty years ago. I had a heart-to-heart talk with her about the way things were. She paid attention for a few minutes and then wanted down to play with all the stuff in the box of toys that Beth had brought over. I sighed. "I see. Well, I guess I'll just have to see what's in my box then."

It was just an old chocolate box. It was sealed with scotch tape. My name was on an envelope inside. It was short and to the point.

My Dear Lady Vienna,

I am beseeching your assistance once more. You will not remember a time before when I asked you if you could intervene in a dire situation with the Donnelly family. I knew you were a caring person as I saw it in your eyes at the fete. I was only seven years old then. My mother said it was what one Gibson woman would do for another one. You came to their assistance as you did the McCracken child. I pray you will now as I am dying and my baby girl needs someone to love and care for her…please let it be you Lady Vienna.

I have nothing to give you or her, or my beloved sister but this small pittance. May the good Lord bless and keep you. I will be ever in your debt.

Marianne Gibson

I did not remember the Donnelly family or helping them in any way. I put the letter down and opened the next envelope. A wad of large bills fell out. The next envelope was addressed to Ada. By the feel of it I guess that it also held money. I was interrupted by Evan and Johnny as I was counting out the quid.

"We thought we'd come down and meet the new arrival … what have you there Vienna?"

"Well Evan, I don't exactly know."

"Looks like moola to me." Johnny said sitting down on the floor beside Pixie.

I watched the two of them make friends before I passed the stash and the letter to Evan. "She likes you Johnny."

He grinned. "What's not to like?"

"Where do you think she got ten thousand quid from?" Evan asked.

"From the wages at her job I guess, and, by the feel of it, there may be another ten or more in Ada's envelope. I guess I'll track her down and have her open it and maybe she can shed some light on the money and the note. I mean, suppose it's stolen … that's a lot of money for a hostess to make. Ada told me that Mari had assured her that their mother's stay at the nursing home had been paid for a year, so there's that too."

"Just a minute Vienna; let's not jump the gun here as Ada may not know anything."

"What do you mean Johnny; anything about what?"

"What her sister actually did for a living."

"She was a hostess at some fancy hotel … I forgot the name."

"It's The Blue Parrot Roadhouse. It caters to men who pay for sex."

"Johnny O'Shea, are you saying Mari worked at a house of ill repute?" I said astounded.

"That's a very polite way of describing it Vienna. I'm sorry, but Johnny's right."

"And just how is it that you and Johnny know about this place Evan? Is that why you two looked at each other so oddly in the heli when Ada told us where Mari worked? Have you both been there?"

"Don't go painting us into that picture Vienna, but word gets out, and we do have a workforce of men in our employ you know. Ada may have no idea what her sister did for a living, and maybe she was just a hostess so let's not go jumping to conclusions, okay?"

"I won't, but I'll have to go to this resort as that is the only way I can clear this up."

"Like hell you will!" Johnny exclaimed.

"What's going on in here?" Amma asked surprising us.

"Not much Amma; Vienna says she's going to a brothel and Johnny forbade her to go."

"What…that's not funny Evan." She picked Pixie up and walked to the door with her. "Did you all forget that there's a baby here and what if the girls are listening?"

"It's nothing to worry about Amma. You know how Vienna goes on."

"Thanks Evan." I said sarcastically. "Johnny, where are Mari's declaration papers?"

"I'm not sure."

"Well think…"

"Don't have a conniption fit Milady." He said fishing them out of his back pocket.

I took them from him roughly and scanned quickly. "I heard her say it, I read it in both papers, and now in the letter she wrote me…it's all there in black and white…the name Gibson. What did she mean from one Gibson woman to another…here, look."

"Why are you asking me? I have no idea what you're talking about."

"You know that's my mother's and Jannie's mother's maiden name. You know that Johnny."

"I'm not sure I do, and anyhow that doesn't mean anything Vienna. Gibson is a very popular name and that was Mari's last name so the gender doesn't fit does it because as I remember your mother and Jannie had no brothers."

"Remember Johnny, Vienna told us that her mother's maiden name was Gibson and not Lane as everyone thought because she was known as Lily Lane. I don't think I ever asked Jannie what her maiden name was. Anyhow, Vienna told us and Rainey at the bonfire the night before they left for Spain…oh dear, I shouldn't have gone there; back there when you went missing and now he's missing…"

"It's all right Amma, I'm used to all the comparisons so don't you go fretting. Let's just focus on the future and that is that I could be related to this darling little girl that I am adopting. Wouldn't that be something? I need to call Jannie as I have a lot of questions for her, and Johnny, you know I have to go to this Blue Parrot place. There might be some clue there…oh, suppose if Pixie's father is there?"

"I think you are running on empty right now so you need to give it a rest and go phone Jannie. Amma and I'll entertain Pixie. We'll talk later."

"You mean about the Blue Parrot?"

"Yes, if we must, and you know damn well that I'll take you if you're insistent upon going."

"Not without me you don't! I think a helicopter landing on the front lawn should get some answers don't you think?" Evan laughed.

"Answers to what? I think someone better tell me what's going on and what a blue parrot has to do with anything?" Amma demanded.

"Bring Pixie Honey, let's sit down and I'll explain it all." Johnny promised.

"Wish me luck with Jannie." I said as I hugged my best friends.

"The girls are upstairs unpacking Pixie's stuff but who knows how long they'll be there so let's make the calls from the library where we will have some privacy." Evan suggested.

He put the call through to Rosy. She said something must be wrong if he was calling her in the afternoon. He passed me the phone saying I would explain everything. I assured her that all was well with everyone but an unforeseen incident had happened this morning. I briefly described the unravelling of events that had taken place saying that Evan would explain in greater detail, but yes, she had heard me right. I had agreed to take Mari's daughter and raise her as my own, but where I was going to go was undecided at the moment. She asked me what I meant. I told her I loved her and passed the phone back to Evan. I heard him say to Rose as I walked out the door to take no mind to what I had said because I didn't know what I was talking about.

I found the girls in the kitchen with Mary. I asked Ada if she would come with me for a minute. She followed me into the media room. I gave her the letter that Mari had left for her. She broke into tears astonished at the monetary treasure that her sister had left her. She asked me where I thought the money came from because Mari couldn't possibly have that much. I told her I didn't know but she could be assured that I'd find out. I asked her about the Gibson name. She said it was her mother's maiden name. I told her it was my mother's too.

"How...how?" she stammered. "Could we be related remotely do you think?"

"I do, but first I need to know why Gibson is yours and Mari's last name. Why did you not go by your dad's name?"

"My name is Ada Spencer and my mom is Evelyn Spencer. Why Mari had her name legally changed to Gibson was never clear to me."

"Did your mother ever talk about her family?"

"She said she had two sisters, but along with her parents had passed on. She said she didn't have any pictures of any of them, but after she went off to the rest-home I found a photo of three little girls in the bottom of her knitting satchel. It is very old and has no names on it."

"Do you have the photo with you?"

She said it was in her overnight bag and would get it for me if I liked. I waited anxiously while she went to retrieve it.

It didn't take me but two seconds to realise that it was indeed a picture of my mother and Aunt Jannie. The third, a much younger girl must be

Ada's and Maryanne's mother Evelyn. "I know who two of these young

girls are Ada. One is my mother Lily and the other is my aunt Jannie. They would be your aunts, sisters to your mom who is the youngest here. and if it is so that would make you my niece and Pixie my great niece. My Mother lives in Arizona, but Jannie lives in London and I am going to call her right now and get this dilemma straightened out. There has to be a reason I never knew there was a third sister. I can't imagine what it could be."

"You might be my aunt?" Ada said through tears.

I hugged her and said it didn't really matter if we were blood related or not because she was already part of my family.

Evan found us sharing a box of tissues. "Well if this isn't just a fine kettle of fish. Now I've got three women all crying their eyes out. Thankfully, Amma isn't the fourth. Here, Rose wants to talk to you."

The conversation was what I expected. It ended with her saying that she was coming home because she wanted me to know what a selfish thing I had done and that my thinking of leaving Avanloch was preposterous. She wanted to meet her new niece and home is where she needed to be so she would get to Waverly and Evan would pick her up there. I asked her to wait until after I had talked with Jannie. She agreed reluctantly.

After pleasantries were exchanged I went right to the crux of the matter. "Why is it that you and Mother never told me about your sister Evelyn?"

There was silence at the end of the line for a few seconds before she responded.

"Where is this coming from Vienna?"

"It's a story that enfolded today. A young girl named Ada came to the door this morning and informed me that her sister was dying and she needed my help. The sister went by the name Marianne Gibson. I sat with her at the hospital until the angels came for her. I was totally unaware that she might be my niece. With her dying breath she asked me to care for her baby. I did not refuse. It wasn't until I was back home and read a note that Mari had left for me did it dawn on me that her last name was Gibson, just like yours and Mom's. It hadn't resonated with me at the hospital even though she had spoken it in her dying testament. Ada and her mother's last name is Spencer. Evelyn's maiden name is Gibson. For some reason Mari chose to change her name to that. Ada has a picture of three little girls. One is Lily and one is you. I'm assuming that the third and youngest is Evelyn. Am I wrong about this Jannie? Before you answer I will tell you that Evelyn is alive and right here in Scotland."

"Oh my God Vienna," she gasped. "you have just answered my prayers. I have looked for her for many a year with no results and now you are telling me that you have found her right next door?"

"I did not find her as I never knew she existed. The question is why has she been banished by you and Mother? What could possibly have happened that you both eliminated her from your lives?"

"I cannot explain it over the phone, but I will tell you that I have regretted what happened between us all my adult life. Now I must come and see my sister and beg her to forgive me. Where is she?"

"Evelyn is in a nursing home outside of Stirling. Ada and I are going there tomorrow to inform her of Mari's death. How much of it she will understand I do not know as she has dementia."

"I must come. She will know me; she just has to."

"I know this has been a shock to you so please just let me talk to her first and get a feeling of what and who she remembers. I promise I will keep you informed. It would mean a long trip for you and your health…"

She cut me off laughing a little. "My health is just fine. Do you not think I won't take advantage of McAllister's resources to get what I want, like transportation? I am going tomorrow whether you like it or not my dear girl!"

"I do like it, but you are not coming alone. Rosalyn is in London and is coming home tomorrow. As I said Ada and I will be going to Stirling, so let's have Rosalyn look after the flight plans as Evan will be with me. I need to get more info on the nursing home so will call you later with the details. I will let Rosy know of the change of plans. Are you okay with that?"

She said she was but she wouldn't have been alone as John would have accompanied her. I thought as much. I had two last questions for my aunt. I asked her when she had last seen Evelyn and what was the age difference.

"I am 8 years older so that would make her 71. She was barely sixteen when she up and went to Germany with that Nazi so that is the last time we saw her, so roughly 60 years ago. You said that her married name was Spencer…that is not the name of the man she ran away with. I will have to think of his name or maybe Lily will remember."

Sometimes Jannie's language was very colorful so I did not comment on the Nazi reference. There would be lots of time for discussion another day.

"She must have had the girls very late in life as Mari was only 25 and Ada is 20. Oh, suppose the girls were adopted?"

"That is not for me to offer an opinion on, but it would be very easy to verify don't you think?"

I agreed that it would be and left it at that. I needed to find Evan and tell him of my plans for tomorrow and hoped he'd agree. With little information I had insinuated that Mari and Ada were my nieces and Pixie my grand niece. It was yet to be proven and if I was wrong that would mean there would be no blood line, but that would be okay because I loved her even before this possibility existed. But, suppose if I had never chose to come here to Avanloch? Suppose if Ada hadn't brought Mari here? Suppose if I hadn't been home…oh dear, I'd better go find Evan.

He was all alone relaxing on the sofa with his feet up on the hassock. His eyes were closed. I sat down beside him and asked if he was sleeping. He said he was. I moved closer and leaned my head on his shoulder.

"So Milady, it is not all good news?"

"It's not bad news, but you may not like or agree with my plans for tomorrow. It appears that Evelyn is Jannie's long-lost sister. She did not elaborate on what happened sixty years ago. She does want to come to

Stirling tomorrow, in fact she insisted that she was coming. Rosalyn is feeling left out of everything so I suggested that the two of them could come together and meet us all there. It's no problem for Rosy to acquire transportation because you can't pick them up because you will be with me." I sat up and waited uneasily for his reaction.

"So you think I would rather be with you than my wife?"

"Don't be daft. It just seemed like a better fit to have them meet us there. It doesn't have to be though as Ada and I can drive to Sterling and you can fly to London and pick them up. We can put our plans on hold to visit the Blue Parrot. I'm sure Johnny will insist on driving us."

"The original plan was for the three of us to fly to Stirling. You and Ada would visit with her mother and Johnny and I would go to the Blue Parrot, right?"

"Now you're just being silly. You know damn well you're not going there without me! The only change is that I am buying Ada a car, and Rosy is coming with us to the resort and then we will fly home and you and your Rose can spend a few days alone together away from all the madnesses. I suggest you make plans to go somewhere besides here."

"Can I have that in writing?"

"What?"

"That there's a place in our lives where madness doesn't exist."

"I should have said senseless foolishness."

"A little more to my liking. The heli is fueled and ready for take-off."

I gave him a hug and went to find my new daughter. She was sitting on the floor with the girls in the family room amongst a mountain of vintage toys.

The next morning I hugged Amma and Pixie and promised to be back by dinner. Amma had designated herself as Pixie's Godmother. She said Evan and Johnny could argue over which one could be her Godfather. I suggested that they could be co-Godfathers. Ada and I joined Johnny and Evan at the hangar. It was 8 a.m. Johnny held the passenger door open. "I'll ride with you Ada as Vienna likes to ride shotgun."

"You're the co-pilot Johnny, so I'll ride with Ada." I disagreed.

"Are you two arguing already? Well, I'll settle it; Ada you're with me." Evan stated.

"Oh no, Mr. Evan, it's not my place."

"Nonsense and there is no mister in my name, remember?"

"He prefers Laird anyhow." Johnny teased winking at me. I nodded.

"I suppose you think you've pulled one over on me don't you?"

"Don't know what you're talking about Boss, do you Vienna?" Johnny answered.

"No I don't. Enjoy the view Ada."

Evan had found an air strip that catered to small aircraft five kilometers from Aberdeen, the care home that Evelyn was in. We would land and hopefully the rental car would be waiting for us. All I knew was that Rosy had made the plans for her and Jannie and would meet us there about ten.

I thought I had prepared myself for meeting my aunt. I expected to see a frail, helpless, unresponsive woman. Obviously she had been informed that Ada was coming because she was waiting at the front entrance with a care giver for us. Her joy at seeing her daughter was obvious. She was in a wheelchair but stood up when Ada burst into tears. I guess I reacted to her standing and suggested that they sit on the sofa. The nurse smiled and left saying she would give us some privacy.

"What…oh you think I need that chair?" Evelyn directed her question towards me. "It's just for show as I don't want them knowing how strong I am getting. Now, I fear something has upset you Ada as this is not like you to be weeping so. Now, what has happened? Tell me it's not Darlana?"

"No Mama, it's Mari…she's gone."

"I know, I know my darling. Let these be tears of relief then for she is liberated from the fetters that held her captive. She is flying now."

I backed off watching mother rocking her daughter in her arms. This was not a woman with dementia. What had gone wrong with her diagnosis?

Ada managed to ask her mother how she knew. "Did Doctor Shelia call you?"

"No, Marianne called me two days ago. You were outside packing the car. She said that she was on her way to heaven, but before she went she had to look after Darlana and she was going to the castle where miracles happened to do just that. She said not to be in any hurry but she would see me on cloud nine. She told me she loved me and that all was right. She said her angels were waiting for her so she must go as she didn't want to be late for the launch."

I tried to restrain myself from an emotional outburst but I was not successful.

"Isn't it time that you introduce me to your friend Ada?" She beckoned me to join them. "I hardly need an introduction though as I know her as Lady Vela McAllister of Avanloch. It has been many years since the fete at the Fairy Bridge but I never forget a face and surely not one as lovely as yours. I am puzzled though as another image keeps appearing in my vision. Am I wrong; have we crossed paths more recently? Come, come sit with us."

Ada began rambling on about how they came to be going to the castle and discovering we had the same name and Darlana was back at the castle with Amma and was now Pixie and I was her auntie and…

"Slow down child. Take a breather and let Lady McAllister tell the story."

"Thankyou Mrs. Spenser. I will explain everything in a minute, but first I must ask you a question. Is Gibson your maiden name, and did you have two sisters?"

I was afraid that I had shocked her into aphasia. She was definitely startled, but not to the point of being alarmed. Ada asked her if she was all right.

"Two days ago I was informed that I had been misdiagnosed. My forgetfulness, inability to make decisions, and lack of verbal comment was not dementia. It was of my own doing. I had put myself into that state because I was unable to cope with Maryanne's cancer. I had dealt with trauma when Wilf was ill because I had no choice and I had two girls to care for, but I couldn't do it again, so I just dropped out. A week ago I decided to open my eyes and my heart as Ada and Darlana were going to need me, and now you stand before me My Lady and I know why I feel I know you. Sixty years ago I left my family and the country. The details are not important right now, but yes, I did have two sisters whom I am sure are long gone and I had a mother, a beautiful mother. I thought my eyes were playing tricks on me when I first saw you because you are the living reflection of her. How is that My Lady?"

I took her hand. "I have been told many times throughout the years by my mother Lily and Aunt Jannie that my likeness to my grandmother Fannita is astounding. I have also been told that I look exactly like my grandmother on my father's side so I guess it is all in the eyes of the beholder. I did not know either as they both passed away before I was born. If Lily and Jannie are your sisters and Fannita was your mother that would mean that you are my aunt and Ada is my niece and Mari's daughter, the little pixie that I am adopting is my great niece. I came to live with Jannie in 1962 when I was eighteen and married Lord Jeremy McAllister. We had no children as our marriage was only one of convenience. I adopted his daughter Rosalyn and she is now the rightful lady of Avanloch. I have not been Lady McAllister for many years. My husband Rainey Quinn and I moved back to Canada in1984. It is an outright shame that I was never told about you. If you were living in Melton all those years that I was at Avanloch…"

She patted my hand. "You must not fret my dear. It was a much different life back in the forties. No one approved of the life I choose so I guess one might say I exiled myself to Germany, so I wasn't even here. I did not return to Scotland until I was in my forties with my new husband. Chances are we would never have met. I was childless, but a miracle happened when I was 46 and Maryanne was born and four years later Adelaine came along. You would have been long moved on by then."

"Mari wrote me a letter and she mentions meeting me so I must have been at Avanloch. We can take up that gauntlet another day because Jannie will be here any minute…"

"What, she's still alive? I think I'm going to pass out."

I assured her that she wouldn't and told her Lily was still alive also. We heard her before we saw her. My normally sedate aunt burst into the room.

"Where is she, where is my sister…oh, is this really you my little Evaney?" Jannie gushed as she rushed to Evelyn's side. She kneeled down and took her hand and held it to her face. "Where have you been…where have you been?"

My newly discovered aunt patted my forever aunt's head. "Apparently, I haven't been very far Janey, and Vienna tells me that Laney is still of this world. Come sit with me and tell me everything."

I brushed the remaining tears from eyes and realised that Evelyn did have moments of confusion as she had referred to her sisters as Janey and Laney. I voiced this to Rosalyn. She said that she had heard Uncle John call Jannie Jane before.

"In all my years I have never heard him call her Jane." I replied rather harshly. "Where is Uncle John anyhow?"

"He's outside. He thought it best if he gave Jannie a few minutes alone with her sister. He said he'd wait for the all-clear."

"You mean after all the crying? Evan will be here soon so come along and I will introduce you to Evelyn."

"Jannie called her Evaney didn't she?"

"I think so. Maybe it was just a pet name or else she truly is confused. I have to admit that I am a little confused myself Rosy. Look at them holding hands and chatting and laughing as if this was yesterday sixty years ago."

I placed my hand on Jannie's shoulder and apologised for interrupting.

"There is no need for apology my dear. Rosalyn, come say hello to Evy."

Oh dear, another name. I gave them time to get acquainted before I spoke. "We must make our excuses now as Evan will be here to take us to an appointment but hopefully we'll back in a few hours. I imagine you will still be here?"

"Not if I can convince Evy to come home with me we won't." Aunt Jannie said.

"Oh, that sounds like a wonderful idea." I exclaimed dubiously. "What do you think Ada?"

"I am all for it. Mom still needs some nursing aide and Janey said she can supply it so that will give Mom the chance to decide what she wants to do when her health is better."

I was silently wondering what Uncle John would say. "And, what do you say Evelyn?"

"You may as well call me Evy my dear. You have graciously taken Ada and my granddaughter into your fold so we will be forever joined. But, back to your question. I cannot see how I could refuse such an offer and it is a tempting one, but there is the matter of Janey's husband John. and I understand that the house belongs to his son and fiancé. I fear I would be intruding on all their lives and I would be many miles away from Ada and Darlana."

"I can attest that you will not be in anyone's way. The house is a seventeenth century mansion and has rooms that have hardly been used; much like Avanloch Castle. I am sure there will be rooms just for you and you will be much welcomed. Rosy's husband is a pilot and has his own helicopter and the company plane is his to command so travel will never be a problem. I will let Rosy weigh in on this, but first I must ask you why you call Jannie, Janey?"

My aunt's both twittered. "You're the oldest Janey so you tell her." Evelyn said.

"Our mother, Fannie, God bless her soul, had this thing for double n's and there were two in her name so we were all named accordingly. Evy was Evannie, your mother was Lannie and I was Jannie. Evy says she became Evelyn when she returned to Scotland. Your mother changed hers legally to Lily Lane when she was still a teenager working in the cannery at Bristol. I never had mine altered so have always been Jannie. Evy always called me Janey so if it isn't too much trouble I'd like to be just Jane again."

I laughed and hugged her. "It might take a little while but I can definitely call you Jane. Who would I be to object? I was once known as V and then Vela and Lady this or that and now, just Vienna. I hope you will be calling Lily later?"

"Oh, you can count on that. There's Evan, and that rascal Johnny. Bring them over here to meet Evy."

The guys welcomed Evy into the family. Evan apologised saying we had to borrow Ada for a bit. He handed her the car keys.

"Come along girl; we need a ride to the hanger."

"Why are you handing me the keys? Oh, you need me to return the car to the rental agency after I drop you off?"

"Sure, something like that."

"Be safe my loves. I have a feeling that you are all up to no good." Jane said throwing us kisses. "And you know Vienna that Rainey is always in my thoughts and prayers don't you?"

I nodded tearfully. Johnny took my arm and escorted me out.

We left an astonished Ada at the airfield. She stammered that she couldn't accept such a gift as a new car. I told her that of course she could as she needed one to get around and how else did she expect to visit Pixie and all of us. She accepted tearfully and we set off for the Blue Parrot.

Chapter 6

The Blue Parrot

It was a short trip to the Blue Parrot. Evan circled the lodge several times before he put the copter down on a paved parking lot at the back of what I assumed was the rear entrance to the building. He turned to Rosy and me.

"Now there's a possibility that I may be recognised by one of the guards as I have been here before."

"What are you saying Evan?"

"Not what you're thinking Vienna. I was here a year or so ago with Dr. Shelia to attend a guest who had suffered a heart attack on the golf greens. I was at no time inside the building as Shelia handled all that."

"Why would Mom be thinking anything else Evan?" My daughter asked.

"Do you want to fill her in Vienna?"

"I can't believe you've left this up to me." I answered grumbly.

"When would I have had time to tell her?"

"Maybe when you told her about Pixie would have been a good time don't you think?"

"Ah guys, we're being approached by two burly armed fellows holstering guns." Johnny warned.

Evan opened his door and asked the two men if he could alight. One of the men asked him to state his business. He said it was regarding one of the lodge's employees and it was a highly personal and delicate matter and we would like to talk to the manager. No, we did not have an appointment. He stated his and Johnny's name and that he was here on behalf of Lady Rosalyn and Lady Vienna of Avanloch Castle. He did not refer to himself as Laird. He said they were not armed. I knew that was a lie as he had a secure undetectable hideaway amongst his first aid equipment. I had a chuckle to myself thinking that he and Johnny could take these two hands down if push came to shove. I'd be more confident if Jack was here. Rainey never entered the picture. After a brief conversation with someone on the other side of the walky-talky we were granted admittance to the main office.

I patted Rosy's hand. "Keep your cool Sweetie as we are about to enter a house that caters to the perversions of rich dirty ole men and not so old ones too."

Evan helped her down blaming me for the venture.

"These last two days are the most bizarre days of my life. First my sixty-year old mother adopts a child, then I find out that Aunt Jannie has a whole other family that actually has a connection to the child and now here I am standing in front of a house of ill repute."

Johnny laughed. "And this from a woman who has lived all her life in a haunted castle!"

I reminded her that I was not quite sixty yet and I thought my birthdate was out by five or six years.

We were escorted to the welcome desk. Evan introduced Rosy and I as royalty, stepped back and said, "You're up Milady."

The girl behind the counter was trembling saying she didn't know how to address us. She couldn't have been more then twenty. Her name tag read Cindy so I addressed her as such saying that I was Vienna and that Rosalyn was my daughter, and we were here for no other reason then to inquire about a former employee who had passed away. "Perhaps you knew her. Her name is Marianne Gibson."

Cindy was alarmed. "No, no she isn't dead. She just went home to care for her mother."

"I'm so sorry to be the bearer of such sad news. Perhaps it's best if you call your supervisor."

She broke into tears. "Mari *is* my supervisor!"

One of the guards who had met us had taken a position at the door rushed over and asked her what was wrong and glared at us. She told him what I had said. His body language registered concern. He told us to take a seat, took Cindy's hand and walked across the room to a double door and knocked.

"It's Frank Ma'am, sorry to bother you but there's been an incident and Mr. Marquie is not back."

"Come in Frank." The voice behind the door beckoned. "Cindy… what's wrong?"

"She said she's dead, but she's not, she's not, tell me she's not." Cindy wailed.

"Frank, what is she carrying on about?"

"Marianne Ma'am; there's a group of people who arrived by helicopter with news regarding Marianne and it isn't good. They are waiting in the lobby for you. I believe they are royalty Ma'am."

"Take Cindy to the parlor and send Beverly to me and for God's sake show the visitors in!"

She met us halfway across the room. She was a tall dark woman attired in navy blue garb from top to bottom. Streaks of red seemed out of place filtering through her short black hair. Her scarlet lipstick was a perfect match. She wore no jewelry except for a silver medallion around her neck. Perhaps it was a medal as her gait and posture reminded me of an army drill sergeant. Her voice was soft though, not like the one we had heard through the doors, and apologetic. Her nametag read Marguerita and that is how she introduced herself, no last name. She said we could call her Rita. She asked who was in charge.

Evan extended his hand and she took it saying she felt that they had met before.

"Yes, very briefly a year or so ago. I flew Dr. Shelia to this establishment to attend to one of your guests who'd suffered a heart attack on the golf course. You came out and thanked us."

She smiled. "I never forget a face as charming as yours. Sadly. Mr. Hedly did not survive, but your swift response enabled the family to spend a few hours with him. Now what is this news regarding our Marianna? I'm sensing it is not good Sir. I'm sorry that I don't recall your name."

"Evan Govern Ms. Rita; my co-pilot Johnny O'Shea and the ladies of Avanloch, Lady Rosalyn and Lady Vienna, who is the reason we are here."

"Ah, the royalty."

"We are not of royal blood Marguerita, but I will add that Evan is too modest to refer to himself as Liard of Avanloch but he and my daughter Rosalyn are the Lord and Lady of Avanloch Castle. She, being the daughter of Lord Jeremy McAllister is the only one who can rightfully claim lady status. However, that has nothing to do with why we have come to The Blue Parrot. It is apparent that you have not been notified of Marianne's passing. We had never met before but her sister Ada brought her to me as it was Mari's last wish and that was that she wanted me to care for her daughter because she was dying. We did manage to get her to the hospital thanks to Evan and Johnny. She lived long enough to sign an affidavit that saw me take legal guardianship of her daughter until adoption papers are completed. This all took place just yesterday. It is a complicated series of events. The sole reason we are here is to find out if there is a father of her child in the picture that you or any of the staff may know about."

"I thank you for your straightforwardness Lady Vienna. I am not privy to any such information regarding parentage as I had no such knowledge of her pregnancy. She left here six months or more…let me bring her information up. My mistake it was December 12th, 2002. The reason for her leave of absence was to care for her ailing mother. I have had no further contact with her, but it is not a dead end as she was very popular with the rest of the staff and surely one of them will have further insight into her private life. There will be many tears shed over her sudden passing. May I ask what the circumstances of her death were?"

"It is not a secret, she had stage four cervical cancer."

Marguerette was visibly shaken. "How… how would that have gone unnoticed? Surely, it takes longer than twelve months to get to that point. How would we not be aware of such a condition?"

"I have no knowledge of the symptoms or the duration of such a condition to comment on it. We are only here hoping to shed some light on the father of her child who is now my child."

"I am sorry Lady Vienna that I can not. I will tell you that she was a valued member of our staff and was respected by all. Cindy, whom you have already met was her protégé so perhaps she will have some insight into Marianna's private life. However she does appear to be deeply affected by this news of her death so I will summon another employee whom I believe will have the information you are seeking. I must attend to another matter so will leave you in the hands of Pangea, my trusted right hand. Please enjoy the refreshments I have ordered Beverly to deliver for your leisure. I hope Pangea will have the information you are seeking and I trust that you will relay my personal condolences to the family."

She got up, shook all our hands and wished us luck and exited through a red door behind us. Coffee and tea and pastries arrived a few minutes before Pangea. She was a beautiful dark- skinned woman somewhere in her mid thirties I guessed. She had a melodious and soothing voice and made us feel comfortable as she expressed her sympathies and apologised for her tardiness but it had been a great shock to learn of Mari's passing so had stopped to get a brief synopsis from Margarette. Apparently she and Mari were close. She had even accompanied her several times to the care home where her mother Evelyn resided. Mari was always saddened for days afterwards, but it never interfered with her work ethics. She went on and on singing her praises never actually saying what Mari's job actually was. I figured enough was enough and it was time to get to the crux of the matter.

I boldly interrupted her. "Thankyou Pangea for providing us with a lovely picture of Mari as she only came into our lives on the day she was to die. I am not sure if Margaretta relayed the circumstances sufficiently to you, but we are only here for one reason and that is to know if you have any knowledge as to whom the father of her child might be. It is of no consequence to what her occupation was which I have assumed was in the capacity of Hostess, but perhaps I am wrong as it's no secret that the Blue Parrot caters to men. So, if you were such good friends you should know if Mari had a special relationship with one certain individual wouldn't you? Perhaps she had a boyfriend that she met up with on her days off?"

Pangea's friendly and compassionate attitude suddenly changed to one of anger and defiance.

"Mari was not one of *the* girls! She did not have a male companion of any sort. She didn't even like men so there is no way she could have been pregnant. She would have told me if she had been defiled as we had a special relationship. She must have brought someone else's baby home and claimed it as hers. Yes, that must have been what happened."

Not wanting to ruffle her feathers anymore I decided to try another avenue. "Thankyou for your candor Pangea. Had you and Mari ever talked about your future, say away from here and maybe even having a family? Was it possible that she may have undergone artificial insemination?"

I think Rosy gasped at my insinuation.

Pangea shook her head. "Never. We were going to leave here as soon as we had saved enough money, but then she got sick and went home. No one else here knew she was ill. She quit answering my calls soon afterwards. I did not know where she lived and the facility where her mother was would not give me that information and the address that was listed here was fake so for over a year I have had no word from her and have been deeply worried and now you say she has died ... I cannot fathom any of this and this story that she had a baby does not jive. I think you may have been duped." She bowed to me and said she had nothing more to say and walked out.

"Well, that's that then." Johnny stated as he helped me up. "It's time to vacate this so-called retreat. May I escort you to your carriage Milady?"

"With pleasure." I answered.

We exited through the same door that we had been escorted through. We saw no one and none of us spoke until we were all settled into the heli. Rosalyn broke the silence.

"That was a joke right? Where do we go from here Mom?"

"Nowhere Dear, I am satisfied that there is no father who will ever come forward to claim Pixie as his."

"What will you tell her when she is old enough to ask about her father?"

"How about he died in a car accident in Italy?" Johnny volunteered flippantly.

Rose laughed. "You know that was Mom's story regarding Rainey don't you?"

"I do, and it worked didn't it?"

"Everyone thought it was true, but Ava and I knew different."

"There will be no story because I will raise her as Rainey's child. Subject closed." I asserted.

Evan turned around and gave me the thumbs up and winked. "That's my girl."

Chapter 7

Pixie

Iawoke to find Pixie sitting up in her crib talking to the little rag doll that she had taken to bed with her. How I wished that Rainey was here to see her. There had been no more babies for us after the twins were born. He had not been present when Ava or Liliana had been born so finally he was going to be with me at the twins' birth, but where was I … alone in the operating room due to a placenta abruption. I could not give him another child and yet I felt I owed him one for reasons that didn't even make sense and now here was Pixie, but he wasn't here again and may never be. Today was her first birthday and we would be celebrating it with my Avanloch family who had all fallen in love with her just as I had. I picked her up and sat her down beside me. We chatted for a while in her language making plans for the day. I reached for the picture of Rainey that I kept on my night table and introduced her to him. I told her all about him and that she was going to help heal the hole in my heart that got bigger and bigger every day I was without him.

Thankfully Rosalyn hadn't passed all of Collene's and Beth's baby clothes on. She had kept a dozen or so sleepers and dresses and had given them to the girls to dress their dolls in. They had taken very good care of them and now years later they had been resurrected again and happily given them to Pixie so I would have something nice to dress her in for her birthday.

She had been with us for seven days now. I was going to be sixty in a month so what was I doing raising another child I asked myself. With Rainey gone I couldn't imagine how I could do it without my Avanloch family. Amma and Johnny were close to my age, Evan was fifty-six, Mary was eighty-seven and Rosalyn was the baby at forty-four. Colleen and Beth would both be off to university soon which meant that Pixie would be raised in a house full of people who were old enough to be her grandparents or great grandparents. My children were all grown up. Zander and Novia were the youngest, having just had their twentieth birthdays a few weeks ago. We'd had a little celebration for Zander here and I had had a tearfully long phone call with Novia. Thankfully, she wasn't alone as Sammie, Ava's son, and my grandson, was with her. Novia was the quiet and shyest one in the family. I would have worried more about her going to college had it not been for Sammie.

I had planned on going into Waverly to shop for the party and buy Pixie a new wardrobe, but Rosy had taken that out of my hands as she was coming home for the celebration and was doing all of the shopping. She'd only spent one night with us after our visit to the Blue Parrot as she had wanted to meet the new addition to the family. It was love at first sight just as it had been with all of us. She promised that she would be home for the whole weekend. She had abandoned all other aspects of the intended takeover of McAllister Enterprises since Chandler had returned to the company. Her focus now was dealing with the shareholders and convincing them that McAllister was still in full control. She hadn't said precisely what that number was, but in my day, it had been in the thousands and that was twenty-five years ago. More and more people were investing their monies in what they thought were sure things. I couldn't even fathom what that number would be now. Her absence was not one that I could fill entirely, but I was more than happy to be a substitute mother to the girls and a confidant to Evan. I worried more about his emotional health than I did about hers. He had said to me at the end of one of our midnight sessions that sometimes he wished they had never moved to Avanloch. Even though he hated city life he'd at least see his Rose every night.

Pixie called Mary, Amma and me Mama. I supposed that all women were Mama to her and yet she had called Ada something like Aia. We'd have to work on names for everyone else. I didn't want her calling Evan Daddy but maybe she would call him Dad like Colleen and Beth did. It would take some time so there was no need to fret.

After our bath I dressed Pixie in a blue gingham for the day and left the fancy pink dress for the party. Pink had never been my favorite color. Rainey had bought me a pink Banlon sweater set when I had spent the weekend with him in 1960. I told him I loved it and wore it, but I think he could tell I didn't. He never bought me anything pink ever again that I remembered. I suppose Ava and Rosy had pink outfits as most girls do.

While I was having my own meager breakfast which consisted of coffee, a glass of orange dress and a slice of toast with marmalade I helped Pixie with her breakfast of apple juice and a bowl of Amma's special hot cereal with milk and mashed bananas. She did not get along with a spoon and threw it to the floor. Just because she could handle a sippy cup didn't mean that she could handle silverware. I fed her the cereal as I usually did, and she made grimacing faces which she usually did. She did not have her milk in a bottle and was well on her way to being toilet trained. I could see Mari spending hours and hours with her, and it saddened me that her life had been cut short. I vowed to raise her daughter just as she would have.

I picked Pixie up from her highchair, poured myself another cup of coffee and walked with her to the playroom. I heard the telephone ringing but ignored it. Unfortunately, Amma didn't. She handed me the portable saying I had a call. I sighed and answered. It was Hawk.

After pleasantries were exchanged, he asked me if there was any chance that I may be in London on the weekend of the twenty eighth. I asked him if he had spoken to Johnny lately. He said that his cousin was his next call, I told Hawk how things had changed and made the circumstances of Pixie's arrival as brief as I could. I told him that she was my priority and that there would be no socializing for me for a while and to have a good holiday and thanked him for the invitation. He was still talking when I disengaged. I figured Johnny would give him a detailed account of the events not that I cared one way or the other.

I heard Evan talking and went to the door to ask him when he was going to pick Rosy up. I felt her as she brushed past me. "Where do you think you're going young lady?"

She ignored me and continued wobbling down the hallway until she reached the parlor door.

Evan beat me to her, scooped her up and said, "I think we've got a runner here Mum."

The celebration began at five p.m. Colleen and Beth had blown up three dozen balloons and strewn red and green streamers that were left over from Christmas all around the family room as soon as they had arrived home from school. Pixie had watched with wide open eyes as the balloons danced around the room. Rosy insisted that Pixie wear one of the new outfits that she had bought along with things that were needed for a one-year-old plus gifts for us all to give to her. Amma had made a delicious pot roast dinner for the adults and a special one for Pixie that consisted of pureed potatoes and rutabagas and apple sauce. None of it was digested by her but she did manage to spray me with samples of everything. I mashed a bit of the three-layer vanilla cake which had strawberry filling that I had made with milk and a tiny amount of ice cream and gave her a spoonful. She didn't spit it out, so that and a cup of milk we called it supper.

Aunt Jane and Grandmother Evelyn phoned to wish our little girl loving wishes. Ev had indeed gone to live with her sister and family. Just for awhile she said. Everything seemed to be going just fine. My mother said she would come over to the Isle in the summer. I was pretty sure she wouldn't.

The gates at the tops and bottoms of the stairways had been put in place once more and we soon learned to keep all the doors shut on both floors as Pixie was very inquisitive. As soon as I'd open the bedroom door she'd be out toddling along down the hall as fast as she could go, falling down half a dozen times. Sometimes she'd look to see if I was coming. She loved to ride in the lift and push the button for up or down. I had Johnny make a cover for the roof floor button that she was unable to operate because we had entered up there more than once.

March and April were the months of rebirth at the farm, so we spent many an hour there. Evan or Johhny would accompany us opening gates and lifting Pixie up to pet the horses or the llamas who were a new addition last year. Of course, there were baby bunnies and kittens. Aunt Becky as Beth had so named her, was the gentle mother hen and she would let us peek under her to see her baby chicks. It was hard to draw Pixie away from them. Letting her pick up an egg from a nest and place it in my basket usually did the trick even if it cost us an egg now and then.

Hawk called again and again I said no to a dinner and show in London, He said he'd keep trying. It was harder for me to say no to Chandler's invitation to the opera in Edinburgh, mostly because I wanted to see Carmen, but maybe I wanted to see him too and I didn't like that.

May was bursting at the seams with spring vegetation. Tulips and daffodils were popping up everywhere. The roses were budding, and the meadows were alive with wildflowers. Most significantly, the pathways had dried. I felt that it was safe for me to take Pixie down to the ponds. I'd had qualms about putting Pixie in the little cart that Butch had made for her remembering how Ava had fallen out of the one Rosy was pulling. This cart was a lot sturdier, so one sunny day we ventured out on our own without incident. The pools were teeming with fish and waterfowl. We fed grain to the ducks and a few scraps to the two geese that showed up. Pixie's amazement was a wonder to behold. I was sure that this outing would be on our weekly calendar as I enjoyed it just as much as she had.

Suddenly, it was June. I have been at Avanloch for seven months now.

Duffy took a turn for the worse and passed away June 11th. He hadn't wanted a funeral but of course we had a celebration of his life and laid him to rest in the family sepulcher.

There was still nothing new about Rainey's abduction. Though it was still an active case I feared it would soon be a dead one. I kept my fears to myself.

Chapter 8

The Proposition

Ioffered to take Amma into Waverly for her dentist appointment on June 23rd because Johnny was busy haying. Rosalyn was home and was delighted that she'd have some alone time with the little angel who called her Mammy. She had only been with us for four months but everyday she had learned a new name or word to our amazement.

I did a little shopping until it was time to pick Amma up. We decided to have lunch at a new café that had just opened. It was operated by two former female employees of Avanloch, Jeanette and Caron. They greeted us warmly.

"Lady Vienna, I can't believe it's you. It's been many a year."

"That it has been Jeanette. I'm pleased to see that you are still in Scotland."

"I can't believe that you remember us! We did go back to Ireland where we met our husbands who now have jobs here in Waverly. Our children are all grown and off on their own so here we are too."

I hugged them and said I had never forget any of my staff and especially the two mischievous Irish lasses. They greeted Amma calling her Ms. O'Shea and asked how Johnny and the girls were. Caron turned ack to me with a tear in her eye saying she was so sorry to hear of Lord Quinn's abduction and that they were praying for his safe return.

I thanked her and said the first thing he'd say to her when he came home was, "It's Rainey; none of this Lord business you hear!" You must come out and see us at the castle. It's always open for you."

Jeanette seated us at a table near an open door that led out to the patio and brought us iced tea and the menu saying that lunch was complimentary. I thanked her with a smile. A few minutes later a young man came by, stooped over at our table and picked something up and handed it to me.

"I believe this fell out of your bag Ma'am." He said and moved on.

I thanked him as I took it. I was sure that I hadn't dropped anything and told Amma so. She asked what it was. I unfolded the piece of paper to a printed black print note.

Lady Vienna do not acknowledge me to your dining partner. I know who killed Walt Oshea. The reward money and I tell you. I will wait two minutes on the bench across the road from the patio and no longer.

I didn't bat an eyelash. "Amma, don't react to what I am going to do, just order me the spinach wrap and I will explain later." I got up walked outside and crossed the road. He looked like a decent enough young man. I deemed he was in his mid twenties. I sat down on the bench a foot or so away from him.

"It is not me who is offering the reward but I will gladly double it if your information is believable so out with it."

"His name is Arthurus Carr alias Alec Carruthers who was once employed at your estate and I know where he can be found."

The name sounded vaguely familiar. "Why are you coming to me with this information and not calling the number on the wanted poster?"

"Because I don't trust that I will not be implicated. I have a record, but I'm straight now and I want to go to Canada and make a new start but I need money to do so. I don't even have enough for bus fare or food so am appealing to your known generosity to see me through the night so I can get you his whereabouts. I know you are a fair and honest lady but I did not know how to reach you without being arrested and I had not made up my mind whether I would rat on my mate or not and then I heard your name as you came in the café and I took my chances."

"How do you know anything about me?"

"A man told me you did him a favor a very long time ago."

"Does this man have a name?"

"Samson."

I took a deep breath. "How do you know him? As far as I know he is still in jail."

"Yes Ma'am."

He needn't say anymore. "All right, how do you want to proceed with this?"

"This has to stay between you and me, understand? I do not want the rozzers involved or anyone else. If you agree to this I will make the arrangements to meet with him and then I will call you."

"And then, what?"

"I get the reward and you get Arty."

"So, you expect me to just hand fifty grand off to a stranger and one that admits he's a felon no less? You're a little naïve don't you think?"

"This is taking too long. Are you in or not?"

"You haven't even told me your name?"

"It's Willie Wallace."

I wanted to laugh out loud but kept it inside. "All right Willie Wallace, I'll bite. Do you have a cell phone…no, okay you can call me from a public phone booth. I need a lot more information before I commit to what may be trickery. In good faith I will spot you a few quid but I don't carry cash so I will have to see if my companion has any to spare so I will have to cross the street." I waited for him to object but he told me to be quick.

I told Amma I would explain all in a minute but I needed whatever she had for cash as it was very important. She passed me five twenty brown pound notes and two red fifties from her pocketbook. I couldn't help but notice that she had a few other bills in a little see through envelope. I asked her what they were. I was curious as I could see a castle on one. She closed her purse and said she'd tell me when I told her what was going on with that young man.

Willie thanked me and said he'd talk to me sometime tomorrow. I gave him my cell number but suspected that I'd never hear from him again. I rejoined Amma. She waited until I'd ate most of my lunch before she pressed me for details. I replied with "He says he knows who killed Uncle Walt."

She gasped almost choking on her tea. "What?"

I told her most of the conversation except I left the names of the people involved out. I was pretty sure of what she would say and I wasn't wrong.

"Johnny will be so happy. I can't imagine what he'll say, can you?"

"He'll say nothing because we are not going to tell him."

"Don't be silly; of course we are."

"It is not a done deal Amma so why would we get his hopes up until after he calls tomorrow and suppose if he doesn't then it would all be for naught."

"I can't keep this from him Vienna."

"What are you going to tell him? You don't even know the name of the informant or the suspect or anything else do you?"

"No I don't but Johnny will get it out of you."

"Maybe I have nothing to tell."

"And Maybe I took a picture of you and this stranger." She said baiting me.

"Amma O'Shea, are you calling my bluff?" I asked amusedly.

"Maybe I am. How about if we make a pact…I won't tell Johnny if you tell me?"

"It will be a long and uncomfortable trip home if I don't share with you so I will, but I am hesitant to do so because I know you have a hard time keeping a secret."

"Let's not call it a secret as it's just unproven information isn't it?"

I reiterated the whole conversation with her. She smirked at the name Willie Wallace, did not react to the Carruthers name, but the mention of the name Samson was another thing.

"I never thought I'd hear that name again. He's dead to Johnny you know. I haven't heard his name for thirty years ever since he was convicted of manslaughter. You were on the threshold of moving to Canada when it all happened. I don't ever remember talking about it with you so why did you feel it was your job to look after the family of the bank guard that he shot?"

"It wasn't my job to do so Amma but Johnny was so distraught that his uncle had taken away the victim's family livelihood and I could help and I did in the only way I could and that was financially. I really didn't pay much attention to the ordeal as I was to busy making the final arrangements for our trip back to Bridge Falls. However, Rainey followed the whole legal proceedings and he believed that Samson took the fall for his accomplice. I know no more but it was Rainey's suggestion that we see that the family was looked after. He sought Uncle John's expertise and it was done. Johnny acknowledged the gesture and so did Samson."

"What did Samson do?"

"I think he sent a note. It may have been during one of my convalescing periods from one of the surgeries so I really don't remember. It's all a blur to me so if you want to know more you'll just have to ask Rainey when he gets home. For now Samson's name is unmentionable all right? Now weren't you going to tell me about those bills in your purse?"

Tears were in Amma's eyes when I mentioned Rainey. She opened her purse, removed them from their envelope that was dated 1987, and laid them on the table. "Yes, you were long gone back to Canada when they were issued. Here, have a look; they are the castle series and are out of print and probably no longer legal tender."

Invermere Castle was depicted on the back of the 50 lb. note, Balmoral on the 100lb, and Edinburgh on the one dollar. She said more castles were featured but printing was halted before it was Avanloch's time. She had a whole set that she had kept for me but had forgotten about them until she had found them a few days ago in an old trunk. She had popped these few in her purse for luck.

"I guess it worked because we may have found Walt's murderer." I conceded.

The girls had asked us to bring Matzo's You Bake Pizza home for dinner so we made the stop after we left Two Irish Gals Café. Their signature dessert was cheesecake and luckily they generously let us purchase a Key Lime, a blackberry and a chocolate one. I chuckled that they were the perfect confections to serve after pizza. All that had to be done for dinner was turn the oven on. Over the meal Rosalyn relayed Pixie's escapades and Colleen and Beth informed us of their summer plans. Johnny and Evan's day was humdrum. We were asked about our day. Amma got up to get the coffee. I recapped my shopping excursion and our lovely lunch and visit with Caron and Jeanette. Johnny asked his wife how her dentist appointment went.

"Great, no cavities or issues. Vienna knows who killed Uncle Walt."

I covered my face with my hands but was smiling underneath. Everyone was staring at me but only one had a question.

"What the hell have you done Vienna?" Johhny roared.

"Don't you dare use that demanding tone of voice with her! She's my best friend in the whole wide world and has been before the dawn of time, even before you! She would do anything for you Johnny O'Shea and you know it. She offered to double the reward money to this complete stranger when she went off to meet with him just in case he really did have information on *your* uncle's murder so put that in your pipe and smoke it!"

You could have heard a feather drop. This was not the Amma we all knew and loved. She came over with the coffee pot in her hands. "I'm sorry Vienna, you were right, you should never have told me. Oh, I hope I haven't woken Pixie."

"Colleen and I will go check on her." Beth offered. "You coming Zander?"

"Do you need me to stay Mom?"

"No, of course not. Give Pixie a kiss for me. I'll talk to you later." I waited until they were out of earshot. "I don't want any coffee thankyou Amma, but I would like a drop or two of Johnny's best whiskey." I winked at him.

He was still stunned from his wife's uncharacteristic blowup but got up and took the bottle down from the top cupboard. "Anyone else?" He asked. Mary nodded and Evan said he could use a shot. He passed them all out and handed me my glass touching my hand.

"I'm not sure who I should apologise to first, you or my wife."

"Not me." Amma stated.

"I am not offended. It was so unexpected and you all know how impulsive I am. If Rainey was here he'd rake me over the coals before letting me explain so I see you as just filling in for him Johnny. Amma is not to blame for me wanting to keep what happened secret but I didn't want to get your hopes up. Anyhow, this is how it all went down and no Rosalyn, I was never in any danger."

I took my time retelling the encounter because I only wanted to tell it once. They all scoffed at the name Willie Wallace as I knew they would. Johnny and Evan both reacted to the name Carruthers. Johnny asked about Willie's appearance and age. I said he was a little scruffy but clean and I thought he might be somewhere around twenty-three. Evan said Carruthers was older than that, maybe forty, and at anytime did I think they may have shared a cell in prison. I said that I had no idea but it was a possibility.

"And he never mentioned the name of the friend who said you had helped out did he? I doubt if it would be any help anyhow and you have come to the aide of so many so I guess there is no use in speculating and we'll just have to wait for his call tomorrow and maybe we'll be able to draw more information out of him." Johnny concurred.

I looked at Amma with a question in my eyes. She frowned and shrugged her shoulders.

"It's your call Amma."

"What's this then?" Her husband asked suspiciously.

"Don't kill the messengers, but the friend was your other uncle, Samson O'Shea."

"You have to be fucking kidding me!"

"This is not the barnyard so watch your language!" Amma scolded again.

"Sorry for the language ladies." Johnny apologised looking at Mary. "This has to be some sort of demented prank. Mentioning *his* name with Walt's is blasphemy!"

"No need for apology Johnny Boy. I have heard it all and then some. Yous just reacting to an upsetting time in your life but it was a long, long time ago and me thinks it's time to let the anger go. He been paying three decades for his sins and if his involvement somehow helps find his brother's slayer, who are we to judge? And, isn't it just like our Lady Vienna to solve another dilemma? Shall we not say thanks?" Mary suggested calmly.

"Thankyou for putting me in my place Mary and I will do just that. Vienna, do you think that you might join me in a stroll through the rose gardens?"

"Yes, I think I might."

"Put a sweater on as it's cooling." Amma suggested.

"And please put a decent pair of shoes on" Evan said tenderly.

We sat on the bench in front of the flourishing red roses. Johnny picked one and handed it to me. He lit a cigarette and passed it to me. I said thankyou but no as Pixie was waiting for me.

"I'll make this quick then. You know I love you and that nothing you ever do or say will change that. You may not feel like I owe you an apology but I do. I'm sorry if I yelled at you but my first reaction was one of fear that you had done something dangerous."

"I know that Johnny and I also knew that Amma would spill the beans so to speak, and I knew what your reaction would be. What surprised me was her reaction to you, so please don't be too harsh with her."

He laughed. "As if I could be. And, Mary's right, it's time I let my anger go and maybe I'll even make a trip into Edinburgh and visit Samson."

I said that maybe it was time.

Will did not call the next day or the next. After two months I concluded that I had indeed been duped. It didn't upset me that I was out a few bucks but that my intuition had been wrong did. I had whole heartedly believed that Will's intentions had been honorable. I think that the encounter had given Johnny false hope bothered me the most.

Stranger at the Door

Zander went home at the end of June. He wanted to be there for Nash for the haying season seeing his father couldn't be. I was saddened to see him go as was everyone else but respected his choice to return to Hawthorne. I had been well aware of how much he missed Novia and Sammie over the past year. They would both be back at school in September so he would at least have most of the summer to spend with them. He lamented over leaving me and Pixie and hoped that I'd come home soon. I said I would just as soon as his dad did.

Novia and Calla arrived on July 3rd and were to stay for four weeks. It didn't seem like that would be long enough. Life was never going to be any different. I'd always be separated from having all my family together by an ocean, and only the good Lord knew if Rainey was further away than just a cruel sea.

There were days when it seemed like I was the only one in the house and such was July 14th. I was in a mood anyhow as it was Rainey's birthday and I had been reminiscing of how he had rescued me from Anton that very day twenty-one years ago. Pixie had been playing quietly on the floor in the family room in front of me when she suddenly stood up and was out the door. I was a prisoner in the recliner as it refused to lower. I yelled for someone to catch Pixie while I fought my way out of the chair.

No one answered as I heard her giggles getting further and further away down the long corridor. By the time I caught up to her she was sitting on the floor looking up at the front door.

"You little rascal." I scolded picking her up just as the door knocker sounded. "Oh, what hell is this?" I whispered out loud as I opened the door to a beautiful young lady with long brown ringlets crowning her head standing there. She was dressed in a long emerald green 18th century gown. I gasped "Vivienne?"

I obviously startled her. "Actually, it's Genevie."

"Sorry, but your resemblance to her is astonishing. Actually, she isn't even a real person … oh dear, I am just confusing you. Please excuse my ramblings and tell me what I can do for you."

"I'm looking for my aunt Lady Vienna whom I'm thinking might be you?"

"Why would you think that? I am Vienna, but your aunt I'm sure I am not."

"I am Genevie LaFontaine, your brother Joseph's daughter."

The closest chairs were in the informal tearoom so I invited her in. I needed to sit down but first I pushed "2" on the call panel. Pixie wanted down so I sat her on the floor where she had several toys and went out in the hallway asking to be excused for a minute. Where was everyone?

I returned took a seat across from this young lady who said she was my niece. "Excuse my astonishment but I assure you it is genuine. Not only do you resemble my daughter Novia, but you are an exact facsimile to a young woman on the cover of a book that she has had for many a year and now you tell me I'm your aunt …"

Janet burst into the room. "Are you all right Ana? We heard the bell but Jane was up the ladder …"

I interrupted her excuse. "It's all right Dear but I need for you to find Novia and send her to me, just her you hear, and ask Amma for refreshments please."

"Amma's not here I'm afraid but I can see to tea. Shall I bring it down here?"

"Yes thankyou; but find Novy first." I ordered as I turned to my supposedly new niece. "How is that you are here Genevie? I have never met my brothers and have been led to believe that they wanted it that way so how did you come to find me?"

"I only found out that you were my aunt a week ago. My grandmother knew about you and she knew where you lived. Believe it or not but my dad and uncle didn't even know of your existence. My grandmother's name is Anne and it seems as if she was married to your father Joseph LaFontaine. She wanted to move back to France but he didn't so she dissolved the marriage and took my dad and Jamie with her. She said the boys believed their father had died and had no family, so this was a big surprise to them to find out that their dad had a whole other family. She said she would have taken this secret to the grave with her but her conscience got the better of her and she confessed. That is all I know as I had to leave the very next day for the tour. She is quite ill so may not even be alive when I get home. I'm so sorry for this."

"My Dear, you are not responsible for someone else's actions so you can't be sorry for what you didn't know. I too did not know I had two brothers until some twenty years ago when circumstances revealed it. My father said he tried to find the boys in a town in France where he thought their mother was from but was not successful. It was a big wide world out there in the 1940's, no search engines and internet like we have now. You said your grandmother dissolved the marriage but to my knowledge they didn't divorce because they were both Catholic. My father passed away a few years back but had said goodbye to the religion before I was born. I'm surprised that your grandmother kept the name LaFontaine. Did she remarry?"

"I don't know why she kept the name. She didn't remarry but she had suitors."

I was about to comment when Novia appeared. She was breathing hard.

"What's happened Mommy...oh..." She gasped as she saw Genevie.

They stared at each other for a few seconds and then they both said, "Hi." at the same time.

I introduced them telling Novy who her look alike was. She didn't even sound surprised.

"I always felt that I had a twin somewhere and now to meet her wearing the very same dress that she wore on my book cover. Oh, that must sounds so cryptic."

Genevie laughed. "Your mom explained a little but I can't wait to hear the whole story. I only have a few hours and then I have to go back to Waverly for a rehearsal so I hope that's long enough. I came here hoping to find my aunt and discovered I have a cousin too so I am without words."

"I am not the only cousin as there are eight of us and four of them are right here. You've already met Pixie and Mama just found her a few months ago so she's new too. Let's go find the others." Novia said taking her new cousin's hand.

Tears slid down Genevie's face. "I don't have any cousins; I don't even have a sister or brother or…"

I put my arm around her. "You do now, and aunts and uncles too. Now before I let you go off with Novy I'd like an explanation of why you are here dressed in a 1800's outfit and what's this about a rehearsal?"

"That's why I am here. I belong to a minstrel acting troupe in Montpellier and we do performances in the district. This is the first year that we have taken our act on the road and Waverly Hall was chosen as one of our stops. When I told my Grandmother all the cities we would be visiting and mentioned Waverly she said that I must make a visit to Avanloch Castle because there was someone there I needed to meet. She told me to call my Dad and Uncle Jamie to come over and she confessed all. They were very upset but had to let it go because of Grandmother's health. They will be calling you if they have your permission. They speak English but French is their first language as it is mine. Do you find my accent too much?" She asked. Apologetically.

"I am also of French heritage and I love your accent just as I do the Scottish and Irish ones. I will send a thankyou note to your grandmother for sending you to us and having the courage to tell the truth about a time that was painful and uncertain to her. There is no forgiveness needed and I look forward to talking to and meeting my long-lost brothers. Now about this performance of yours … may we attend?"

"Oh yes, I would love that! How many seats should I reserve?"

"I'm counting heads and I think maybe eight. Is that too many?"

"Oh no; it's a big hall as you probably know. I will have vouchers for you at the door."

"Okay, I will look forward to the concert, but before you go off with Novy I'm wondering if Montpellier is anywhere near Sete ?"

"It is only about 40 kilometers away. Do you know the town?"

"Not very well, but my daughter Tanny works and lives there so maybe the two of you can meet. Novy will give you all her information."

"Oh, that would be wonderful. I'm sorry but I'm not too sure what I should I call you? Somone called you Anna but your name is Vienna so…"

"You may call me either. My children call me Mama or Mom or Mommy and sometimes Mother when they are angry with me. The grandchildren and others like Janet, who you met and Jane and who work here call me Ana. Everyone else calls me Vienna so I am good with either."

"My Uncle Evan and Johnny call her Milady." Novy added mischievously.

I laughed and told them to be off because the clock was ticking. Janet arrived with the tea which included a pot of coffee just as the girls were leaving. I told her to leave it as Novia would look after our guest.

I knew it was Evan even before he stuck his head in the door as he was whistling Waltzing Matilda.

"You rang Milady?"

"And you just heard it now?"

"Didn't even hear it as I was on the mower up the hill. I saw a car leave and thought I'd see who I had missed. Novia said you needed me so here I am. What's happened?"

"I didn't tell her that, but seeing you are here I have something to tell you."

"I'm listening."

"I've decided to go back to Hawthorne where it's quiet and no one can find me."

He laughed. "You think you can hide there; well you can't and you'll go home when I say you can and that will be when Rain returns. Now pour me a cup of that coffee and talk to me."

I ended the soliloquy stating that I had no idea how I was going to get everyone to the concert and supposed that we'd have to take two vehicles and maybe we would stay overnight, but then there would be no one to stay with Mary and maybe I shouldn't go because it would be too much for Pixie.

"How much coffee have you had anyway? Your talking like a mad Nellie. Never mind the cars as you can take the bus."

"He says that like we have a bus, and who is this Nellie anyhow?"

"We *have* a bus. Johnny and Butch finished repairing it last week. It's all ready for action when needed next year so there, transportation problem solved."

"Don't be daft Evan, we can't take something that belongs to the district school board."

"*We* are the school board Vienna. Now that's settled, where is this new niece of yours? I guess I'll have to claim her as mine too as we all know that a blood relative of mine will never just drop in on me."

"I think it's time we took Dr. Shelia up on the offer to connect you with Doc Holliday who says he has found someone who knows the story of your parent's disappearance don't you?"

"I guess it wouldn't hurt to exchange a few emails."

"To heck with that, I say, let's **go** to Australia!"

"What was in that coffee you've been drinking anyhow, or have you changed to a different kind of cigarette? Before you get any higher you best return Hawk's call. It appears as though he's accepted your offer to visit you next week."

"I do not recall inviting him and there is no way he can come when Novia is here, so yes, I had best return the call and disinvite him."

The day ended on a high note as Genevie's concert was delightful. We promised to keep in touch.

There had been half a dozen pleasant phone calls from Hawk over the last three months. He always inquired about my schedule and travels and asked if I might be in London during the summer as he had several forums there regarding his projected mission to the Antarctic. I had always put him off as I had no such plans until now. Novia's and Calla's flight home was on July the twenty-eighth from Edinburgh. Without them knowing I had managed to get their flight moved to London for the thirty-first. As a treat I had booked passage for them and Pixie and myself on a scenic train from Edinburgh to London. They were ecstatic. Evan would fly us into Edinburgh to catch the train and then pick Pixie and I up in London on August first when he came for Rosy. We would stay the three nights with her. Auntie Jane and family were within walking distance so there would be many visits with them. I made the move and told Hawk that I could have dinner with him on the thirty-first if it suited his plans. It did. To be perfectly honest I had hoped that it wouldn't be feasible for him. I guessed I thought I was being unfaithful to Rainey.

Before I knew it the girl's visit was over and we were on our way to London via a luxury coach. Amma had been worried that the day long trip would be too much for Pixie and advised me to leave her at home with her. I did not take her advice. Pixie loved the train and marveled at all the passing scenery as much as any seventeen month old child could. Of course there was an aisle for her to scoot up and down in and the passengers encouraged her to visit with them. She did not make strange with anyone. I was glad to have Novia and Calla to chase after her. I think she slept once for forty-five minutes.

Our three day holiday seemed to fly by. At three in the afternoon on Saturday we had a tearful goodbye at the airport. Novia wanted me to come home at Christmas. I made no promises. At six o'clock Hawk picked me up at Rosy's. He had big hugs for Rosy and me. I introduced

Pixie to him. She was not impressed and hid behind me the whole time. Rose rescued her and sent us on our way.

Luckily for me Hawk was a great conversationalist and entertained me with more adventures of working in remote locales. His six month assignment in Antarctica was now definite. He would be leaving on the first of November and hoped we could meet again before that. I told him I would not be coming back to London in the fall but that didn't matter because he had already made plans to come to Avanloch for three days before he shipped off to the south pole. Johnny had been pleased to put him up.

As promised Hawk arrived at the end of September. His visit did not interfere with my everyday plans with Pixie which included our morning visit to the farm, hikes to the ponds and working in the rose gardens or picking vegetables. He accompanied us on our walks to the ponds and practically everything else we did. After lunch it was Pixie's and my alone time for two hours or so. She napped and I puttered around upstairs. It was also the time I wrote in my diary to Rainey. If I mentioned Hawk at all it was just to say that Johnnys cousin was here visiting.

I knew that he was interested in me as more than just a friend but it wasn't going to go any further on my part so I didn't worry about it. When he left he said he'd keep in touch as often as he could and that I'd be the first person he would want to see when he got back in the spring. He kissed me and told me that he was going to miss me. I felt nothing.

Chapter 10

Gracie Darling's Grave

October 30th

There, six dozen orange rice crispy balls finished. They would go nicely in the treat bags with Evan's candied red apples and Amma's chocolate and vanilla ghost and goblin cookies. I hung up my apron, scribbled a note to Mary saying that I'd gone for a walk and would be home around three or so, grabbed one of Evan's tartan shirts and a cigarette and retreated outside. It was a little past two. It was a glorious autumn day. I had cut my unhealthy habit down to one a day and it was usually with Johnny in the evening just before I put Pixie to bed. It was Amma's day to take Pixie to the village to have a playdate with her sister Emma's grandson Benji and several other children about the same age. They usually went at eleven and were home by two, but seeing today was a Halloween party at the school, the young ones had been invited to join in the festivities from one to four, so it would be a late day. I had a few hours to kill so what was I going to do? I spotted one of the girl's bikes lying in the grass by the pergola. Did I dare…sure, what the heck?

I hadn't ridden a bike for years so thought it best to walk it to the bottom of the hill not wanting to start off at fifty miles an hour. Thankfully, there was no one around to see me zigzagging back and forth across Mill

Street. Half-way up I saw Amma's Mom, Granny Kaye sitting in her rocker on the front porch and stopped to say hello. A quick visit to the new Village Creamery, Mr. Macintosh's woodworking shoppe and chats with several villagers out for their afternoon strolls I thought I'd start for home. I glanced at the clock that towered above the community hall. Seeing it was only 3 o'clock I decided to take the long way back down Holy Cross. This had always been the name of the street as the Catholic Church and Convent had once been here when the religion was in favor many years ago. The community hall, a horseshow pit, and lawn bowling park now occupied that property. The ten new prefab homes took up the next street over. No one was outside so there was no reason to stop but stop abruptly I did as I had to swerve to avoid colliding with a large boulder. Just ahead and to my right a shape scuttling out from Primrose Street caught my eye. It was definitely a person, but I couldn't make out whether it was a woman, man, or perhaps even a child. I believed it was a woman as the figure appeared to be dressed in a long black dress and hooded cloak. I think she may have spotted me because her pace quickened as she made her way to the main road. She turned left at the intersection. I wondered where she was going as there weren't any more houses in that direction. I climbed back on the bike and followed after her.

I stopped at the junction. She was nowhere to be seen. Well, that was crazy. She had to go one way or the other. I was only a few minutes behind her so she couldn't have just disappeared. Avanloch was to my right and to my knowledge there wasn't another road on the left before Thistle, and that was a good five miles away. Wait, there was a maintenance and landfill road … but why would she go there and I would see her wouldn't I? The other side of the road was nothing but thick bushes and trees and there was nothing behind them that I knew of. I crossed over anyhow. Maybe there's a path further down that leads somewhere, but where? A little chill enveloped me. Don't do it Vienna. I laughed and climbed back on the bike and peddled to where I thought the path might be.

I parked the bike in the ditch and tried to remember Johnny's directions from last summer when he had come to the "forbidden cemetery" as Amma called it, to free Evan and Rainey from the tunnel. I followed what looked more like a deer trail than a pathway. It led me down an embankment where I came face to face with a barb wire fence and signs that read: NO ENTRY, DANGER, INTRUDERS WILL BE PROSECUTED, HIGH VOLTAGE WIRE, DANGER. I didn't believe the high voltage sign for one second. I continued down the rugged pathway. I knew I was in the right place from what I could see but was hesitant to climb through the barb wire. Was that a gate down there…it was, but it was padlocked. Damn.

"Who goes there?"

What…who talks like that?

"Who goes there?" The voice called out again.

Okay, what the hell. "I am Vienna of Avanloch. Who be you?"

"I am Dalezza of the Dales. What business do you have here?"

"I am here to see you."

"Approach then."

"I cannot as the gate is locked."

"Look beyond."

"Beyond what?" Was this some eleven-year-old girl playing some sort of game?

"Look just beyond the gate and you will see an opening into the warren."

What…a warren is a rabbit's den isn't it? I found the opening in the fence that led to another opening. Oh, it's a maze of sorts. Okay, I got it, but anyone could probably figure it out in time so why the lock on the gate? Was Haworth, the caretaker so obsessed with keeping people out that he had devised this?

I saw a figure crouched behind a headstone. I asked her if I could approach.

"If you must. This is sacred ground, so what is your business here? Do you come to visit a lost soul? This is a very old resting place so perhaps you are in the wrong cemetery."

She was not such a young girl as I had thought, but a woman in her twenties perhaps. It was hard to get a good look at her because of the hooded cape.

"I told you that I came to find you."

"Do we know one another?"

"No, I saw you walking at a brisk pace and wondered where you were going to so quickly so just followed you. I have not been here before but it has been on my list of places to visit."

"Why?"

"Just curious I guess. Who is it that you are visiting?" I asked respectively as I took a few steps towards her. The headstone read:

Eisla McKenzie 1533–1599 October 31st
Wife, Mother, Daughter

"Was she kin from another time?"

"No, she is not of my family."

"I see. It is just something you do then, bring flowers to unknown souls. That is very kind of you. Where did that pail of water come from?"

"I got it from the cistern." She gestured behind her.

"I didn't know there was one here. Is there some significance to bringing water to a grave?"

"It is Holy Water and is for protection."

"Protection from what, and why to someone you didn't know who died four hundred years ago?"

"Did I say I didn't know her?"

"You said she was not your family."

"Eisla was not, but she keeps my great, great, great, great, great aunt from the huntsmen."

What had I stepped into? I told myself not to ask, but I did. "Huntsmen?"

"Just because *he* is gone doesn't mean that his evil does not live on in others and they are still searching for the remains of the sacred because they believe that the only way to rid the world of them is to hang them and then burn them on the stake."

"Was your great aunt a witch?"

She laughed. "Witches revered her. No, she was a warrior, a great warrior."

I thought I might have just put two and two together or maybe I'd gone over the edge. What the heck, I'd go fishing. "This grave does not hold the remains of Eisla does it? It is masquerading for the resting place of your aunt who was hunted by the King because she was a Dame and was a member of the Knights Templar? I am acquainted with that era and a Dame who was named Gracie Darling"

"Grace Darling lived long after the crypt's date and she was not a warrior."

"I didn't say Grace Darling, the heroine from the lighthouse who saved 9 lives from their capsized ship in the 1800's. I said Gracie Darling who lived a covert life as handmaiden to Avaleena McAllister, Mistress of Avanloch Castle in the 1500's."

She stood up and looked at me with fire in her eyes and pulled a

baton out from under her cape and waved at me. "Step back…how did you find me? Who sent you? It was that evil Mercede McCambridge pretending to be a witch wasn't it?"

I put up my hands. "I do not know anyone who masquerades as a witch but it is Halloween so I just might meet one or two. I mean you and your great aunt no harm. It is as I said, I am Vienna Quinn from Avanloch Castle. I followed you because I wanted to see what you were up to. I know that Luke Haworth, the caretaker of this place tries to keep intruders out. I hoped you weren't up to any mischief. I will leave you be and I will return another day to search for my friends."

"You are really Lady Vienna…" She said lowering her head and almost bowing. "Please forgive me as I should not have threatened you. Luke is my father and he knows I am here as I come every year at this time to lay flowers at my great aunt's resting place as my relatives have been doing so since her death. You said your last name was Quinn…."

"It is, and coincidentally, it is the name of one of my friends whose gravestone I am thinking might be here also as Gracie Darling was his lady, and they were inseparable."

I thought she was going to faint. I asked her if she was all right.

"How can you call them friends? They lived and died five hundred years ago? I'm thinking that it is *you* who is masquerading as Lady Vienna but underneath you are a witch of that dreaded sect."

"I do not know what this 'sect' is you are referring to, but I am definitely not familiar with it and I am not masquerading as anyone but myself. I have lived at the castle on and off for almost fifty years. I found a diary that Lady Avaleena wrote and through the pages I came to know Gracie Darling and Quinn. So, tell me if she was your great, great, aunt from another time and is buried here, and if she is, where is Quinn?"

"You need to prove to me that you are who you say you are."

"I do not have to prove anything to you, but you are on private property and for all I know you are a grave robber so I can have you evicted."

She laughed. "Touche; I was just testing you. Lady Vienna you are, and I apologise for my impudence. I must know what you know."

"I am no longer Lady Vienna, just Vienna. You will know all that I know Dalezza of the Dales, and I am looking forward to exchanging stories with you, but not today as it is late and I must take my leave. How long will you be at your father's?"

"Just until the first of November because my work will be done then."

"What kind of work?"

"Protecting Gracie Darling from Mercedes Macabre."

"I thought you said her name was McCambridge?"

"I did, but macabre, malevolent, wicked, all her. She comes every October thirty first to desecrate the graveyard because she knows that Gracie lies beneath a stone somewhere here."

"You said that witches revered her."

"Not this faction; she is from one of the blackest covens in history that date back before time. They practice black magic for the purpose of evil. Rumor has it that they were under the protection of King Phillip and that their accusations along with the poison pen of William of Tyre in 1307 were instrumental in the execution of the Knight's Templar in the prison in Domme France. It was also rumored that some of the Knights escaped right here and changed the village's name to Domme because it represented their victory over their persecutors. I do not know when or why the spelling has been altered to Domne. Anyhow Gracie Darling was a known Templar Dame so it's obvious why her remains are thought to be here. It is only speculation though on their part, but we, kin of Gracie know and keep her consecrated remains secret."

"To my knowledge none of those so-called insinuations have ever been proven but I do respect your devotion. It was pointed out to me in my early years here that the residents of Domne did not like the name and it was rarely used and spelled differently from the French town. There was never any mention of the Templars or Gracie Darling. Like I said I would be very interested in future discussions with you so we will keep in touch."

"I am most fascinated by your knowledge regarding my great aunt and look forward to hearing all you know. I will walk with you but first we must lay down protection. Here, take this atomizer that contains Holy water from the cistern and oils of rosemary and peppermint and spray all the headstones around Gracie's. Then we will walk a serpentine path to the entrance gate and you will shower everything as we go while I brush out footfalls away. You may call me Lezza."

She said her promises to Gracie, picked up a huge branch that looked like a broom, took my arm, and led me through the graveyard sweeping behind us as I sprayed. As we zigzagged our way around the long forgotten dilapidated gravestones I wondered about my sanity. I guessed I'd just look at it all as a game.

I found my bike and chose to push it so I could walk beside Lezza. The town clock announced that it was 5 O'clock. Darkness was falling quickly. Just before we reached Mill Street where we would part I asked her how old she was. I was surprised by her response.

"I will be thirty-one on the thirty first. Isn't that interesting? Gracie died on the thirty first and if you turn the number around then thirty-one becomes thirteen, a very witchy and Templar number." She laughed.

"Gracie died on the thirty-first of October and you were born on the same day…that is interesting and I am very aware of the number thirteen."

"Actually, my birthdate is December the thirty-first, but it's the numbers that are portentous."

A light shone in front of us. It was from Evan's jeep. I told her that I would call her tomorrow.

Johnny got out, told me to get in and asked Lezza if she wanted a ride. She said she didn't. He said to say hello to her father, put the bike in the back of the jeep and slid in next to me. No one said a word, but I felt some tension. When Evan stopped I asked if I was in trouble.

"Why do you think you are?" Johnny asked.

"Because no one is saying anything."

"Nothing to say Milady. Go on in and warm up. Tell Amma I'll be in shortly."

With that he started up the rose garden path. I looked pleadingly at Evan.

"He was worried about you."

"I best go and have a word then don't you think?"

He nodded that I should. Johnny was sitting on one of the benches at the top of the hill. I sat down beside him. He passed me his cigarette. I took a long drag and passed it back to him.

"I cannot have you angry with me so I will apologise for being out after dark."

He snickered. "It's not that dark and you're not one of my wayward daughters so there is no need for an apology. I know where you were though, but I don't know why. I am guessing that you ran into the Haworth girl and got to talking and somehow ended up at the graveyard, but why?"

I explained how it all came about. "Now we should go in and you can think about what punishment you have in store for me. Oh, one little tidbit; the grave that Lezza visits is none other than Gracie Darling's." I teased as I ran off down the hill to the house.

"Get back here Vienna!"

I heard Rainey reprimanding me in Johnny's voice.

"Did you two kiss and make up?" Amma asked.

I walked over and gave her a peck on her cheek. I looked back at Johnny who was grinning from ear to ear. "You'll have to ask your husband, but I'm sure he has a punishment in store for me because I was a naughty girl and went off without him and Evan and stayed out too late at the graveyard. Thank-you for looking after my baby all day,"

"You're welcome, but you know it's no chore. You don't know anyone who is interred there so why would you go there…oh, please tell me that you weren't at the forbidden one?"

I picked Pixie up from Duffy's chair and sat back down with her on my lap. "I was and I discovered something very interesting that I will share with you all after dinner."

"I can't imagine, but by the look on my husband's face I guess that he already knows and that's why he was so worried?"

"I did not know Amma until I saw her with the Haworth girl. Here come the girls so let's table this discussion until later, okay?"

"Ana, you're back! Did you have a good time visiting the Village? We had so much fun with Pixie. Everyone loves her and Auntie Emma's grandson Benji. I think they will be invited back for the Christmas party. Benji says that they should be the school's mascots. That's funny don't you think?" Beth beamed with enthusiasm.

And so, the graveyard adventure was on hold for another day.

Evan found me writing in my dairy in my upstairs parlor that evening. He knocked on the open door.

"Am I disturbing you Vienna?

"You certainly are not. Do you want to talk? Are you coming in or do you want me to come out?"

"How about we sit in the foyer?"

"Oh yes because we wouldn't want anyone to get the wrong idea." I joked.

He laughed as he pulled a chair out for me at the table. "I guess it's my turn to find out why you spent your day at the cemetery, that is if you so care to enlighten me."

"Did Johnny ask you to talk to me?"

"He didn't, but I got the feeling that there is more to the story than you told him."

"I guess I left him guessing. Anyhow, I wasn't there all day Evan, an hour at the most, and it turned out to be a most interesting and knowledgeable hour. I never felt like I was in any danger and you'll hear why as I tell you how it all went down." I responded and relayed my whole encounter to him. "It's a little bizarre I must admit; what do you think?" I asked when I had finished.

"I'm thinking that Miss Hayward has a great imagination, but then who am I to challenge the validity of her story. I knew you were curious about the cemetery and who might be buried there but you never mentioned it last year so I thought that with everything else going on around here that you had pushed it aside. I would have escorted you there anytime if you had asked you know."

"I know that Evan, and it wasn't in my plans today but … well, things just happen."

"Yes, with you they certainly do. I worry about you and hope you'll give me or Johhny a heads up before your next venture."

"In other words you want me to report my plans for my days to you every morning?"

"Primarily, yes."

I got up, hugged him, told him I loved him and to get to bed.

He said the feeling was mutual and at least he could view my encounter with Lezza if he wanted to.

I turned back. "What?"

"There are several hidden cameras there in the yard so I am sure one has picked you up."

"Isn't that fringing on privacy?" I replied dumbfounded.

"You can take that up with Johnboy."

I shook my head. "He doesn't do anything without your approval."

"Don't be too sure about that Milady. Good night and sweet dreams."

"You know damn well I'm going to dream of graveyards and witches and everything else that goes bump in the night."

"Better then having nightmares about Jorja."

"I'll get you for that Evan Govern." I promised.

"Can't wait. Love you."

I had to have the last word. "Can't wait to view the tapes and see if this Mercedes woman does indeed haunt the graveyard on Halloween searching for Gracie Darling's bones." His response was to throw his hands up in the air.

As we exited the lift on Halloween morning I got a firm grip on Pixie so she couldn't run down the hallway. Everyone was still seated around the kitchen table. Evan relieved me of Pixie and put her in her highchair that was between him and Rosy. After our good mornings Johnny got up saying he had some work to do on the yard decorations. I asked him if I could accompany him. He said of course I could and to dress warmly as it was cold outside. Amma automatically put my coffee in a go cup and told us not to get into any trouble.

"How much trouble could we get into Amma as we aren't going anywhere else are we Johnny?" I asked.

"No, just the yard." He answered.

"Are you sure about that John?" Evan grinned.

"Do you have other plans for me Vienna?"

"Evan thinks I'm going to stir the cauldron." I said.

"I didn't know that there was one to be stirred, but seeing it's All Hallow's Eve and the moon is still full I'm game for whatever Milady."

I took his arm, blew a kiss to my daughter, made a disapproving face at Evan and left while the discussion of what Evan knew was going on. As I was putting my boots on I heard my daughter tell her husband to spill and tell her what her mother was up to now.

Johnny was waiting for me in the golf cart. He had loaded the portable tire inflator in the back as he said some of the Halloween decorations need a top up of air. He drove straight to the gate where two welcoming ghosts were bowing in the breeze. They were weighted down so hopefully they couldn't fly away. The driveway consisted of straw scarecrows, bony skeletons sitting on benches, cackling witches on brooms, spiders and their webs dangling on tree branches and dozens of pumpkins that would turn on at dusk to show the visitors the way to the fountain where the water ran red. A tent had been erected over the fountain where the guests would be greeted and treated to all kinds of amusement and treats inside. Two formidable sentries depicting the wicked witch's guards stood at the sides of the entrance were the only ones that needed a little air. The girls had chosen The Wizard of Oz as the Halloween theme.

A lighted walkway and pumpkins that led to the front door had been all the outside decorations that had graced the yard in the days when I was Lady Vela McAllister. I asked Johhny when this outside decorating had started.

"I'd say ten years ago. Colleen and Beth were the instigators of course. It started off relatively small but every year more was added. The population of the village has quadrupled in the past few years so it was no longer feasible to use the grand entry room as a party room. This is the second year for this tent formation and the fourth or fifth for fireworks with Evan as the pyrotechnician who has assured me that it's going to be a spectacular display this year. They are set up on the hilltop at Willowisp Manor so everyone around for miles can see them, but there will definitely be a crowd outside the gates. People will be setting up their chairs well before nine."

"Umm, I wonder where Pixie and I will sit." I mused.

"You will have the best seats in the house, so to speak, as will the rest of the family. Do you think Pixie will last that long?"

"Time will tell. Johnny, do you know Mercedes McCambridge?"

"No, who is she?"

"According to Leesa she is a very bad witch."

"Well, my knowledge of witches is limited but if she's an enemy of Lessa's I would take everything she says with a grain of salt as she lives in her own world of make believe."

"I'm sure she does but I do so want to believe that Gracie Darling's remains do lie beneath the stone that Lessa says she protects."

"I think that we all concluded when we did all the investigating after Uncle Walt's murder that it was a definite possibility that she and Quinn may be buried in that cemetery. So, it could very well be the grave that Lessa protects with what she calls Holy water and all her incantations. If it brings you closure then it's a good thing."

"You know about all of that and Lezza too?"

"Yeah for several years now."

"When did you set up the cameras?"

"Hayward and I installed them about that time. There had been half a dozen graves desecrated so it was Haywards idea to install them and that's when I found out about Leeza. He says she is harmless and I believe him. There has been no further mischief since it was posted as being under surveillance."

"I didn't see any such postings. Did you view the tapes last night?"

"Why would I do that?"

"Because you knew I was there"

"I don't have access to the tapes and I would only look at them if I thought you were in danger. I did not know where you were and you told me what happened so I had no need to look at the tape but if you'd like to see it we could get Hayward to show us."

"I do not. I guess I overreacted with Evan last night thinking I was being spied on."

"You are not being spied on and we can't keep a watch on you twenty four seven even if we probably should seeing you have this tendency to wander off with strange men like Willie Wallace."

"Speaking of strange men, Evan's probably wondering what you and I are doing down here without him."

Johnny laughed. I told him he had done a wonderful job on the yard and now I had better get back to the house and see what was left for me to do.

At three I dressed Pixie in her Munchkin costume and donned my designated character outfit which was Dorothy. We went downstairs and met up with the rest of the cast. Amma was Aunt Em and Johnny was Uncle Henry. Rosalyn was Glinda the good witch and Evan dressed as the Wizard. Colleen, Beth, Janet and Jane were Munchkins like Pixie. They would be the ones receiving all the guests in the tent. Mary wanted to be part of the cast and seeing she would be in her wheelchair we decorated it like a bicycle and called her Miss Gulch. Butch was in charge of security and he and his crew would be circulating the grounds and aiding Evan with the fireworks disguised as Dorothy's companions from the yellow brick road journey. The only character who was missing was the wicked witch of the west, or so I thought.

At four o'clock Pixie and I were ready to join the others in the tent. I had hold of Pixie's hand and opened the door and was met by the ugliest and scariest witch I had ever seen. She was laughing in the spine chilling cackle that witches are known for. Pixie yelled, broke free from me and went running down the hallway screaming and crying. I kicked my silly shoes off, left the uninvited stranger at the door and ran after my daughter catching up with her just as she was attempting to crawl under the divan in the library. I scooped her up in my arms and talked as soothingly as I could but she kept right on sobbing and shivering. I had planned on shielding her from all the scary getups which were bound to show up but I was not prepared for the nightmare at the door. I managed to get her up and into the rocking chair thinking I could rock the fear out of it but it didn't seem to help any. Someone was coming down the hall whistling. Pixie stopped fussing. She looked to the door and said, "Dada."

"Where's my big girl?" He held his arms out. "Does someone need a hug?"

"I think we both do. Did you see her?"

"Yeah and Johnny's dismantling her, or maybe it's a he."

"That screech definitely came from a woman."

Pixie was all calmed down when Johnny arrived. He asked if he could see me in the hall. He was not alone. She was faced away from me holding something in her hands. She turned.

"I'm so sorry Lady Vienna … I didn't know your daughter would be with you. I just wanted to surprise you … I never thought, oh, I'm no better than any of them …" She sobbed.

I walked out into the hall not knowing what I was going to do or say. I shocked myself. "Would you like to meet my daughter? She's a little anxious right now because there was a real scary witch at the door so you are going to have speak very softly. Leave that costume on the floor for Johnny to dispose of please."

She pulled something out of her bag. "I have a present for her."

"May I ask what it is?"

She tore the wrapping paper off and held it up for me to see. It was a little blonde rag doll dressed in a fairy dress with wings and a magical wand. I said that she would love it and invited her to follow me. Pixie was sitting on Evan's lap pulling on his fake moustache. I asked her if she would like to meet my new friend Lezza and then we could all go find a seat to view the fireworks. Evan was not pleased that I invited her and told me so with his eyes. I nodded and told him that I'd make it right.

It had been a long time since I had reprimanded any of my children. Lezza was not a child but had acted like one and so I was going to talk to her like one. I called her back out into the hallway and lectured her about boundaries. The castle was not open to Halloweener's and the front door was posted as such so I asked her why she though it that didn't apply to her. Her reason was hard to discern through her sobbing and pleas for me to forgive her. When I was sure that she had understood that her actions were insensitive and unacceptable I told her that Evan was Pixie's surrogate father and it was him that she needed to apologise to and Johnny was her Godfather so a word to him would be appreciated. I sent her in to do see Evan. I guess he accepted her apology because she came back smiling. He handed Pixie over to me and told us to enjoy the evening's festivities.

While we were waiting for the family to join us for the fireworks display I asked Lezza why she wasn't at the graveyard protecting Gracie Darling from Mercedes. She said there was no such person and that she had made her up and it made for good story telling. I was not amused. Thankfully she was going back where she had come from tomorrow.

The fireworks were fantastic. Pixie clapped along with the rest of us at each burst and only jumped a few times at the loud explosions. Rosalyn carried her upstairs and put her to bed while the girls and I looked after Mary. I waited awhile for Evan and Johnny with Amma but the sleep bug got the best of me and the compliments for such a glorious night would have to wait until the next day. I slept on the whole Lezza event overnight and wondered why I had been so taken in by her story. Maybe it was all a ruse and only alive in her mind. Maybe Gracie didn't even lie beneath that stone. There was only one way to find out and that was never going to happen so maybe someone else held the answer. It was worth a try and one day I'd get Johnny to take me to see Lezza's father.

November and December were busy as usual with the baking and shopping and organizing of the Village gift baskets. It was a quieter Christmas as Jannie and family didn't come. Ada went to London to be with her mother and new family. Evan offered to take me down for a few days but I declined as I had just wanted to be here with my Avanloch family. It was my second Christmas without Rainey.

And so we said goodbye to another winter. The spring of 2005 came early. Hawk was due to arrive in April. We had been corresponding regularly while he was in Antarctic but now that tour was over and his first stop home was to see me. His texts had become much too personal and I had not corrected him and told him that there was no future for us in the way that he thought there was going to be. I would have to deal with that and I was not looking forward to it at all.

Maybe I had read too much into his words because I found our visit to be quite enjoyable. He was a great storyteller and had us all listening intently to his adventures and misadventures over the three days he was with us. He brought gifts for everyone. Pixie was not overly enthused with the stuffed penguin. The rest of us all received the typical souvenirs. I was not alone with him much except when he insisted on taking me to dinner in Waverly. I enjoyed the dinner but put a kibosh on dancing citing an old injury. It was then he presented me with a little box and asked if I would consider it as a friendship token. It was a ring. I was never much lost for words but I was then. He must have spent a half an hour apologising if he had offended me or overstepped the boundaries. It was not meant to be an engagement or promise ring or meant to replace any of my other rings that I no longer wore. I felt as if I had to explain why I didn't wear them. There was a valid reason and that was that I had a circulation problem so sometimes the rings would fall right off and other times my fingers would swell so the tightness pained me. If I would only remember to take my water medication I wouldn't have the problem. I didn't tell him that and was sorry I hadn't worn them today. He looked so forlorn that I said I'd keep it. I did not put it on.

Chapter 11

The Abduction

The morning had seen Amma and Pixie leave for their weekly playdate with Emma and her grandson Benji. Johnny had business at the mill so he had walked down to the village with them. It was 10 a.m. Mary had gone into her room to watch TV. Evan was on the telephone complaining to someone about shabby work. I told him I was on my way out. He waved and whispered over the phone. "Have a good outing and don't get into any trouble."

"I'll try not to." I answered as I grabbed a bottle of water and my phone.

It had become customary for me to make my rounds around the Village on Wednesdays when Pixie would be away. I had purchased a new bike last year in Waverly. It was blue and had no special features or extra gears. It usually took me three to four hours depending on how chatty everyone was that I met along the way. I'd usually stop at the little gift shop and visit with Marcia and have a brew of some sort. Occasionally I'd have a quick lunch at the new snack mobile truck if it was stationed on my route.

The Village clock rang out as I left Piccadilly Lane and headed for home. It was two o'clock. It had been a busy day. I had met up with

Johnny at the mill and we had shared a strawberry milkshake. It was a lovely end of May day. Everyone was out and about, working in their gardens or sitting on their porches. I was talked out. I heard a vehicle behind me and moved over closer to the edge of the road. The car hit my rear wheel and I was thrown to the ground. Before I could even right myself I was grabbed roughly, pulled up and tossed into the backseat of a car. Just before my head hit the arm rest I got a look at the driver. It was Willie Wallace. He made eye contact with me.

"I am so sorry Miss Vienna, I…"

"Shut your big ugly mouth you rotten double-crosser!" My abductor yelled. "Get this bloody car turned around NOW!"

He turned to me and told me to be quiet or he'd gag me. I didn't recognise him but I was pretty sure who he was. I managed to ask what he wanted from me dreading that he'd gag me as promised.

He laughed rudely. "What do men usually want from a woman? Don't excite yourself as I'm not that hard up. I'm only here for the money that you promised the alter boy, but what say we triple it?"

"I'll give you whatever you want so let's get it done so I can go home to my daughter.'

"How's that going to work lady; do you happen to have two million on you? Naw, I doubt it so we'll just have to hit the bank after we take a little side trip. Make yourself comfy as it'll be awhile."

I pulled my knees up to my chest so that no part of me would be touching him. I closed my eyes.

If we had reversed direction like he'd ordered then we would be heading towards Waverly and we'd be on a paved road, but we weren't. How far had we gone before I realised that I wondered. Had we passed Thistle? Why would we be going there anyhow? No, we must be miles past that. Now and then I opened my eyes and glanced out the window. All I could see were trees. There was no conversation. The only noise was the crunching of the gravel and my abductor's wheezing as he exhaled the fumes from his cigarette. At least the window was open.

After what I believed was thirty or forty minutes the car came to an abrupt stop. My abductor leaned forward and told Willie to get out and not to make any funny moves. It was then that I saw he had a gun tucked into his pants. He produced zip-tie handcuffs, regular handcuffs and a dog leash from a bag on the floor. He asked me which one I preferred. I told him he didn't need anything to restrain me as I wasn't going to do anything to jeopardise my life.

"You're my meal ticket sweetheart so trust me when I say you're safe for the time being. You need to be aware of the consequences though if you don't obey me."

I nodded. He knew nothing about me and if he did he would never have used the word *obey*."

He pulled me up by yanking on my pant legs until I was in a sitting position. He told me to get myself up and into the building. I recognised it as I had been here before. It was Johnny's Uncle Walt's house and we had been on Thistle Road all the time. Armand Janzen, Johnny's cop friend was right…criminals always come back to the scene of their crime. I wished Armand was here now.

The man I believed to be Carruthers held the leash in his hands like a whip and kept snapping it as he followed behind me. Willie was waiting at the open door. He didn't speak but silently mimed, "I'm so sorry." I tried to smile. I was told to sit in a hard backed wooden chair which had once been in the living room and that my behavior would determine how I'd be treated.

It was exactly the same as it was two years ago; a total mess of wall board and insulation lying on the remains of torn up carpet. Ceiling tiles still looked as if they could fall any second. The damage had all been done by Carruthers prior to, or after he had murdered Walt. Johnny believed he'd been looking for something of great value that his uncle had hidden. Johnny didn't know what it was but his uncle had hinted at it many times. Maps of the Thistle Legacy had been found and were investigated, but no treasure had been found. Johnny had thought that the tunnel from the cellar that led to the woodpile outside held something or at least a clue. I knew where the entrance was and wondered if Carruthers did too. I doubted that he had found anything of great value here so now he saw me as the source of easy money. How it had all come about I may never know but I believed that Willie had been an uncooperative ally, but why now? It was over a year ago that I had been approached by Wille and made a deal with him for the reward money, so what had kept him from cashing in?

I heard something that sounded like a motor running loudly. Carruthers heard it too and looked out the window and ordered Will to tie me up. "Silverton must be here. Get a move on kid and tie her up."

I had thought that the sound had come from the other side of the room, somewhere near the vicinity of the trap door to the cellar. I cringed at the thought of restraints. Willie refused.

"You sucky little piss ant Wallace! I'll do it myself."

He approached me with the handcuffs in his hand and snapped one on my left wrist and attempted to attach it to the arm of the chair. I saw red and kicked him as hard as I could and yelled. "No one ties me down, NO ONE!"

He recovered quicky and grabbed me by my hair and yanked me up. "You stupid little bitch! I'll show you who's boss once and for all!"

Willie jumped on his back beating on him and yelling at him to leave me alone. With one hand Carruthers threw me to the floor and started beating Willie with the other. I was dazed by the fall and felt pain in my neck and head. I managed to get to my knees not knowing what I was going to do to save Willie, and then I saw it lying on the floor. I reached for it and aimed it at the ceiling and pulled the trigger. Carruthers turned and laughed.

"What's ya gonna do with that gramma?"

"Shoot ya, that's what I'm gonna do!"

He took a step towards me. Just as I pulled back the hammer and took aim a flash of a form darted across the room and took him down. I thought a piece of the ceiling had fallen in on him. Arms were around me. I wasn't frightened as I knew his scent.

"It's me Vienna."

I touched his hand. "I know Evan. Where did you come from?"

"The heli." He helped me up and took the gun from me. "I'll just leave it here for Johnny."

"Johhny, where is he?"

"Right there Hon. He's got Carruthers in a choke hold."

"That's Johnny…I thought it was a piece of the ceiling. Where did he come from?"

"The tunnel. Come on, let's get you out of here."

"No, Willie needs help and Johnny might too."

"You need help John?" Evan called out.

"What do you think Boss? Get Vienna out of here."

"Right you are. Let's get you to the car." Evan led me out saying he'd come back for Will.

The only car in the yard was the one I had come in. I felt like my head was going to explode as dizziness was washing over me. I stumbled but Evan had a firm grip on me and managed to open the car door and sit me down. I told him that my ears were ringing. He was examining my head and neck.

"You may have a concussion. Did you hit your head?"

"Not intentionally, but I hit the arm rest when I was thrown into the back seat and I smashed into the wall when he tossed me to the floor in the house. I don't think I hit my head when the car knocked me off my bicycle."

"You were hit by the car?"

"Yes but Willie was driving so it was gentle."

"He had a part in this so don't be crediting him with any heroics. Now let's get you over to the heli and I'll get you some cold compresses for your head and neck. You'll stay there and stay still because motion can cause the brain to slide back and forth. Ringing in the ears can be another symptom of a concussion but I'm thinking that the resounding from the gun may be the culprit. I lost another one of the lives allotted to me when I heard that gun shot Vienna."

"I would have shot him Evan. I'm a pretty good shot you know. I was his meal ticket so he needed to keep me alive so I never believed he was going to harm me. He tried to cuff me to the chair and I lost it and went a little berserk. No one was ever going to do that to me again Evan, but he was a lot stronger then Jorja and my kick didn't quite hit the mark but my next shot would have, you can be sure of that."

"I have no doubt about that Mrs. Quinn but I'm glad it didn't come to that."

The heli was sitting on the other side of the house. I guessed that was the whirring I heard. Carruthers thought it was a car and someone named what … I couldn't think. Evan reclined my seat and snapped two ice packs behind me for my neck and one for my head. He kissed my forehead and said he'd be back with Will just as soon as Butch turned up. I asked why Butch was coming.

"Johnny and I were in the hangar when he got the call from Amma that you had been abducted so he called Butch to find Bear and Buck and meet us here as we might need help."

"I didn't know the Boone brothers were back. How did Amma know where I was?"

"Some woman who knows Emma saw it happen and called her to relay the message. Johnny and I took off and called Butch to grab whoever he found and hightail it to Walt's cabin."

"There are no houses or anyone around where I was grabbed so that is curious as to who she is and what she saw. Why would you assume that I was brought here?"

"You can take that up with John later." He grinned.

"Go on then, go and check on Johnny and see how Willie is. Oh, Carruthers was expecting someone else to show up so beware and get the key to unlock this damn handcuff1" I said closing my eyes. I heard a click. I guessed that he'd locked me in.

Fifteen minutes or so went by before I heard the snapping of the door locks. Evan was two feet away holding on to Willie who was limping along. I did not like the looks of him at all. Both his eyes were swollen and blackening. I imagined that his nose was broken. What once was blood now formed ugly clusters from ear to ear across his face and cut lip. Evan managed to get him into the back cautioning him not to move or talk but talk he did calling me Lady Vienna and crying that it wasn't supposed to happen this way. I told him in a soothing voice that I knew and that I wasn't hurt so not to worry, but I had a question for him and asked him why he hadn't followed through with the plans we had made last year. His answer was a little disturbing even though he laughed about it. He had been picked up by two Waverly police officers and escorted to jail. There had been a robbery and he had been seen in the vicinity and he had once been convicted of a petty theft so he was a likely suspect. He spent seven months behind bars as a guest of the county before the real crooks were found. He said he had a good lawyer. It took him six months to track down Carruthers who had his own agenda and make friends with him again. Will assisted Carruthers in some con game and next thing he knew he was on the wrong side of a gun when his big mouth gave him away. He said he'd give me the whole story when we were both in better shape. I said I could wait.

Evan repositioned my cold compresses, took his seat behind the wheel, started the heli and picked up the airphone. It was answered immediately by Jerry at the other end.

"Evan Govern here Jerry. Coming in hot, two casualties, one suspected concussion, one severe injuries from a beating, suspected broken ribs, eta fourteen minutes."

"I hope you're not considering me as one of your patients as I am not going to the hospital."

He grinned at me from the corner of his mouth. "Of course not Milady."

"Miss Quinn?"

"Actually, it's Mrs. Quinn."

"My apologies; I'm Doctor John Holliday."

"Doc Holliday, by way of Tombstone Arizona I presume."

He laughed a little. "Tombstone Australia in fact."

"I doubt very much that there is a Tombstone in Australia. You must know Shelia and Evan then?"

"If you mean Dr. Shelia, I do, but no Evan."

"He's another Aussie and the man who rescued me and then dumped me here."

"He rescued you from what or from whom?"

"The man who abducted me for the reward money that was offered for information regarding Johnny's uncle's murder. He was the assassin so in essence he wanted to be paid for committing murder. And I had the money and was a nice person and I knew Willie wouldn't hurt me…" I put my head down and closed my eyes just as Evan came through the curtain.

"How is she Doc? Sorry for the intrusion but I had to secure the heli. Evan Govern here."

"So you're the one who dumped her here?"

"I wouldn't say dumped. I put her in a wheelchair and a nurse wheeled her off. She does have a colorful way of describing things so I am not surprised that she said I dumped her."

"This rambling is normal for her then and not because of a suspected head injury? I take it that you are familiar with Mrs. Quinn and can give me some info on her?"

"We live together, so ask away."

"Are you married or just cohabitating?"

I heard Evan laugh. "You might say that we are cohabitating as I am married to her daughter and we all live together in a very big house."

"So you are her son-in-law?"

"I never think of myself as her son-in-law as she is so much more than that to me. Vienna, and I along with Johnny O'Shea have a unique friendship and alliance, and I have no idea why I found it necessary to tell you that. How long has she been sleeping?"

"I don't think she's sleeping Mr. Govern…just a minute; did you say your name was Evan Govern? Are you THE Evan Govern?"

"THE Evan, I hardly doubt it. You must have me mixed up with someone else Doc."

"You're not the Evan Govern from Western Australia whose family disappeared after their house was burnt down some fifty years ago?"

I couldn't feign sleep anymore. "Yes, he *is* the one."

For some ungodly reason Dr. Shelia chose that exact moment to enter the ER and started to fuss over me. She made sure that Doc Holliday knew exactly who I was and that I was to receive the best care possible. A private room was waiting for me as soon as I was done with the x-rays and whatever other tests he had ordered for me. I told her that he hadn't ordered any tests and was yet to examine me.

He smiled amusedly. "What do you think I was doing Madame while you were napping?"

"I was not napping. I heard every word you said."

"Then you heard me say you had a slight concussion and a shoulder sprain?"

"I did not."

"The x-rays are precautionary. I do not believe the shoulder will have any lasting affects. The tenderness and painful movement you are experiencing will disappear when the swelling goes down. Mr. Govern knew what he was doing when he applied the ice so you may want to thank him."

"Evan always knows what he's doing…where is he?" I blurted out realising he was gone.

"He said he'd see you later as there was something he had to tend to. I will see you when you are resting comfortably in your room." Shelia answered.

"Okay, but just for a little while as I have to get home to Pixie." I agreed.

"I'll leave you in Doc Holliday's care then." Shelia said, squeezed my hand, whispered something to the doctor and left.

Two nurses came in and escorted me to the x-ray lab and then to my room. I was given something for pain, had icepacks positioned from my shoulder to halfway down my back and more on my neck. I was told I was on concussion watch for the next 12 to 24 hours. I protested vehemently.

I felt warm hands on my shoulder nudging me. "Time to wake up Vienna."

I opened my eyes to see Johnny. "I didn't realise I was sleeping."

"I guess that's what happens when one has a concussion. Try and stay awake for a bit okay?"

"I'm awake. Can you find my clothes for me?" I asked throwing the ice packs to the floor.

"Those are still good you know. They were just changed when I came in so lets put them back."

"What, why, I'm going home so…" I said swinging my legs over the bed. I regretted it immediately as the pain in my shoulder escalated. "Damn it!"

Johnny put his arm around my waist and lowered me back down. "Easy does it Milady."

"I need to get home Johnny."

"You will, but front and foremost you need to look after yourself so how about you follow the doctor's orders and stay still for the night? Anyhow, we have no way home until tomorrow."

"What do you mean…where's Evan?"

"He had an emergency run."

"What? He wouldn't just leave without telling me where he was going. Just a minute…did you say you weren't going home today? Who's manning the estate then?"

"The gates are locked, Haworth and crew are manning the sentry, Butch and the Boones have the castle so all's good. I never had any plans to go home. I've been at the police station for the last few hours and on the phone with Detective Armand Janzen. He'll be here first thing in the morning to escort Carruthers and Will to Edinburgh so I'll be meeting up with him. You remember Janzen don't you?" Johnny smirked.

"The bump on my head didn't erase my memory Johnny. I don't have to see him do I?"

"He'll want to hear things firsthand from you while everything is still fresh in your mind, but if you're not up to it he'll just have to wait until you are won't he? He did say he was looking forward to seeing you."

"I am in no mood to put up with his flirting so you best warn him. Do you know where my phone is? I need to phone home and say goodnight to Pixie. Oh, Amma must be exhausted…"

"She is not. Jane and Janet have been helping all day long and are spending the night so no worries there. I'm afraid your phone was damaged so you can use mine, but Pixie is probably already in bed."

"Why would she be in bed so early?"

"It's 8:15."

"You mean I've slept right through the whole day?"

"Looks like it doesn't it? Have you eaten at all because I can get you something if you're hungry."

"I remember eating soup and pudding. I don't know when but I'm not hungry. I asked Evan how he found me and he told me to ask you so I'm asking you now."

"GPS tracker, that's how."

"Well its not on me so it must be on my phone. I didn't know mobiles came with one."

"I don't think they do. You can beat on me tomorrow as I put one on yours without your permission."

"And when did you do that?"

"After your graveyard adventure, so like I said, you can shoot me tomorrow."

"I believe you have the gun and have already turned it in to the police so I will have to find another way to reprimand you, but for now I will just say how happy I am that you did so or else I might be dead or out a few thousand dollars. Thankyou for always looking after me. I think I need a hug. I never even asked how you are after the fight with Carruthers. Are you hurting?"

"A promise is a promise, and it wasn't much of a fight so no wounds." He said squeezing me gently.

"I'm glad to hear that. Have you seen Will?"

"He's resting comfortably down the hall."

"Good. Now what's this about a promise and whom did you make it to?"

"Forty or fifty years ago I told your husband that I'd look after you whenever he wasn't around to do so. At the time I didn't know it was going to be such a chore. Thankfully Evan signed on too." Johnny laughed looking at me for a reaction.

What could I do but smile. "You know you're not out of the woods yet don't you as something else will surely come up. It appears that Rainey had a premonition that he wouldn't always be around so I'll take that up with him and pray that it's sooner then later."

"Amen to that. I'll send a nurse in to see to you and I'll see you at noon tomorrow. Be good."

"Noon, why so late? You'll have to bring me something to wear. You're staying at the suite aren't you? There should be an ugly brown pantsuit in the closet that will have to do. You still haven't told me where Evan is?"

"Tomorrow is another day. Get some rest Milady."

Johnny arrived at eleven the next morning with the pants and jacket and a white cotton blouse and even underwear. He said that there was a pretty yellow dress in the closet and wondered why I hadn't asked for that. I told him that it was Katarina's dress and that I had thought Rainey had thrown it out.

"What do you mean Katarina's dress and why would it be here?"

"It's a long story so I'll just say that somehow it made it home from Spain and Rosy mistakenly brought it to me last summer…oh, I guess it was two summers ago. Anyhow, I put it on and I became Kat again."

"What? That's preposterous Vienna!"

"I didn't literally become her but the essence was there and she could do things that Vienna couldn't."

"Like what?"

"I could suddenly knit." I asserted.

"You're one damn strange lady Vienna Quinn. I should know better than to be surprised by anything you do or say but there's just no end to your revelations is there?"

"That's why you love me right?"

He laughed and we walked arm and arm to the nurse's station where I was outfitted with a sling. Doc Holliday said he'd see me in a few days and to have Evan call him. I doubted it.

Evan and Detective Janzen were waiting for us at Two Irish Gals Café. After pleasantries were exchanged Evan said he had something to tell me.

"It had better be good for you to leave me alone at the hospital." I said expecting a dull reason.

"You were in good hands. Now just remember that you are in a public place so don't have a meltdown when I tell you where I was. Do I have your word that you won't jump to conclusions or have a tantrum before you've heard the full story?"

"You're scaring me Evan."

"All is well and there is no reason for you to be afraid. Rose called me not having any knowledge of what had just gone down here with your abduction and asked me to bring you to London as Jannie had a little episode and you would want to be there."

"What kind of episode?" I asked anticipating the worst.

"She had a mild stroke known as a TIA, a transient ischemic attack. She spent the night in the hospital just as a precaution due to her age. She protested heatedly just as you did about your overnight stay here. Anyhow, as I said it was very mild and there was no permanent damage to the brain, the spinal cord or the retina. I brought you some brochures that you can read regarding strokes. I hope you understand that with your suspected concussion there was no way I was going to subject you to flying."

I interpreted his last remark as a question and answered candidly. "I know that Evan though at the time I probably wouldn't have because

I was in denial of my own condition. Many years ago when Rainey had an episode which caused him to black out momentarily I read every pamphlet that was in the hospital as I anxiously waited for his diagnosis and one of them was regarding strokes so I am already familiar with the consequences. I am glad you were able to be there when I couldn't be. I suppose you knew didn't you Johnny so thankyou for not telling me which would have kept me up all night worrying. Please put some jam on my toast as I seem to be a little awkward with my right hand. Anything else to add Evan?"

"Jannie suggested I refrain from telling you as there was no need to add to your worries. I did not tell anyone except Rose what had happened here. She is staying with the family until I pick her up in a few days, and no you can not come with me." He asserted grinning at me from across the table. "Now Armand has a few questions for you if you feel up to it."

"I'm sure Johnny has told you everything Detective so I really don't know what more I can add."

"I will need to take a statement from you but it can wait for a few days. My biggest concern was not only for your injuries Vienna but for your emotional state. It's not everyday that someone gets abducted and with no word on Rainey's disappearance it must be doubly frightening for you. I know you are in good hands with Johnny and Evan but there is no shame in seeking help from a professional if you have any recurring fears or nightmares. If there is anyway I can help please feel free to ask."

"I did not like being treated roughly but I did not fear for my life at anytime. I have no shame in telling you that if Johnny hadn't appeared at the exact moment he did I would have shot my assailment dead. I have no idea how many bullets were in the gun but I'm pretty sure I would have emptied it on him. So if you want to charge me with conscious attempted murder you may."

The three men were all grinning as if I had said something amusing. I continued. "Now Detective Armand, if you really want to do something for me you can see that Will does not see any jail time."

"That might be beyond my control My Lady, but I will put in a good word for him on your word. It may be best if we see what charges will be brought against him before either of us intercede formally. Say in three or four days I drop by and we have our tete-a-tete then?"

"I will look forward to discussing the matter with you. If there is nothing further I would really like to get home to my daughter. Am I allowed to fly Evan? He said that I was.

Aunt Jane had no after affects from her little stroke but was being monitored closely. Except for a few bruises and a sore shoulder for a week I rebounded from the harrowing encounter only to be accosted by another health calamity at the end of June. Evan, Johnny and I had been out on a trail ride. It was a long day and I was getting saddle sore when my horse CindyLou stepped in a hole and I was thrown forward. I felt a pain in my right hip when I bounced back into the saddle. I had gone on ahead of the boys who were fixing a broken gate so they had not seen my horse stumbling. I absorb the pain and plugged on. Fifteen minutes later we arrived home. I dismounted quickly and cried out when I hit the ground. Evan and Johnny were both at my side and caught me before I fell. They were sympathetic but still gave me hell for not telling them what had happened. I was able to make it with their help into the house without them putting me in the "farm ambulance" which was just an old Volkswagen equipped with medical supplies and adapted for rough terrain. A few Advil and Tylenol and the heating pad were at my beck and call again. Unfortunately, that was just the beginning of the age old hip crisis again. It wasn't long before I made the connection to the injury I had sustained during the earthquake in Andorra. I had thought the surgery to dislodge the bone fragments twenty years ago had taken care of that, but here was the same pain back again. It came and went but was enough for me to seek help. Evan flew me into Waverly for an appointment with Doc Holiday. X-rays didn't show anything so he suggested an ultrasound. I told him I would make the appointment. Thankfully I was prescribed a pain medication which did the job so I never made the appointment.

I had sort of promised my family back in Hawthorne that I would come for a visit in the summer. I changed my mind and promised for real that I would be home for Christmas. Pixie and I did go to London with Beth and Colleen at the end of July. We stayed with Rosalyn but I spent most of the time with my aunts. Ada even joined us for the weekend. Of course Hawk made an appearance. I had dinner with him and attended a fun gala at the opera house. He was off again for a four month engagement. This time it was in Japan. I tentatively agreed to accompany him on a vacation to France and Sicily in November.

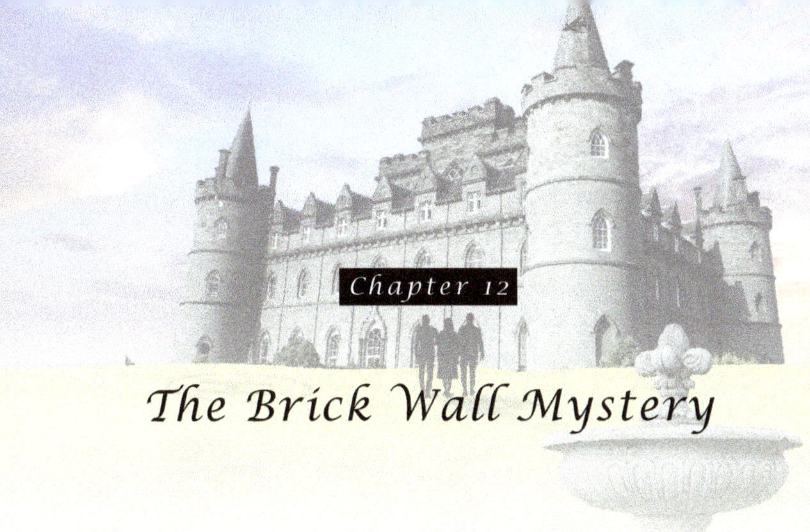

The Brick Wall Mystery

September 7ᵗʰ

The castle was mine. Rosy was in London and Evan was on a rescue mission somewhere. It was Pixie's playdate in the village at Amma's niece's. Amma had talked Mary into accompany them which was somewhat of a miracle in itself. She hadn't been anywhere since Duffy had left us in June. Johnny was driving them to the village as Mary would need help with her mobility issues and wheelchair. He would be busy at the workshop until pickup time at two. It was half past ten so I had three hours or so to do my investigation. "What kind of mischief are you planning Milady?" Johnny asked as I gave Pixie a kiss and hug.

"No plans, but I'm sure I'll think of something."

He laughed. "No doubt."

As soon as the car was out of sight I opened the tool kit that always sat under the backstairs. I wasn't sure what I would need but grabbed a handful of various objects making sure I had a hammer and several different sizes of chisels. I lugged them up the stairs, opened the bookcase, turned on the lights and made my way down into the underground.

A few weeks ago my granddaughters had complained to me. They were bored and yet they didn't want summer to end. They had attended a summer camp in Wales and along with Pixie and me had spent a week with Rosey in late July. Evan and Johnny had rebuilt the stairs that led to Avaleena's rooms when we were gone. It was a wonderful surprise to come home to. Rainey had seen to their dismantling in 2003 but at the time I'd had no plans to return to Avanloch so didn't put up a fuss, but the girls did complain that all the secret rooms were off limits to them and there wasn't even a moat. They had been placated for awhile when the bookcase and stairs was reinstated, but that was all over now. I had suggested we make a tea-lunch and take it downstairs to Avaleena's room, dress up in her gowns and read from her memoirs. They agreed and it had been a fun afternoon. On our way back up the stairs I noticed that one of the bricks on the back wall seemed to jut out from the rest. The old stairs had been built right up against the wall so we never really saw the wall but the new stairs were built away from it. I wondered if anyone else had noticed this protruding brick but kept it to myself.

Now, here I was staring at the wall and wondering what if anything could be behind it. It was going to take some work, but I was determined to remove that wayward brick and see if it was harboring anything. I had no idea how long I'd been hammering and chiselling before I heard something and stopped for a few seconds telling myself that it was just the wind whistling down through the open doors in my bedroom. The second time I listened for a longer and heard nothing again and concluded that it was just normal haunted castles vibrations. The third time it was Johnny calling my name.

"What are you doing down there Vienna?" He asked from the top of the stairs.

"Looking for treasure." I answered.

He came down and stood beside me. "I don't think you are going to find any here. What's with all the tools and the brick?"

"I think I've dislodged it enough to pull it out. What do you think?"

"I hope it's not the brick that holds the whole castle together."

"Very funny...here goes."

"What do you expect to find behind it?"

"Another room."

He laughed. "The brick wall is just covering up the exterior wall you know."

"Really Johnny? The outside wall is at least forty or fifty feet beyond."

"How did you come up with that measurement?"

"Well, the foyer is at least twenty feet past the bookcase and then ten feet across the hall and another forty or so to the outside wall through the bedrooms so this wall doesn't make sense. There has to be something between it and the outside."

"You may be off by a few feet."

"So you agree with me?"

"Don't I always?" He agreed taking my hands into his. "How many times did you hit your fingers instead of the brick? Never mind for now but they will need tending to. Let me give it a pull."

It came out easily. He grinned and passed it to me.

"Here's your brick Milady. What are you going to do with it?"

I took my flashlight out of the duffel bag and shone it into the cavity. "I guess I'll have a full-time job removing enough bricks to gain entry won't I?"

"Entry into what?"

I passed him the flashlight. "Take a look yourself."

He took his time moving the light around just as I had.

"I thought I told you not to get into any trouble and what have you done but open up a new mystery, an underground one at that. The ladies will be home in a few hours so hand me that chisel. We need to remove a few more bricks to get a better view. I think we'll need a pickaxe but this will do for now."

"Don't you have to pick them up and why are you here anyway? I thought you and Butch had a new gate to build."

"Millie's bringing them home. After I dropped the ladies off I had a quick tour of the mill and met up with Haworth. He asked if you knew that Lezza was coming on October the 29th, so I just dropped by to inform you. I might have just thought that you'd gone for a walk when you didn't answer me but the open toolbox and the wind echoing down from your bedroom gave me reason to check upstairs. I saw the open bookcase, and here I am involved with another caper of yours and wondering what Evan will think."

"Well, you pulled the brick out so you're my accomplice. We don't have to tell him right away anyhow."

"Have you ever been banished before?"

It was my turn to laugh. "He can fire you I guess, but I'm the mother-in-law so I have leverage. Won't Butch coming looking for you?"

"Maybe. You own you're son-in-law my dear, but I'm willing to have a little fun with him at the dinner table tonight."

I had no idea what Johnny had in mind but it didn't matter anyhow. An hour or so later we had removed two dozen more bricks. Another ten or more and I'd be able to fit through the hole and into the void of what appeared to be a completely empty space. Of course Johnny nixed that idea. I was disappointed that there appeared to be nothing in the room behind the wall. He said we should see it through as there might be some clue in a corner that we couldn't see.

I put my hand on his shoulder. "Did you hear that?"

We listened but heard nothing and dismissed it as the wind whistling again. Johnny kept pulling out the bricks and I kept piling them up. He said he was going "in" just as we heard the slamming of a door and thundering footfalls on the stairs. We stood with our backs against the hole in the wall waiting to be found. I knew it was Evan even before he called my name.

"Are you down there Vienna?"

I needn't answer as he was already halfway down and could see me.

"You too O'Shea … what are you two up to?"

We stepped away from the wall in unison.

His reaction wasn't what I expected. "I wondered how long it would take you to find that loose brick."

"You knew about it? Why didn't you say something?"

"Why didn't you?"

"I only noticed it a few days ago when the girls and I had our little tea party. You never come down here so when did you notice it?"

"When we built the staircase. I didn't say anything because I didn't want to start something that I had no time for, but I have been thinking about it."

"Why didn't you mention it to me Boss?"

"Because I knew exactly what you would do John. You'd say something to Vienna and well, here you are so I wasn't wrong."

"I found her the same way you found us." Johnny said as he passed Evan the torch. "Have a look."

Evan peered into the hole just as Johnny and I had. He backed up and said that we were going to need a bigger torch. I asked him if he was angry with me for not consulting with him first before attempting to bring the castle down. He put his arm around me.

"No Milady, I am not. It's really not a job for you so I'm glad Johnny found you before you did anymore damage to your hands. Let's go upstairs and get you cleaned up."

"I'm not in any pain and I'm not going anywhere until I see what's inside that hole."

"From what I can see there isn't anything except four walls."

"I agree, but just because we can't see anything from here doesn't mean there isn't something there that would warrant the room being walled up."

"I'm worried that the floor may have settled over the years and may be unsafe to set foot on."

I picked up a brick and threw it as far as I could across the empty room. It landed with a loud thud. I slammed another down right in front of me. "I think it's safe." I bent down ready to crawl through the opening we had made.

Evan stopped me. "It's yours and John's discovery to explore but I'd be more at ease if you would let him enter first. What'd you say John?"

"That's the plan." Johnny bowed to me and wiggled his way into the hole. He bounced up and down on the floor. "Feels sturdy to me Boss." He reached out his hand. "Come on in Milady; easy does it."

I stood up in a completely empty room and dusted myself off. Johnny shone the torch around the room.

"Do you see anything?" Evan asked.

"Not yet but I think we need to check each wall and corner for what I don't know, but there has to be something here."

"I agree but be careful of any pitfalls in the floor." Evan encouraged from the outside.

It didn't take us long to scour the perimeter of the room. The results were nil. I sighed and turned to leave disappointed that it was just an empty chamber much like all the other rooms that Rainey had discovered. Those rooms did seem to have a purpose though as this one did not. Oh well, nothing ventured, nothing gained. "Owww, what's this? I just stubbed my toe on something."

Johnny shone the light down at my feet and bent down to examine it. "Looks like a pin of sorts. It appears to have a coating of some kind of powder around it. Here, hold the light while I brush it off."

"Stop! It may be hazardous. Evan, can you throw that little broom over here?"

"Vienna's right John; don't be touching anything unknown. Can you tell what it is yet? Damn, I should have insisted you wear masks and gloves."

"We should have thought of that ourselves Ev so no blame on you." I stood back as Johnny brushed the unknown substance off what appeared to be a large stone imbedded in the floor. He looked up at me. "It's definitely a hook attached to a metal plate. Nope, don't think it's metal. Take a look Vienna…"

"It's shiny. I think it's stone…could it be marble?"

"Don't know, but it's a good size. I'm thinking it's a trap door. I'm going to try and open it."

"I'm coming in John; wait for me."

"You know if you get stuck Evan, Johnny and I'll be imprisoned in here forever."

He was standing beside me before I even finished warning him. "How big do you think I am anyhow? I removed a few more bricks while you two were trapesing around in here. I think you're right John; it's definitely looks like a trap door. It might not open easily."

"You're right about that. It probably hasn't been opened for a few years and could be corroded. It hardly budged for me so see what you can do."

"Just a few years eh?" Evan managed to pry it open for a few seconds but it was too heavy for him to open it completely but it was enough to see a couple stone steps. He took his cell phone out. "We need a pulley. Okay, no reception here. I'll go out and give Butch a call."

"Let me do it Boss. We'll have to swear him to secrecy you know. Why don't you and Vienna come out into the daylight and I'll wait for Butch?"

Evan and I crawled out behind Johnny and sat down on the steps sharing a bottle of water. He suggested that I should take a break upstairs for awhile. I said I might just do that when hell froze over. He laughed and said it was worth a try. I asked him what he was doing here anyhow as he was supposed to be out on a rescue mission. He said it went smoothly and no one was injured.

"I'm going to have to tell Rose but I'm wondering how we could keep it from the girls."

"Quit fretting; we haven't even found anything yet. If you get that trapdoor open it might reveal absolutely nothing and may just lead outside."

"Is that what you really think?"

I said it was but my fingers were crossed.

I decided to take a bathroom break when Johnny and Butch arrived armed to the limits with ropes, chains, a ladder, a block and tackle, trouble lights, and other riggings. I washed my face and hands and attempted to comb my hair. I put a heavy sweater and my ball cap on and found a pair of old opera gloves in a drawer. I'd deal with the scraped hands later. I made my way back downstairs noticing that there was an extension cord plugged into a receptacle in the foyer and poked my head into the hole-in-the-wall and asked how things were going.

"Come on in, be careful not to get tangled up in the cord." Evan summoned. "We feel we have secured the door adequately but Butch and I are going to make sure it stays open. It has to weigh half a ton so we're not positive that the chain won't snap. One can never be too cautious. Johnny's almost ready for the descent, just waiting for you to stand guard."

I took my place next to Johnny. The pulley was activated. I suddenly felt fearful. We were about to venture into the unknown. What was down in that underground chamber? Was it another hidden passage? There was only one way to find out. I took one of the large torches from Johnny and shone it behind him. "Be careful Johnny, the rocks might be slippery."

"Not to worry as they're dry" He called as he descended. "Yup, they are all dry. I'm on the eighth step and I can't believe what I'm seeing."

"What is it?"

"Let's just say I know where the McAllister clan kept the alligators." He cajoled.

"What did he say Vienna?"

I repeated it to Evan. He said to tell Johnny to quit fooling around.

I reluctantly forced myself to take a step down. Johnny came up and guided me downward. We stopped on the tenth stone rock. He shone his torch into a room that took my breath away.

"Are those paintings on the walls? How deep do you think the water is?" I asked in awe.

"I'm not sure it's water. Look how different it is over there. We need more light. Let's go up and send Evan down."

"Rainey should be here."

"He should be Hon and we can honor him and name this chamber in his name."

"Well what?" Evan demanded.

I couldn't help it; I had to say it. "We're going to need a bigger boat."

"Are you two screwin with me? Are you saying that it's a bloody swamp down there?"

"Wouldn't go that far Boss, but it might be liquid gold."

"Yeah, yeah, yeah. Give me that torch and I'll see for myself. Give Butch a rest will you John? I can't read you Vienna…you don't look disappointed, yet there's something in your eyes."

"There just might be, come find me after you see."

I was halfway up the stairs when I heard Amma calling for me. I retreated and told Johnny that Amma was home so I was going to shut the bookcase. She eyed me suspiciously when I greeted her. I took Pixie from her so she could help Millie get Mary into the bedroom for a laydown. I asked how the day had gone.

"I might ask you the same. Why the cap and tattered jeans and what's with the gloves?"

"I scraped my knuckles and didn't want Pixie to see the cuts. I didn't know my pants were torn."

"That doesn't explain anything. What were you doing?"

"I was removing bricks. We found something Amma. Johnny will be down, or maybe it's up to explain it all. I'm just going to get a glass of water and take Pixie for a nap."

"I can't even imagine what you two have been up to now."

"Evan and Butch are here too."

"Butch, why would he be here? It's too late to take Pixie for a ride today."

"I told you Johnny would explain. It's all good Amma."

Pixie fell asleep with her head on my bosom almost immediately. I thought I may as well have a nap too. I closed my eyes and a trunk overflowing with colorful jewels opened before me. I picked up a ruby red neckpiece and slid it around my neck. It was very heavy. I took it off and replaced it with an aqua marine chocker. It was the color of Rainey's eyes. I felt the tears clouding my vision as I reached for an alluring gemstone tiara just as a hand on my shoulder brought me back to reality.

"Dreaming of treasures Milady? The dungeon, as Amma calls it is all lit up and it's time to check it out." Evan cradled Pixie in his arms and laid her on the daybed.

"How long was I sleeping for anyhow? I can't leave her alone so you go and I'll see it later."

"She won't be alone as Amma is staying with her."

"What did she have to say about the discovery?"

"You're assuming that she crawled into the wall and had a look into the chamber…well, she did not. I left her and Johnny arguing about you."

"What are you talking about? They never argue and what would I have to do with anything?"

"She thinks Johnny has got you involved in another scheme and she wants no part of him luring you into the dungeon."

"He's never been the instigator of anything. Didn't he tell her it was my idea to take the wall apart?"

"You know he wouldn't paint you as the initiator. She's just worried about you."

"Well, there is nothing to worry about and I'll set her straight on the circumstances. Let's go rescue Johnny and do some investigating before the girls get home. Do I need rubber boots?"

"There is no water. I can see why you thought it was though as from your viewpoint it looked like it. However, as you get closer to the bottom you will see that it's a floor of some type of rock that's even glossier than the one covering the trapdoor. Butch thought that it might be obsidian as it has a reflective surface, but the mineral is known as volcanic glass formed from volcanic ash so that lets that out, but quartz and feldspar can have a glassy luster so maybe it's one of those which would make more sense. Anyhow, he has gone home to do some research into minerals of the area. The rock floor only occupies a small portion as the rest is all packed loam."

"So you've made a thorough investigation already?"

"No, not really, just enough to set up the lighting. I had a gander here and there but didn't open any trunks or rummage through the cubicles. That's for the three of us to do together, so let's get to it."

Amma and Johnny were sitting at the kitchen snapping green and yellow beans. Johnny was grinning boyishly. I put my arms around Amma and asked her if she was going to join us. She asked me if I was daft.

"I think that has already been established as fact, but I'd like you to come with us. You don't want to miss out on an epic discovery do you?"

"Thank you, but no, and who'd be left to look after Pixie?"

"Mary I guess, or she could come with us." I answered inanely.

"No Goddaughter of mine is going to any unexplored dungeon and you shouldn't be going either!"

"It's just a room Amma. Ther is nothing harmful in it." Evan tried explaining.

"There better not be. Get on with you then and let me get to supper."

"It's my day to cook and casseroles are unthawing in the pantry, so that's taken care of and there is nothing more to do but relax." I said.

"You're still eating beans whether you like them or not." Amma asserted and told Johnny to take the camera and document everything and to be alert.

He kissed her and said, "Aye, aye my love."

Chapter 13

The Treasure Room

"Ready?" Evan asked as he beckoned me to join him at the top of the vault. Johnny was waiting for us at the bottom.

I said I was. He connected an electrical cord to another one that ran from the generator that had been set up outside the brick entrance. The room below lit up like a Christmas tree. I gasped.

"Exactly our reaction."

"The floor that looked like water earlier looks like it's made of gold now." I stammered.

"Like I told you, it's some unknown stone. The heat from the lamp enhances the colour. Turn the lamp off John. See, it's opaque again."

"Strange, but then the whole thing is, don't you think?"

He said he did and took my arm as we descended into the treasure room. I counted the steps. I stopped two steps before the bottom. It was the eleventh which meant there were thirteen steps. "Funny how the number thirteen keeps turning up."

Evan said he wasn't aware that it did and it meant nothing anyhow.

I did a quick once over the whole room that fanned out before me. "It's overwhelming!" I gasped.

Evan squeezed my shoulder. "It is, and it isn't going anywhere so there's no need to hurry. Eventually we will need to catalogue everything for our records before we inform the authorities."

"Yes, I suppose we'll have to do that. I made my home here some 44 years ago and the room above has always been my bedroom. It's almost too much for me to fathom that I have been sleeping above a treasure room for all that time."

"This castle just keeps on giving doesn't it? Sometimes weirdly like when Johnny had his out of body moment and the vanquishing of Taty's soul and the elevator fiasco, but there have been many more positive and informative things that have happened like the discovery of Avaleena's diary and it's all because of you Vienna, and now this amazing room just because you found a wayward brick."

"Do you not think that everything would have transpired anyhow without me being here?"

They both laughed. "You're kidding right? You're the catalyst Milady. Now take my hand and let's put this next quest into motion." Evan handed me off to Johnny who presented me with a walking stick.

"Where did you get this?"

"There's a whole basket of them down the aisle. Some have heads of cats or birds and serpents. Mine has the head of a jackal I think."

"Yes, it's a jackal. Thanks for giving me Anubis and not a serpent. They are all Egyptian you know which brings me to the question, what are Egyptian walking sticks doing in a Scottish dungeon?"

Evan said that it seemed unlikely but as yet we knew nothing about anything, but surely by the end of day we'd have made discoveries as to who had furnished this room and the how, why, when and where.

I glanced back at the stairway. "What's holding it up? The stairs seem to be suspended in mid air."

"From here they do, but they are supported by balusters at the sides and back." Evan explained.

I stepped down onto the gold mat. Johnny said that it was not as smooth as it looked and had some jagged edges. He asked me which row

I wanted to start on. Before I had stepped down I had noted that the wall to my left was covered in what appeared to be fabrics of some sort. The center row was divided by a 3-foot walkway. One side had an array of trunks, crates and barrels. I had even noticed a giant birdcage that looked like it was made of a wicker-like material. The other side was the long pigeon-hole cupboard that Evan had mentioned and two wooden tables. The one directly in front of me looked as if it might have been a dining table because it held different sized bowls, goblets, pitchers, spoons and two-pronged forks and half a dozen knives ranging from paring size to machete-like. They were all wooden or a metal like bronze or copper I presumed. I decided to go right. Johnny took the lead stating that some of the stones on the path were unstable so he'd point them out. Evan walked beside me as usual. The pathway was mainly hard packed loam. The wall across from the cubbyhole cabinet was timber framed. Metal-like panels were secured to them every few feet. These sheets were about five feet square roughly etched and painted with illustrations. The one before me was of a battle scene with what looked to be a castle in the background. I wondered out loud what the artists used for paint as there was a lot of red depicting blood. It was dated 1242.

"Considering the time frame I imagine that nature supplied the coloring, but you're the artist so what do you think?" Johnny answered,

"My attempt at painting did not pan out as you know. I did very little research on the subject of past coloring. It would be much easier to do now that we have the internet if one had the time or inclination to do so. You are right Johnny as plants like flowers and berries were instrumental in producing different colors as we still use them today like beet and blueberry dyes for Easter egg coloring. There is one thing I do remember though is that besides earth contributions, minerals were also used like lead in white and red coloring and maybe that's what was used to depict the blood."

Johnny laughed. "Yeah, I still have the pink shirt courtesy of the beet overboil."

Evan added that his was purple. We moved on to the next two sheets which had rough drawings of sea battles and maps. There was always a castle in the background. One showed Scotland, England, the North Sea, Wales, Sweden and Norway. The other was of countries to the east like France and Spain. Then there was a whole panel of upside-down Roman numerals and letters. Evan thought it was a code of some sort. The next one portrayed a monastery and priests and the last one was a castle complete with a moat and a graveyard in the background. The date was 1500.

"Do you think this is what Avanloch used to look like?" I asked.

"Could be as it seems likely that whoever was occupying this room would illustrate it along with all the others. It's obvious that it was painted before the destruction. Why don't you and John move on to the treasure aisle and I'll start pulling these scroll-like tubes and see what's on them." Evan suggested.

"Yes, I'm anxious to see what's in all those receptacles too. I'm wondering if Edward constructed these rooms the same time that he built the room for his mistress."

"Don't ask me why but I'm thinking it was before his time and that he didn't even know this and the empty room above existed." Evan predicted.

"Okay I won't ask you why, but how come you think that?"

He laughed. "Just an assumption based on nothing, but who was in charge to the era will surely be revealed through our investigating."

"I'm inclined to go along with you Boss." Johnny agreed. "We'll leave you to your nooks and crannies. I'm anxious to get to that crate with the sisal straps."

"I think I'm going to see what is holding those cloth hangings up before I tackle a chest. What's this; why do you think all these logs are strapped together? Could they be remnants of bed parts?"

"Looks like it. See these holes and pegs in the wall? I think they were to hold bunk beds."

I moved on to the south wall, the wall of many colors. I imagined that these cloth panels had been much brighter originally. Time had faded them to pastel hues of beige, greens and yellows. I tried to pull the thin whitish sheet before me back from the wall so I could examine it further but it was attached to the wall and did not budge. There were a dozen such hangings all of materials much like silk or satin. A few were crinkly to the touch but none came away from the wall for further inspection. The last three were heavier, brownish and rough like burlap. I found that I could part them and when I did I stepped back and yelled, "You'll never guess what I found!"

Johnny arrived first. "I knew there had to be one somewhere. Leave it to you to find it."

He was trying his best to open it but to no avail as Evan joined us. "Give us a hand here Boss."

"If you manage to get it open you know what will be on the other side don't you?"

Evan made a face at me. "No, but I'm sure you are going to tell us."

"I think that my balcony is right above us and you know that a wall of Yew trees and Scotch pine line it right up to the formal dining room patio so it is probably impenetrable."

"She's right Evan. I'm going to pace this off and then see how it measures up outside."

"Yeah sure as there is no hurry to see what's on the other side. Wasn't there a song about a green door and the secrets it was hiding a few years ago?"

"It was quite a few years ago Evan and though this door does have a green hue I hardly think it's hiding anything as everything is in front of it. Wait…do you here music?"

"Very funny Vienna. What do you make of the hue Johnny?"

"If the door was constructed out of freshly hewn wood that wasn't left to dry then moisture might remain in the wood if it was derived of sunlight and taken on the hue."

"I can see that happening if they were in a hurry to conceal this room. On you go then as there is no need to get the door open if there's nothing on the other side."

"There is…trees." I stated.

"Right you are Vienna." Evan laughed. "What say we get back to work while John investigates?"

"I think I'll start with that open trunk as it looks like it's full of trinkets." I turned to go and was met with a sharp pain in my thigh. "Damn…" I cringed pushing my fist into my leg.

Evan took hold of my arm and yelled at Johnny who was halfway up the stairs. "Grab a pain pill for Vienna will you on your way back?"

I bellowed. "Don't you dare Johnathan O'Shea. She'll curse you out again…do you hear me?"

There was no answer. Evan asked me how bad it was.

"Tolerable; I'm going to go sit on that marbled bench and you can drag that trunk over for me please."

He walked me over to the bench but stopped me from sitting down. "Just a sec, I think it's a chest." He lifted the marble cover up. "Ha, it's full of parchments. I hope they will be more interesting and decipherable than my maps."

"What kind of maps?"

"Hand drawn in charcoal, some smudged beyond recognition, but those that are legible are mostly of the sea, Scotland and the Isles and one which I haven't figured out yet but I think it's a drawing of an overland road from here to the ocean. Have you ever heard of one?"

"Not that I remember. It stands to reason though because all this loot had to get here somehow."

"So you're assuming that this is all plunder?"

"Well I don't think it was just hanging around for the taking, do you?"

"No, of course not as the Scots were always at war with some country so as they were marauding say, France, maybe Norway was marauding here, so retaliation. We're also assuming that this might be Templar related aren't we?"

"That would just be speculation unless we find some evidence pointing to them wouldn't it?"

He agreed and unrolled one of the scrolls and asked me what it said.

"I'm not a translator of other languages Evan."

"You know French and Spanish so is it penned in one of them?"

"It is not any script that I recognise. I'll check out more rolls later but I'm curious as to see what jewels are in that overflowing chest right now."

He dragged the chest over. We each grabbed a handful of colorful baubles. I ran the strands of a green jeweled necklace through my hands wondering if it was an emerald. Evan said that he cold see Rose in the tiara that was bedecked in jewels that might be ruby and diamonds. The question was: were they genuine or imitation? A jewel expert would have to determine that. I slid a variety of sparkly bracelets on my arm. Maybe these would be mine now that I no longer had the Infinity ones.

Johnny arrived carrying a thermos, a jug of water, three cups and a bag of treats. He poured me a glass of water and handed me a pill. I asked him what was in the thermos. He said coffee but Amma said I had to drink a whole cup of water first.

"Does she think that we need substance and hydration after just one hour?"

"You know she's just mollycoddling. I could use a cup of mojo." Evan said as he sat down beside me. "I assume you never made it outside did you John?"

"Nope, met up with Butch. Seems he's been busy on the internet and has discovered that there have been earthquakes here in the outback many years ago so this plate might just be obsidian after all. He was going to take Pixie to the farm but Amma said it's too late so he's waiting for me to do the measuring. If I can squeeze between the trees I'll hammer on the wall where I figure the door is. Hopefully you'll hear it. Have you found anything interesting yet?"

"It's all just a little too much to take in with just one walk around, but so far nothing earth shattering and nothing Templar related. I think I'll call it a day and go spend some time with my daughter." I answered.

Evan said he'd wait for Johnny's knocking and keep on with the cabinet files. He'd be up before Colleen and Beth got home from school and together we'd decide what to tell them about the discovery. He slid a turquoise bracelet on my arm and said the jewel was the color of my true love's eyes and he was going to look for something that would fit Pixie.

"We should catalogue them first." I reminded him.

"All in good time, but first we're going to have a good time with the loot."

"Chose something delicate for Mary and make sure Johnny brings the pearl necklace up for Amma. See you when the girls get home." I put 5 scrolls under my arm that I would examine more thoroughly when Pixie was playing or asleep, picked up my walking stick and climbed the stairs out of the subterranean cave.

Colleen and Beth found me unrolling one of the scrolls and asked me what it was. I rolled it back up and asked them if they had seen their father yet. They hadn't. They noticed my shiny bracelet.

Thankfully, Evan arrived. He said he had something to tell them but he was going to have to swear them to secrecy as to what we had discovered it could not leave the castle, at least not until we had thoroughly explored the findings for ourselves. They were very excited and promised that nothing they heard or saw would leave the castle citing that they had never revealed anything regarding Gracie Darling had they. Secrets were safe with them. Then Evan said it was best to start at the very beginning and that was when the new bookcase stairs were built and a part of a wall was exposed that hadn't been before. "Ana discovered a wayward brick so I pass the baton over to her as she is a much better storyteller than me. He passed me a decorated eight inch stick."

"This is an Australian Aboriginal Talking stick isn't it? Why are you giving it to me?" I asked dumbfounded.

"Never had a ceremony where I felt it would be useful before."

"This is not a ceremony Evan. I think the stank dungeon air has taken hold of you. Rosalyn should be here and Amma and Mary so let's move this assembly to the kitchen."

Evan took his phone out of his pocket when we got to the kitchen. He turned it on to speaker. "Rose is right here Vienna. Are you sitting down Honey? As I told you before this is for your ears only and us here at the roundtable."

"It's not round Dad." Beth corrected him.

"You're on Milady."

"Hi Honey. It appears s though we have a little discovery to tell you about. Your husband seems to think that I am a better storyteller than he is which is doubtful. Anyhow, first off I will tell you it is not a story that has an ending but an ongoing one of how and when it all took place, and who and what is to be discovered. It appears as we, the caretakers of Avanloch have another mystery on our hands. It is not dangerous and so far has excited us so if you are prepared we will begin the journey which starts again behind the bookcase."

The girls were on their feet at the first mention of treasure. There wasn't much use in continuing the narrative when all the props were downstairs. "A picture is worth a thousand words so there is no use talking about it when you can see it. I've had enough stimulation for the day so your Dad and Johnny can do the honors. Put on a jacket as it's a little cool down there. Enjoy and we'll see you at supper."

The excitement of the find wore off a little in a few days time. However, we were determined to document everything before we announced the discovery to anyone. Rosalyn was the business expert so she drew up category charts as was needed. The plan was for us all to work on the documentation in our own time. We'd make rough copies and Amma who wanted to be a part of it all, would enter everything into the computer and print hard copies. She did manage one trip into the dungeon and that was enough for her. It would be an arduous task, but hopefully we would have answers to all the questions we'd been asking. There wasn't a time limit as to when it had to be completed and there was a long winter ahead of us.

Chapter 14

Beth's Apparition

October 20th

It was midnight. A lovely Hunter's full moon brightened up the sky. I thought I'd go down the patio stairs and take a walk around the grounds. I was just about to open the glass doors when a light knocking on the connecting lavatory door stopped me. Thinking that Pixie must have woken I asked her if she needed me. A surprise voice answered.

"It's me Ana." She said entering my room.

"What are you doing up so late Honey?"

"I need you to come with me."

"Where do you want to go Beth? Can't it wait until morning?" I was thinking that she may be sleepwalking, but then I didn't think somnambulists talk to anyone, and why was she in Pixie's room?

"She'll be gone by then. She only comes out at night."

Oh dear. "Who is *she* Sweetie?"

"I don't know her but she may be one of your friends. I think she needs help. We have to go through your parlor door as it is quieter than this one." She pointed to the bedroom door and took my hand. "We have to be very quiet Ana."

I let her lead me through the parlor. She stopped me at the door whispering for me to be very still as she gently opened the door.

"Shh." She cautioned me as the spectre seven feet in front of us turned and then evaporated into the stairway. "Oh no, she's gone again." She sighed. "Do you know her Ana?"

"I didn't actually see her face as she disappeared so quickly but I'm assuming it was Maveryn."

"It wasn't my Grandmother. She doesn't come anymore and besides this spectre has blond hair, not red and is way younger than Maveryn."

I didn't comment on the hair color but asked her how old she thought she was.

"Young."

"Your age?"

"No, older; twenty-five or so."

"How many times have you seen her Beth?"

"Three times. The first was two weeks ago on Thursday just before midnight like tonight. Something woke me up that sounded like it was in the hall so I got out of bed and went to see what it was and I saw her floating at the bookcase. I did think like you did that it was Maveryn, but when she turned I could see that it wasn't. I also thought I was dreaming, but then the same thing happened last Thursday. She looked right at me Ana and hovered for a brief few seconds before sailing down the staircase just as she did tonight. I think she was crying. I wondered if she might come back tonight so I went to bed in Ada's room and set the clock for eleven forty-five in case I fell asleep. I left the door open and sure enough she came and I snuck through Pixie's room to get you. She needs our help Ana."

"There isn't anything we can do about it tonight so how about we go back to bed and sleep on it? I know you have an exam tomorrow so you need your rest."

"Can I sleep with you Ana?"

"Of course you can."

"I think we should get Pixie too."

"Okay, I'll get her. You climb into bed and we'll talk more tomorrow after school. You know we are going to have to tell your parents don't you?"

"I don't want to as Dad will just say I'm imagining things and Mom has enough problems already."

"How about if I break the ice with your father first?"

"Okay, he'll believe you because he knows all about your other encounters."

"Are you forgetting how Maveryn appeared to him that night when I lay hemorrhaging on the path to the crypt? Before that he'd had no sightings, not even of Maveryn but he accepted that some of us did or that we thought we did. But a twist of fate that night made him believe that there is an unknown presence that can manifest itself when the need be, so yes he will be supportive."

"If you say so. Goodnight Ana."

The next morning after the girls had left for school I asked Evan if I might have a word with him.

Grinning, he answered. "Of course Milady. Are you up for a brisk morning walk?"

I said I was and where were we going. He said there was something between Willowisp and the mausoleum that he'd been curious about for awhile and thought that it was time to check it out more thoroughly. I left Pixie with Amma, put on my hiking boots and a warm jacket and followed Evan.

"I think I might just know what you are wondering about. It's the mound isn't it?"

"So you've wondered about it too?"

"I never gave it much thought except that it was much larger than any of the other knolls around the estate and didn't have a rounded top but a very flat one. Are you thinking about removing it?"

"No, not really but the question has come up as to why it is so different than all the other hillocks. We're wondering if it has anything to do with the dungeon."

"And just who is this *we*?"

He laughed. "Who do you think?"

"And where is he?"

"He and Butch are bringing some equipment over."

"When did you two come up with this idea…never mind I have something I need you to do for me. You are still going to pick Rosey up this afternoon aren't you?"

"Of course; did you want to come?"

"No, I want you to take Beth."

"Well, that's an odd request and I doubt if she would want to come, so what's up?"

"She needs to tell you something, but she is scared to, so I think a few hours alone together will show her that you're not as tyrannical as she thinks you are."

"Excuse me; she thinks I'm tyrannical?"

"My words, not hers. Anyhow, she asked me to break the ice with you first so here goes. It appears as if we have a new visitor. Beth discovered her and is determined to find out who she is and what she wants."

"Are you trying to tell me in that round about way of yours that we have a new ghost"

"I am. Beth and she found each other so she is Beth's revelation. She believes this vision is looking for something and she is determined to solve the enigma."

"Have you seen this apparition?"

"Yes, last night at the bookcase. Beth has seen her twice before. I don't believe that she's been around long as you and I would surely have seen her on the stairs as she vanishes like a mist down them."

"Is it not Maveryn?"

"No Evan, it is not."

"Is Beth afraid?"

"She is not."

"Will you call the school and let them know that I'll be picking her up at two?"

"I will. Promise me that you and Johnny won't dig your way into another mystery."

"Wouldn't think of infringing on your modus operandi Milady." He cajoled.

"And, see that you don't. Just be the supportive parent that I know you are just like Rose will be. See you at dinner." I hugged him. "Have a good safe trip."

We monitored the grand staircase and foyer all week long. Nothing appeared. Then it was Thursday again. Beth was certain that the spectre of the woman would not present herself if she saw Evan and me so he and I stayed behind closed doors in my bedroom waiting, just in case. It was a very long five minutes until Beth knocked on the door and said we could come out as Marianne was gone.

"Marianne… are you saying that you think this spirit is Pixie's mother?" I asked astonished.

"She is, and she has come to find her daughter. She looked right at me Ana. She touched her heart and cupped her hands to it like she was showing me that her arms were empty. A tear slid down her cheek and then she was gone."

Evan and I put our arms around her and sat her down on the settee. Though her body was trembling we could see that she was mesmerized.

"Sweetie, you never even met Mari so why are you thinking it's her? I'm sure some other woman who lived here many years ago lost her child and maybe she has always been searching but it wasn't until now that she made herself visible. Ghosts don't travel to other places and Mari never lived here so I'm pretty sure it couldn't be her."

"She didn't live here but she almost died on the sofa downstairs and she rests in the mausoleum. You brought her here Ana so she would always be close to Pixie. And one other thing, she looks exactly like her portrait, only sadder."

"That makes sense don't you think Vienna?" Evan asked hopefully.

"I believe Beth has had an experience of a lifetime." I said taking her hands in mine. "You've made me believe that she is Mari and she channeled you to speak for her because she's seen that you are a clever and caring person. She will come again and we will find a way for her to see Pixie and to know that her daughter is cared for and loved."

"We will, won't we. You know I think she came to find you Ana but somehow I got in the way."

I laughed a little. "I'm glad she found you instead my darling."

"Well, it appears as though this cagey old castle isn't just keeping secrets from the past but monitors the present also and probably the future too. I hope to catch a glimpse of this fair spirit one day." Evan alluded.

"You will Daddy because she knows you too."

"Come on, the magical hour is over, let you're ole dad walk you to your room."

Amma was in tears when I entered the kitchen the next morning. "Oh, what's happened now?" I asked transferring Pixie to Evan's outstretched arms.

Johnny was flipping pancakes. "You know she cries whether the news be good or bad Vienna. Beth has just informed us of the outcome of the midnight vigil so it's all good."

I smiled. "It is. I assume she is talking to Rosalyn."

Beth handed me the phone. "Mom wants to talk to you Ana."

I hugged her as she passed me the phone. "Good morning Dear; how are you this morning?"

"I should have been there Mom. It must have been a tense time for you and Evan waiting in the wings while she insisted that she had to face the unknown spectre by herself. I am so thankful that you were there and I know you wouldn't have let her do it alone if you had thought that it was a menacing spirit. Thank God it was Marianne! I mean that is so wonderful Mom, but what now? How do you expect to introduce her to Pixie? Beth says you will know what to do so I am trusting that you do. I've missed so much these past few years that I find the guilt bug has found me. I think I will have to make a decision about this job before it consumes me. Once more I am so grateful that you are there to look after my family."

"I wouldn't be anywhere else Sweetie. They are all my family too. We will discuss your anxieties when you get home on Sunday. There is always an answer to everything and together we will find it."

"That's something Daddy would say. Ask Evan if he can come and get me today?"

I relayed the request to him. He laughed and said. "What do you think?"

"He said he'll see you at noon. Is that too early? Okay, see you in a few hours. Love you."

"I love you too Mom."

On Thursday evening October the 27th at precisely the stroke of midnight Marianne was reunited with her daughter. How to fulfill the mission hadn't taken too much thought or planning. Beth would be sitting in the rocking chair holding Pixie who would no doubt be asleep. I would be in the shadows. Hopefully, Mari would make her usual appearance and see them. After a minute or so Beth would get up and nod for Mari to follow her into Pixie's bedroom where she would kiss her as she lay her into her bed and cover her up thus showing Mari that her daughter was loved. It was a simple plan. There was no book that gave us instructions as how to implement such an undertaking…so, what could go wrong?

Nothing did; it all happened exactly as planned, with one exception. I witnessed the phenomenon cautiously from a safe distance. Evan was behind my bedroom door. We really didn't know what to expect but what happened was truly wondrous. Mari floated out from Pixie's room in front of Beth. I expected to see her flitter away down the stairs, but she stopped at the top and looked back. I tapped lightly on my bedroom door and stepped out of the darkness. My heart fluttered as our souls met. It was the exact same feeling I'd had when I had my first encounter with Maveryn all those years ago. Evan and Beth were at my side as we watched her disappear back into the unknown.

"We'll have to warn all the household so they won't be startled when they see her because she will be living here now. I believe she will look at Avanloch as her home because her daughter's here. It's a much nicer place to rest than the old crypt anyway, don't you think Ana?"

"Yes it is."

Chapter 15

The Blue Moon That Wasn't

I put my coffee cup down saying I'd had enough to last the whole day. Rosy laughed and said that would be the day, and maybe she wouldn't put a fresh pot on at lunch.

It was my turn to laugh. "I won't be privy to Evan asking for a divorce."

"He'd be divorcing you too now wouldn't he because who caters to his every whim if it's not you?"

"She's right Vienna and we all know it. The rapport that you and Evan have is ever increasing and even more since the Mari encounter. It's always been there for all of us to see, but these last two years has brought your connection to a whole new level, and Johnny is never very far behind is he?" Amma commented.

"If it was any other woman I'd be jealous, but because it's you Mom my heart is warmed. If I haven't told you lately Mom, I'm so glad you are here. I never worry about the girls when I go into London for two or three days like I did before and Evan doesn't brood so much anymore." Rosy smiled lovingly.

"You tell me all the time Honey."

"The same goes for me Vienna. Johnny is never more alive when the three of you are engrossed in some new antic, point in case, the

Dungeon. That should keep you busy all winter so there should be no new adventures right?"

"Hopefully not Amma; but then things just unexpectedly happen don't they?" I hugged them both. "It is I who is indebted to you as you have been my salvation. Now, I am going upstairs and see what Ada and Pixie are up to, get dressed and maybe even clean up Miss Mary's room as I am sure that I have left it in a mess. It's not a priority though but watering all the palm trees is. Johnny topped the rain barrels up so I guess I'll give them one last bath before they have to be brought in. See you at lunch, and Amma, I'm expecting cinnamon buns with that dough you're kneading." I winked.

"They were Daddy's favorite weren't they?" Rosy said nostalgically.

"Yes, as long as they had raisins. You know when I first met him, he didn't even like sweets."

"That's hard to believe Mom."

"Well, it is so." I answered walking over and looking at a calendar on the wall. "I see there isn't a blue moon this month or in December either. I wonder when the next one will be."

"Why is that of interest to you Mom?"

"You know the saying, "once in a blue moon"…well, that's when your dad will be back."

"Oh Mommy; you've had a premonition haven't you?"

"Not really, and not having any idea when there will be another blue moon, it may be a very long wait."

"Give me a minute; let me get rid of these files and I'll see if I can pull up a few calendars. Oh, there doesn't appear to be any blue moons until 2009. That's odd isn't it?"

"I don't know as I have never thought about it before. I'll let you girls get back to your work, and Rosy take a break from those contaminated McAllister e-mails. I am sure all the busy bodies will be caught soon." I threw them kisses and left.

I stopped at Miss Mary's room but decided to leave it for another day. Colleen and Beth enjoyed their Great, Great, Grandmother's room and closets full of vintage clothing and jewellery just as much as my girls had, so I'd wait for them to help me. Pixie was dressing Pixie in her warm pants and parka because they were going to the farmyard to see the chickens and the lambs. That trip down to the hen house and barns would take an hour or so because of course they would have to visit with everyone. Ada would be heading back to Waverly on Friday and then resuming her studies at Stirling College and wouldn't have a break until the Christmas holiday so she wanted to spend as much time as she could with her niece. I always took a step back with Pixie when Ada was visiting which wasn't often enough.

I reminded Pixie to put her new boots on and to have fun and went on to my room. I pulled an old blue dress and long sweater out of my closet and carried them and a pair of flats over to the bed. I dressed and sat down and dangled my feet thinking that if Rainey was here he'd slip the shoes on my feet and say he was glad that I was following Dr. Barb's guidelines about wearing the proper footwear to fit the occasion. Well, he wasn't here was he, so I didn't have to placate him. He'd been gone for two years, two months and two days. I walked out on the terrace sans footwear.

I stood at the balustrade at Diana's sculpture remembering that Tanny had said that Rainey had picked her statue first because she reminded him of me as she was a little bit wild and loved to dance with the moon. I don't think anyone would describe me as being wild and though I had danced a little last holiday season it certainly wasn't under the moon. I said hello to all the other goddesses that Rainey had chosen to complement the balcony that he'd commissioned Johnny to build for me when I was missing for almost two years. Now, he was the one missing. Why did all these things happen to us? Was there any rationality behind it? No, it was our destiny to be star struck lovers condemned to relive their lives over and over again without each other. Time after time we had resisted all the forces against us, but now we had run out of time…what had sparked me down this road of despondency again? I had accepted the fact that Rainey was never coming back but now I had the biggest decision of my life to make. Was I going to meet Hawk in London in two days? Was I going to go to France with him and then on to Sicily where he wanted to retire? Was I going to accept his proposals to find a house for us to live in and eventually get married? Did I really believe that he could be a father to Pixie? That was the biggest question of all. I was pretty sure of my answer wasn't I? The roar of the helicopter brought me back into the reality of the day. No one had said anything about Evan going anywhere. I heard it land and five minutes later there was the sound of thundering footfalls on the metal steps. Well, that was fast. He didn't even have time to put the heli away. I guess I was going to find out where he had been and why he was coming to see me. I had a moment of panic thinking that Hawk was the one on the stairs. No, it had to be Evan. Watering can in hand, I was about to turn and confront him, but before I could I heard the words that started the dead part of my heart into beating again.

"Hi Gorgeous."

It was Rainey's voice, but it couldn't be. I must have projected his voice into Evan's because I'd been thinking about him a few minutes ago, but then Evan would never call me gorgeous. I took a deep breath and slowly turned around. He was standing five feet in front of me. The little curl that he always struggled to banish was drooping above his left brow. His hair was longer than I'd ever seen it. The sandy-brown locks were now immersed with patches of silver. The crooked smile that he was known for flashed at me as he winked and asked me if I had a hug for an old man. I dropped my watering can and ran into his outstretched arms still not believing it was him.

"Oh Rainey, oh Rainey, is it you…is it really you?" I cried as I ran my hands up and down both sides of his face. The tears I hadn't been able to cry since he'd been gone ran down my face shamelessly. His arms tightened around me.

"I'm pretty sure it's me Honey." He said emotionally.

"I never thought I'd ever see you again. Where have you been…where have you been?" I managed to ask between crying spasms.

"I've been in lock-up Honey."

"What could you have possibly done to spend two years in jail?"

"It wasn't that kind of jail Vienna."

"I know, I know. It was Blackie wasn't it? He's *her* brother. Were you with *her* Rainey?"

"No, I'm pretty sure she's still dead." He asserted rather amusedly.

"Are you sure it wasn't *her* masquerading as her sister?"

He laughed a little. "I'm not surprised that you know about the sister but I'm absolutely positive that it wasn't Jorja and you will be too when you hear my story as will everyone else downstairs because I only want to tell it once. I wanted to see you first and Evan spotted you up here so that meant that I'd see you before anyone else, and I needed to. Now I have to get down there as Evan is probably splitting a gut trying to explain to Rosalyn where he was, and I kind of want to see her and everyone else too."

He took my hand and asked me if I was coming. I nodded and followed him through the patio doors. I think I was still in shock. He stopped at the bed seeing my shoes and asked me if I was going to dry my feet and put my shoes on. I said my feet weren't wet and I didn't need shoes. He nodded to where I had been standing where there was a pool of spilled water from the watering can. I just smiled and said I was so shocked from seeing him that I hadn't felt anything but astonishment and that I still wasn't sure that I wasn't dreaming. He squeezed my hand and said I wasn't dreaming and could I just humor him and put the slippers on. I smiled and said I could and followed him towards the main staircase. I looked back at Pixie's room just before we started down the stairs.

"I have something to tell you Rainey."

"I'm sure you do, and there'll be lots of time for that." He pulled me along and then stopped at the landing halfway down and said that nothing had to change just because he was back.

"What do you mean when you say nothing has to change?" I questioned uneasily.

He pointed to the ring on my hand. "I meant for you. I know you have a boyfriend, and I don't expect you to give up the new life you have made for yourself for me."

I was trembling. I tried to speak but the words came out garbled through my spasmodic lips. He steadied them with his fingers and told me to shush because everything was going to be all right.

"Evan told you didn't he?" I managed to gasp. "How long have you been in contact with him?"

"I called him from Waverly and asked him to pick me up, so about an hour or so. He did not tell me anything about you that I didn't already know."

"How, how is that possible?" I couldn't even imagine.

"Come along. You will know everything in a few minutes I promise."

I didn't want to meet up with everyone else and let go of his hand stating my dismay.

"Well, one thing hasn't changed and that's your stubbornness. Come if you like, or not." He questioned pleadingly and extended his hand again.

I wanted to tell him how much I loved and missed him and that I didn't have a boyfriend, but it appeared as if he didn't want to hear anything I had to say so I took his hand and followed him. I lost my balance on the bottom step. He caught me and asked if I was all right. Well, I wasn't. I just wanted to be alone with him, but it was evident he didn't want to be alone with me. I didn't tell him that my hip had been acting up again or that I had adopted another child or a hundred other things because maybe he wouldn't care and that was why nothing had to change for me because he also had a new life. Maybe he hadn't even been Blackie's prisoner. The hallway seemed to be shorter than usual.

Evan was standing behind Mrs. D at the kitchen table. He threw his arms up in the air. "What took you so bloody long man?"

"You told me to go have a few words with my wife so that's what I did Buddy." Rainey said.

Chairs were uprooted and there was a loud clang as something hit the floor.

"Well, I'll be a son of a bitch!" Johnny exclaimed.

"Blessed be." Mary said, hands in the prayer position, eyes looking upward.

Amma was crying and Rosy was holding her hands to her mouth. She ran around the table almost knocking Evan over. I stepped aside quickly as she threw her arms around Rainey.

"Oh, oh, oh, you're alive! Oh my God, oh my God! Where did you come from…Evan is that where you were…why didn't you tell me?" She stammered.

"He didn't know Honey. I called him from Waverly just like I told your mother. I asked him to keep it a secret until after I saw her." Rainey explained.

She hung unto him as she pulled me close. "Oh Mommy, oh Mommy…" She cried ecstatically.

Rainey embraced Amma and shook Johnny's hand as best he could with Rosy holding unto him so tightly. He managed to bend down and hug Mrs. D.

"How's my girl? I'm sorry about the Duff, Mary."

She patted his hand. "It was his time Mr. Rainey, but it wasn't yours. She always said you were alive and you'd be back you know."

He smiled at me. I did not tell him that Rosy was the one who always said that and not me. Amma wanted to make him breakfast. He declined saying that coffee would do for now as he wanted to give us a brief outline of the past two years before he called everyone else.

"To hell with the coffee; this is cause for a celebration!" Johnny stated as he took the "good stuff" down from the top cupboard. He passed us all shot glasses and poured us a dram. "This will do for now, but later we'll do it up good, what'd you say Rain?" He raised his glass as a salute.

I made a face as usual when I downed the whiskey and made eye contact with my husband. I was compelled to correct his concept of time. "You've been missing not just for two years, but two years, two months, two days and…" I paused glancing at the clock on the wall, "approximately seven and a half hours, and three minutes. Maybe it was longer, but I woke up to find you gone at 3:30 a.m. on August 29th. I guess it was actually the 30th, two plus years ago."

The look he gave me I took as amazement and sadness that I would know the time down to minutes. He squeezed my hand again. His voice was low and heart-rending as he spoke.

"I was awakened by a hand shaking me that morning. Of course I thought it was you, but you didn't answer me when I asked if I had been snoring. A man's gruff voice suggested I turn over and if I didn't want to wake my little wife upstairs then I better keep my voice down. I felt a hand on my shoulder, turned over and saw Black Smith holding a gun aimed at me."

"Oh Daddy…" Rosy exclaimed.

"It's okay Red; he never used it, but let's put it this way; I was definitely aware of its capability. I asked him what he was doing. He suggested that I get dressed as we were going for a little ride. I told him to think again as I wasn't going anywhere with him. He told me to suit myself as he'd just as soon take my wife. Well, that woke me up. I threatened him as to what would happen if he touched one hair on your head. Of course he laughed rudely at that. I was never more thankful of your nocturnal walks as I was that night Honey." He said warmly smiling at me.

"I didn't know at the time what he wanted or even where you were but he happily filled me in on your whereabouts. He said you were sleeping soundly upstairs so let's get a move on before you woke up. I asked him how he knew that. He laughed and asked me if I was stupid enough to believe that he'd come alone. He pulled out a walkie-talkie and asked if all was calm upstairs. Satisfied with the answer he got from whoever was on the other end he nudged me with the gun and suggested I speed it up and get dressed. I glanced at my watch on the dresser and saw that it was three a.m. He goes through my wallet and removes all the cash never taking his eyes off me. I'm now afraid that whoever is keeping watch over you is all set to grab you if I make a mistake. He pushes me out of the bedroom with the blunt end of the gun and suggests that we make a quick trip to the basement and to keep my mouth shut. He ordered me to open the safe. Somehow he knows that I keep the money from my blueprint sales in there. I couldn't believe that I would have told him that but I gladly passed it all to him hoping that's all he wanted."

"He wanted the bracelets too didn't he?" I interjected.

"Your bracelets weren't in the safe Vienna; why would you think they were?"

"Because they are missing and I know you've locked them up before so I just assumed that Blackie had taken them."

"Mom, this is the first I am hearing that your bracelets are missing."

"I don't know when I discovered they were missing or even if I linked it to Rainey's disappearance. It's of no consequence though."

"I assure you they were not in the safe, and I have only put them in the safe once."

"I know I was careless with them, but I only wore and took them off in my own house so I never thought someone might steal them. I suppose that Blackie may have found them the same way. Anyhow, they are missing. I just assumed that is one of the reasons he asked for such a little ransom as he had them and could get a small fortune for them."

Rainey seemed surprised. "You know about the ransom?"

"Of course I do, and so does everyone else."

"The only one who knew that besides Black is Owen so I'm assuming he called you even though I asked him not to."

"The reason for that is what Rainey? Didn't you want us to know you were alive?"

"I guess I was too trusting or maybe just friggin gullible to believe that I'd be released as soon as he had the money. I believed I'd be home the next day."

"Well, you weren't. We waited, and we waited, and we waited. We knew the ransom had been paid because Owen called back as soon as it was successfully transferred. We speculated as to what went wrong and thought that another ransom demand was forthcoming. All along I wondered why Owen had been contacted and not me or the girls. Suppose if he couldn't come up with the two million … what would have happened then?"

"But Mom…"

Evan interrupted Rosalyn. "I think that your mom is wondering what Blackie's reasons were for not contacting the family for the ransom and that she would have paid a hell of a lot more."

I nodded and smiled at Evan. It was up to me to inform Rainey that I had paid the ransom and that he hadn't lost anything at Quinn Enterprises, and I would when the time was right.

"I let Black abduct me without putting up a fight so I felt responsible and went along with his plan thinking that the two million was all he wanted. It wasn't as if I had a choice anyhow."

"You have no reason to feel guilty Dad because there was nothing you could have done. He had a gun and you couldn't risk Mom's and the twins' lives."

"He should have taken me because it's my fault that he was even in our lives." I responded.

"Why would you say such a thing?" Rainey demanded.

"If I hadn't befriended Izzy and talked her into moving back to Hawthorne, Black Smith would never have existed in our world, so that's why."

Rainey put his arm around me. "Look at me Honey. You can quit believing that and I never want to hear you speak of it again. He's a mad man and I thank God every day that it was me he chose to abduct and not you. There is no blame here, understand?"

"I'm the one with the money, so why didn't he ask for more? He had to know I would have given up everything to get you back, so why didn't he?"

He smiled at me and wiped a tear from my eye. "I know you would have, but I don't have an answer as none was provided to me. I just assumed after it would be over and done with when the ransom was paid, but for reasons unknown Black wanted me and he wanted to destroy me in every way that he could, and taking me away from you and the kids, holding me hostage and leaving me destitute was his punishment. He never supplied me with a reason. As time went on I came to believe that ransom was just the tip of the iceberg. He wanted revenge for something that I haven't been able to comprehend, but believe me when I say that I am going to find out if it takes me the rest of my life."

"I'm with you on that Rain, but why do you think that he'll be more co-operative in jail?"

"Do you know something that I don't Evan?"

"What do you mean?"

"I've been on a plane for twelve hours so enlighten me please as to how he was found and arrested as it will be music to my ears."

"Oh Christ, that was just an assumption on my part that he was taken into custody when you were found. Sorry, but we haven't heard anything. I'm sure Sergeant Rolph or someone would have contacted us if there was any word."

"No one knows but Mason and Morgan and you guys that I have been rescued and I have been informed that is the way it is going to stay until everything from the compound has been collected and analyzed. I was taken to a police station in Burnaby where I gave a limited account of the abduction and incarceration. I was also given a quick medical before I was escorted to Mason's. I was not surprised to be informed that Black had been on the radar for several years, and especially more since he was a suspect in my abduction. As far as I know he is still a fugitive and where he or his cohorts were the night of the rescue is unknown."

"We were informed that he has been a wanted man for some time. How he has been able to avoid the authorities and the private investigators is a conundrum, but what does it mean for you and our family? If he is anything like his sister he will never give up, and that means we are all in danger." I stammered.

He pulled me into his arms and rocked me. "It's all been taken care of Honey. Amma, can you bring her a glass of water please? I'm sorry, I got ahead of myself and said things out of order and I should have told you from the start that you have nothing to fear. The authorities were well aware of Black's connection to you and me, and all our family. They've been keeping tabs on everyone and now that I have been rescued that protection has intensified. I will correct what I said about no one else knowing I am alive because Novia and Sammie have been taken to Mason's as a precaution and are under round the clock protection as is Morgan, and everyone in Hawthorne. I screwed up and I'm sorry for not telling you from the get-go."

"I asked too many questions so it's my fault as usual for interrupting." I lamented.

"It's not Honey. I was over- anxious and you can ask as many questions as you like. I talked to Novy briefly as I left to catch the plane before she and Sammie arrived at Mason's. I guess I had better get on with the account because I've asked them not to call everyone else as I need to do that myself."

"You do, and you need to do that right now Rain. We're not going anywhere and we'll be right here when you're done." Evan said.

Rosy agreed. "Here's my phone Dad; all their numbers are listed just in case you've forgotten them. Why don't you go into the parlor for some privacy?"

"Thanks Honey. Are you coming with me Vienna?"

"I think you need some private time with them, and I'll just distract you as I'll probably cry."

"I won't mind."

"Go, and tell them I'll talk to them later."

He kissed my forehead and told the rest to look after me. Amma said she was going to make him something to eat. She asked me if she should make breakfast as he probably hadn't eaten yet, or did I think a roast beef sandwich would be enough. I nodded saying a sandwich would be good. I couldn't hide my apprehension anymore and I just blurted it out.

"He knows."

Rosy put her arm around me. "He knows what Mama?"

"He knows about Hawk."

"How could he? Do you think Mason or Morgan told him? Oh, tell me it wasn't you Evan?"

"It wasn't me Rose. I was surprised when he asked me how serious the relationship was. I asked him how he knew, and he said that he just did."

"What did you tell him?" She asked.

"He said that he didn't expect an answer because he knew I was loyal to Vienna, and he'd get the answers from her, and he'd know the second he saw her. So, did he get an answer?"

"He said he knew I had a boyfriend and that I needn't change my life just because he was home. He wouldn't let me explain and said that it was all right." I covered my face with my hands and wept. Rosy tried to comfort me. I looked up at all the eyes that were focused on me, stood up and expressed myself rather loudly. "All right, he said it was all right. What does that mean anyway? It's all right that I have a lover; is that what he means? Well, I don't… I don't!"

"We know you don't Mom, and so will he. You have to give him some room to come to terms with what's happened while he was gone. We have no idea what he's been through and I'm a little fearful of what we are going to find out. One thing is for sure, and that is that he loves you. He caught the first flight over here to see you before he did anything else. I can see the love that shines for you when he looks at you. His feelings for you haven't changed and I know yours haven't either. He's barely been here an hour and we still have no idea what he has been through so we just need to be patient. Can you do that Mommy?"

"Rose is right Vienna." Evan came over and wiped my eyes with a towel. "This isn't new to us is it? For two years we've watched you grieve just as we watched Rain do so when you were missing. It's inconceivable that this could even happen once in a couple's life, but twice is astronomical, but then life has never been normal for the two of you has it? By the end of the day it will be all sorted out, and you can take my word on that."

"Or, what if isn't?" I dared to ask him.

"Then I guess the fixer-upper will have to intervene won't he?"

"You mean like he did with me in the hospital twenty-some odd years ago?"

"That's right Milady."

"He asked you to go with him when he did his phoning…"

I didn't let Rosy finish. "No, he didn't. He asked me if I was coming; he did not invite me and that is because he doesn't want to be alone with me. I'll take the sandwich into him and let the chips fall where they may." I got up and opened the fridge and took the chocolate cake and milk out. I cut a large piece of cake and poured the milk into a tall glass and set it on the tray that Amma had prepared for him. I turned around and asked Johnny why he was so quiet.

"I've seen this movie before and I know how it ends, so just watching and waiting."

"You might just be in for a surprise new ending."

"Don't say that Vienna." Amma said breaking out in a fresh barrage of tears.

"What will be will be." I picked up the tray and started for the parlor.

Evan stopped me holding unto the tray. "How far do you think you'll get before spilling the milk? Your whole body is shaking like a volcano ready to explode. Let me get you a tea trolley."

"Okay; make sure it's not one with squeaky wheels as I don't want him to hear me coming."

He grinned, placed my tray on the cart and put his hands on my shoulder. "Relax will you? Just breathe. That's Rainey down there, not some stranger, so don't treat him like one. He's probably overcome with emotion as are the rest of the family, so cut him a little slack. You've waited two years for this day so make it a day to rejoice. You hold the key to his heart you know."

"Actually, it's two years, two months, two days, eight hours and seventeen minutes."

"That's my girl. Now get a move on."

The back door opened just as I started down the hall. Ada was telling Pixie to take her boots off. I turned back intending to catch her before she did her usual running down the hall. She scooted past me laughing that I couldn't catch her because she had skates on. I caught up to her just short of the parlor doorway where she had stopped. Rainey came out holding the phone to his ear. He scooped her up in his arms and asked her where she had been hiding.

"Me no hiding, you hiding." She said and then spoke into the phone. "Hi."

"That's Ava you are talking to. Do you know Ava?"

"Me talk Aba."

I pushed the cart up to them as I needed it for balance. This wasn't the way I had hoped to introduce my daughter to the man whom I wanted to be her father. On the other hand, maybe she had taken the pressure off me. "Amma insisted that you need to eat. I see you have met Pixie."

"Pixie…I thought her name was Darlana."

"How would you know that?" I asked sternly.

"Ava asked me if I had met Darlana yet, so I'm thinking this might be her?"

"What else did she say about her?"

"Nothing. I heard a noise out here and came to investigate and was immediately relieved of the phone."

Pixie dropped the hold she had on the phone and put her arms out to me. "Mommy, Mommy."

The look on his face was priceless as I took her from him. "Yes, she's mine; she's *my* baby."

"How…why didn't you tell me before?"

"Before, before what? If you remember correctly, you didn't want to hear anything that I had to say."

"Sorry about that. So, you and Hawk have adopted a child?" He asked dubiously.

I pushed the cart at him a little too vigorously and retreated back down the hall recoiling from his ludicrous assumption. I heard him tell Ava he'd call her back.

All eyes were on me as we arrived back in the kitchen. I sat Pixie down in Duffy's old chair under the window and proceeded to remove her boots. As usual, she wanted to comb my hair.

"In a minute Honey. Why did you run away from Ada?"

"Me play game."

Ada apologised for letting her get away. "There is no need to as we all know how cagey this rag-a-muffin is don't we? Oh, I guess you've been told that Rosy's Dad has shown up?"

She hugged me with tears in her eyes and said that she was so happy for me and Rosy and that I must be so relieved. I said I was as I picked Pixie up and sat down with her in my lap. Ada pulled the wheeled table up and placed the coloring books and crayons on it. I looked up and Rainey was standing there smiling down at us. I introduced him to Pixie's aunt.

"I am very pleased to meet you and your niece Ada. It's an unsuspected pleasure to see a little one laughing and running down these halls again. It's just like old times, but I fear I may have jumped to conclusions just like I did in the past so I need to apologise to this lady here. Will you please accept my apologies Vienna?"

"For what I am not sure, but like always, I will. There is no way you can possibly know all the facts about the last two years, so I take no offense and as you said we'll iron it all out later. Now I fear that Ava was only your first call and you need to finish that up before we go any further."

He agreed. "Pixie, eh?" He grinned and started to leave.

She raised her head and handed him a red crayon and stunned him by saying "Wainey."

He recovered quickly, drew a heart with the crayon and told her to be a good girl for Mommy and that he'd be back in a few minutes.

Rosy was all smiles. "See Mommy, he loves her already."

"What's not to love, but I'm not so sure that he'll be as accepting with everything else."

"Is there something specific your referring to?" Evan asked tongue in cheek.

"Oh you know, just the little things like my relationship with Hawk, my trip to the Blue Parrot, my involvement with Uncle Walt's killer, my abduction, finding Gracie Darlings grave or what's behind the brick wall…need I go on?"

"We all had a hand in your shenanigans which are now interesting stories and made for the telling. I'd like to keep the tales for another day though when Rain's had a chance to get accustomed to the castle craziness again." Evan suggested.

"You forgotten to include the new ghost in your resume Milady?" Johnny quipped.

Evan laughed and wished me good luck. Rosy hugged me and Amma said that they were all going to miss me. I asked her where I was going.

"Back to Hawthorne of course." She answered.

"Well, I will probably go, but who says that I'll stay?"

"You'll stay all right because that's where you belong, but you'll be back at the first sign of unrest when the castle calls your name." Evan smirked.

"You mean when one of you summon me. If I go I'll leave you detailed instructions for dealing with the spirit world, but anything else you're on your own. First, I have to get through today, and things may not be as promising as you think they will be. Now, I need to get this little imp fed and down for a nap before Rainey returns so let's hope he isn't too curious about yesterday's events."

"Today is all about him Mom, so don't worry, we know what to do."

As if on cue, Rainey arrived just as we getting into the lift. Funny, I hadn't seen him for over two years and I still felt his presence before I saw him. I asked him if all was well. He said that it was and he had left instructions for Novia to call over here the minute she arrived home. He said he'd wait for my return before carrying on with his ordeal. Ada relieved me of Pixie saying that I should go with Rainey now. I kissed my little darling and followed him back to the kitchen. He thanked Amma for the sandwich and the goodies. Of course she had to tell him the cake was my idea. He said he thought as much because I knew he could never pass up a piece of chocolate cake.

Hesitantly, he said he guessed it was time to get on with the story. "I'll keep it as brief as possible just so you get the picture of the last two plus years. Mason received my email on the day I sent it which was October

29th and he contacted a friend in the RCMP and he took it from there. I was rescued on October 31st at midnight. That's a Halloween I will never forget."

"We have gone from the night it all went down to your rescue Rain. You need to go back to what happened after you were forced to leave the house and fill us in on a few more details like explaining this compound you were held in and the indignities that you've been subjected to for the last two years." Evan suggested.

Chapter 16

The Incarceration

"**S**orry, I wasn't sure if you wanted to hear it all. The first thing I want you to know is that I was not physically abused in any way except for the injection of a drug that was given to me the second I was escorted into the van that night, well morning I guess. It was parked just beyond the stile. My hands were tied so I had one hell of a time getting over it."

Rosy was fretting.

"Look at me Red; do you see any wounds of any sort on me? I'll strip if you like and you can check me over." Rainey said trying to make light of it all.

She managed a little twitter. "I don't think that will be necessary Dad, but I'm not totally convinced. Why did they drug you?"

"It was their way of managing me. I had no sooner been pushed into the back of the van when I was injected. I don't know who the injector was but I assumed it was Black because Lonnie was the one who had a hold on me. Of course I didn't know this man's name at the time or what his involvement was with Black. Just before I lost consciousness I heard a woman's voice. It was dark but I believe she was behind the wheel. She said, "Hi Rainey.""

I asked him if he recognized the voice.

"No, not then. There were several females that made an appearance at the compound and I tried to compare that voice to one of them but I never came up with a definite answer. The only one I actually saw was Black's sister Leslie so I just assumed it was her. I'm getting ahead of myself, but I need Vienna to know that it was not Jorja, and there was no resemblance to her whatsoever." He looked at me hopefully.

Before I could say anything Rosy asked him why he would think that I thought it was Jorja because she had been dead for years.

"That was the first thing she said to me Rosy. She asked me if I had been with *her*."

"Mom, why would you think such a thing?"

Evan was the only one whom I had told about the dream, and as usual he came to my rescue.

"I think I can answer that. The minute Sgt. Rolph told us that Jorja was Black's sister your mother convinced herself that it was her twin sister who had died in prison and not Jorja. No matter what anyone said she had that picture of her etched in her mind and I don't believe she has ever squashed it." He gave me the knowing nod. "Am I right, is that's why you asked Rain if it was so Vienna?"

"You assumption is correct Evan, and even though he denied it, I'm still not sure."

"Vienna, for God's sake you can't possibly believe that?" Rainey questioned anxiously.

"My head knows that she's dead, but sometimes I catch a glimpse of her as she whizzes by on her broom. I smile as I watch her melt as a giant raindrop crashes down on her head." I don't think I stunned anyone except Rainey by my response. Looking around the room and recognizing their compliant grins he nodded. "I have missed you twisted sense of humor Vienna, but I see that it hasn't been lost on everyone else. Still, I'm not sure you believe me."

It was more a question so I placed my hand on his. "I believe you because it is only logical."

"Great; now you've quoting Spock again." Evan said shaking his head.

I laughed slightly. "So, you are in the back of the van and you think that the person behind the wheel is a woman. Did you ever think it was Jorja because you said you recognized the voice, and when did you know that Black was her brother? Never mind, go on with your story. I'm sure it will all become clear as mud when your story unravels. You had just been injected with a toxic drug, so what happened next?"

He squeezed my hand. "Nothing; I knew nothing but queasiness for days. I was not aware of how long I was in that state until I was told. I just remember having a headache that wouldn't go away and I was nauseous all the time. If I lifted my head dizziness overtook me and I had to lie back down. I was conscious of voices now and then, but I couldn't focus on where they were coming from. Like I said, I had no idea how long this went on for. When I could keep my eyes open for more than a minute I saw a man standing over me. I recognised him as the man who had met Black and me outside of the house."

"Well, it's about time Quinn! Did you think you could sleep forever? You smell of sweat and vomit so get up and get over to the sink and clean yourself. Everything you need is there."

"Where the hell are we?" I demanded.

He said that I'd figure it out. I heard what sounded like a heavy metal gate slamming. I sat up cautiously not sure if the vertigo was still with me. I had seen the inside of a jail cell once when I was in high school on an assignment. It pretty much looked the same with one subtle difference and that was the door. It had been left open in the police station, but that was not so here. A big, heavy padlock hung on the steel door. The man was nowhere to be seen and no amount of yelling brought him back. He was right; I stunk. I hobbled over to the sink and shed my clothes. There was a bar of soap, a washcloth, and a skimpy towel. I turned the taps on. They both ran cold. Yup, I was in prison. I looked around, all twelve feet square of it. Besides the cot and the sink there was a toilet, a small table, and a hard-backed chair. There was a curtained off "something" to the left outside my cell, a wall 6 feet across and what appeared to be a long hallway to my right. Before I started to have a stand-up bath I stripped the bed and along with my clothes threw it all out the bars into the hall. You can breathe now Red; it doesn't get any worse."

"I doubt that. It is so inhumane…tell me you were given fresh linen and clothes?" Rose pleaded.

"Half an hour later the jailer returned and found me sitting in the chair in my birthday suit. He whistled and told me to make myself decent as the boss man was on his way. He passed a duffel bag and a plastic bag through the bars and placed a thermos on the little opening that was just large enough to hold a small meal tray. I asked him if there were more drugs in the thermos. He said, "No, but you might wish there was by the end of the day." He laughed and left. I dumped the bag and found a t-shirt, a pair of boxers, socks and what passed for a track suit. I dressed and found all that was required to make up a bed in the duffel bag. Strangely, it included a one-inch foam mattress. I supposed they didn't want me getting bed sores. I made the bed and laid down waiting for Black. He arrived and addressed me as if we were best friends.

"Good to see you up and breathing Quinn. You gave us a scare there for a few days."

"A few days? How long was I out for with that poison you injected into me?"

"Like I said, a few days. It's Labor Day, so figure it out."

I tried to focus. What was the last thing I remembered before being rudely awakened by Black? Why was I seeing Lily? Oh yeah, we'd spent the day settling her, JT, and Rusty into the Palace. But, what day was that… Friday maybe. Okay, Izzy's wedding was on Saturday…hell! I called him a rotten son of a bitch saying that he had no intentions of ever marrying her and that she was just bait in his twisted plot to get to me. I demanded to know what he wanted from me.

"Hold on there Quinn. I genuinely liked the girl, but come on, she's a little far out there don't you think? Anyhow, it was her idea to get married so that made things easier."

"Easier to get to me you mean, but for what purpose…money I'm assuming. Well, you can have all I have, just leave my family out of it. Let's just get on with it."

"Not so fast boy; give me a few days to get the ducks all together and then we'll talk again. Meanwhile Lonnie will look after you. He's a fairly decent cook…"

"That's when I first heard the name Lonnie. I blew up then, so I will leave the rest of the colorful conversation to your imaginations. He commented on my temper saying I was going to be here for awhile so the sooner I accepted things, the better it would be and walked away. Somehow I managed to get the thermos through the bars and throw it at him. Of course it landed three feet short of the mark. He laughed and said I'd be thirsty for the rest of the day then. He didn't make an appearance until Friday. I assumed that today was Monday because he had said that it was Labor Day; you know, my favorite holiday."

He snickered at that, but we all knew the irony of it.

"Oh Daddy, how horrible. He just left you there with no food or water?"

"To be honest, I was glad to see the back of him. I was still weak and tired so laid down again and tried to put the pieces together. A few hours passed before Lonnie showed up with supper. It was a frozen entree of some sort and was lukewarm. He said it would have to do on such short notice whatever the hell that meant and scooted on back down the hallway. I was hungry so ate it all and washed it down with a can of soda. There was also a bottle of water and aspirin on the tray. The next morning he arrived with breakfast which consisted of 2 fried eggs, 3 strips of bacon and 2 slices of buttered toast with strawberry jam in a little cup and a thermos of coffee. I asked him where the cream and sugar were. He laughed and said he knew a few things about me. I guessed that Black had mentioned that I took my coffee black. I wondered what else he knew. Anyhow, that was breakfast. It arrived every morning at eight. Some days there was sausage instead of bacon, hash browns two or three times a week and pancakes once a month or so. I asked for the eggs to be scrambled once in awhile. He told me to scramble them myself."

"He sounds like somewhat of a decent chap despite being your jailer, or is there more to him than what we have seen so far?" Johnny questioned.

"Yeah, he is John. We were cooped up together for two years…yes, I know two years, two months, and three days…something like that, right Vienna?"

"Yes, something like that." I replied. "Now get on with your friendly incarceration."

"Like I was about to say, we did become friends, friends out of necessity. I pretty much got what I asked for. First things were a clock, a calendar, and a newspaper. The first two arrived the next day. A week later I received the Vancouver Sun paper. It was 2 weeks old. I asked for a pen or pencil so I could do the crosswords. He brought me one of each saying that he didn't think I was suicidal. Next I asked for a notebook so I could keep a journal. I wrote in it three or four times everyday. It may surface one day and then I'll probably burn it."

"No you won't Rainey Quinn! I'm going to read every word of it just like you read all of my letters. I'll already know the bare bones so it won't be too upsetting." I asserted.

"There may be a few surprises, but I'll see how things go."

"What does that mean?"

"I may have revealed more than I should have; you know emotional outbursts. Shall we get back to the account. So, that's how I spent my days, reading, writing, and doing puzzles. A snack of fruit and a granola bar or sweet would arrive at one in the afternoon. Dinner was between five and six. There was only an occasional TV dinner. Meals were cooked by Lonnie, or maybe someone I never saw, but I was pretty sure it was him. He was a meat and potato man so that's what I got usually accompanied by a vegetable or a salad once in a blue moon. Lonnie had no answers for me regarding why I was there, or when Black would be back. Then, there he was asking me if I would like to pay my own ransom. I told him I might be able to get a million for my company. He said I was pessimistic and made me write the note to Owen asking for two mill. You all know how that went. At the beginning of December he informed me that Vienna had moved back to Scotland."

"How odd, that you used the phrase "once in a blue moon" as Mom used the same phrase this morning. She said that's when you'd come home next time there was a blue moon. I'm so happy that we didn't have to wait until 2009."

"So am I Rosy." He smiled at me. "You always believed I'd make it back did you?"

"It was more hope than belief." I answered and asked him what he thought of me moving back here.

He said he was surprised because he didn't think that I would have wanted to leave JT.

"I needed to be here." I said bluntly.

"I know what Avanloch and everyone here mean to you so I understand."

"We needed her too Rainey. If it wasn't for Vienna, there would be no Pixie in our lives and we may never have found Uncle Walt's killer." Amma stated emotionally.

We stared at her in disbelief. Rainey's eyes were questioning me. Johnny was livid.

"Jesus Amma, didn't we all agree not to burden Rain with all that today?"

"Sorry, it just came out." Amma apologised. Tears were running down her face.

Johnny got up, hugged her, and said he was sorry for yelling at her. Rainey reached across the table and asker her if he had to come over there. She sobbed "Yes."

I watched my husband walk around the table and take her in his arms and tell her he loved her. He hadn't told me that he loved me yet so I guiltily felt ejected. He then addressed us all making eye contact with each of us as he spoke.

"I've been rotting away in a bloody, boring dungeon for the past two years so believe me I can use some healthy stimulation, and if it involves my wife and I gather it does, bring it on. I've been through hell so I don't require any mollycoddling. Things that happen at Avanloch usually have her name written all over them don't they? I'm anxious to hear all of the stories. It sounds like the place to start is with what went down with Johnny's uncle, so let's get on with it."

I stepped in before anyone could have their say. "You can be assured you will hear about all the shenanigans that have taken place around here, and yes, they have all started with me. Luckily I had accomplices and I will leave you to conclude who they are. Let's see if I can tantalise you a little. First there was the reward I paid to Willie, then there was Dalezza from the grave of Gracie Darling…" I heard Rainey take a deep breath. "Oh, I missed the Blue Parrot investigation. What happened next Evan?"

He laughed. "Nothing much except for the time I came home early and found you and Johnny tearing down the wall behind the stairs in the cellar."

That got Rainey's attention. "Stairway…what stairway?"

"You know the one beyond the bookcase. Surprise, the boys rebuilt it. That's enough for now and you will hear no more until after you have uttered the last word of **your** story, understand?"

"Got it. Curious though, what were you and Amma doing when all this was happening Red?"

"Well Dad, Amma was holding down the fort here and I was chasing down intruders in London."

"I might just have some insight into that Honey. We'll get into it later because your mother is nudging me to get on with my horror story. Where was I…oh yeah, the reveal about you moving back to Scotland. Of course I asked him how he would know that. He said he had his sources. Three days before Christmas he arrived with Lonnie and said he had an early present for me. I naively thought he was sending me home. He laughed as usual and said he wasn't through with me yet and asked me if I had ever wondered what was on the other side of the curtain. I did not appease him with an answer. He told Lonnie to pull it open. It was another cell just as I had thought. It appeared to be larger than the one I was in. Lonnie unlocked it and walked through it pointing out the larger bed and table and the comfy chair. He did a little jig and opened a door into a cubicle which held a toilet, sink and the piece de resistance…a shower. Black asked me what I thought. I answered saying I guessed I was getting a roomie which brought on more laughter. He shoved a pair of handcuffs at me and told me to put them on, backed away and pulled a taser out of his pocket. "You know what these things can do don't you Buddy? Make no mistake as I have no problem in zapping you if you try to get by me. Be a good boy, live another day, and walk quickly to your new digs." Lonnie unlocked my cell and escorted me to the new one. Black said Merry Christmas and walked away chortling. Lonnie told me to check things out and he'd see me in an hour or so. I was used to doing my business on a crude public biffy for the past four months so having a closed in one was less shameful, and a shower…wow, I was livin on easy street!"

He stopped to get his breath. No one said anything, but our dismay was evident. I squeezed his hand letting him know I understood the indignities. He gave me one of his crooked smiles.

"It was obvious I wasn't going home for Christmas, so I made a promise to myself that I'd find a way to break out. Little did I know it would take another two years. But things were looking up weren't they? I had these bright new digs which gave me more room to exercise in and I had a shower with actual hot, well warmish water. The mattress still had its stickers on. I hadn't seen it arrive so assumed it was there before I arrived. I hadn't done anything to earn any gold stars so why I'd been given this luxury accommodation was a mystery."

"Oh Daddy, your sense of humor is priceless." Rosy laughed.

"You think so do you Red? I'm pretty sure I wasn't laughing, but I was thankful for the upgrade. Another surprise was a little refrigerator that was sitting on the table. I opened it and found that the interior was cold. What the hell…that meant electricity. Sure enough the cord was plugged into an extension cord that passed through the cell behind the desk that Lonnie would sit at when he had something to say. From there it meandered down the hall a few feet where an electrical socket was situated. Strange that I had never noticed it from my old cell. Briefly I wondered how I could use this electrical device in my escape plan. I reminded myself that I was no MacGyver."

We had a twitter over that. I felt like he expected it. He continued on amused by our amusement.

"I could also see all the way down the hallway now. I'd keep an eye out for where Lonnie came from. I didn't have long to wait. I heard a clanging like metal on metal. Lonnie appeared with a cart in tow so I assumed that he'd come down some stairs. I asked him when he arrived and he said, "Yeah, you be in the dungeon Quinn." I had thought as much so no news flash. The cart was full of stuff for the fridge; a 6 pack of water, a quart of milk, butter, yeah butter not margarine, mayo, cold cuts, cheese, and greens. There were things for the pantry which were in a cardboard box like cereals, canned beans, tins of salmon, tuna, and bread. You see, he would be gone for 2 days starting tomorrow evening which was Christmas Eve, so I would be on my own. Later he brought me enough Shepherd's pie to last for 2 days, an ice cream treat and 3 frozen TV dinners which fit nicely into the little freezer compartment. I asked him if he was suppling a microwave. He said it wasn't on the list, but I could have a radio if I would like. I liked. He passed it to me through the food tray opening and said I shouldn't worry about being left alone as I was well looked after. I took that to mean that I was being monitored. I did a thorough search of the cell but found no such device. Christmas morning I sat down at the table with a bowl of cornflakes and a banana and opened the new crossword book that Lonnie had given me the day before. An envelope fell out. In it was a card from Black that said Merry Xmas Quinn, enjoy."

"How very thoughtful of him!" Rosy said sarcastically. The rest of us snickered.

"There was something else attached to the card so it wasn't all merciless."

I asked what that could possibly be. He said he'd tell me later and continued on.

"That about does it for the first four months. Nothing much changed in the routine until sometime in July when Black told me that you had a boyfriend."

I stiffened. "I did not, and he had no business assuming that I did!" I denied assertively.

"I didn't think anything of it at the time Hon as I knew it was just one more way he he'd found to torture me. Every so often after that initial reveal he'd greet me with little tidbits regarding you and him. I now knew that his name was Hawk O'Shea. I guessed he was a kin of Johnny's so it couldn't be all that bad."

I was livid. I stood up and looked down at him with razors in my eyes. "That's what you thought did you? It was okay if I had a boyfriend because he was related to Johnny. Did you think that Johnny had control over us so nothing serious would develop? Did you just accept it as fact and have no emotional reactions at all? I was out of sight so out of mind. No, don't touch me…" I fought him as he tried to hold me. His pulled me into his embrace and held me until I quit fighting.

"It was just the opposite Sweetheart. The anguish that racked my body was overwhelming and if I could have I would have choked the living daylights out of him. Do you understand that I couldn't give him the satisfaction of knowing that he'd pushed the one button that would destroy me. That's you, and you know it Vienna. I had to keep playing his demented game and not show the emotional state he had put me in. I wanted to lash out you can be assured of that. I had to keep telling myself that the day was coming when I'd have my revenge, and you can make bet that I will. Let's end this, okay? I can't distress you anymore."

"I always make it about me don't I? I was safe and with my family here in this high and mighty castle and you were in a cold dark cell not knowing if you would ever see the light of day again with no one and so once more, I apologise. You must continue right to the end of your ordeal, and I will try to keep *my* emotions in check, but that all depends on the next revelation."

Rainey laughed a little as he lowered me into my chair. "There's not much more, but just so you all know, it wasn't cold and damp and the lighting was good. There was no daylight and no outside yard for exercise like in real prisons. One thing I know is that I will not repeat much of this to the family back home as once is enough. How are you holding up Red?"

"About as good as Mom is. How would he have gotten that information Dad?"

"Yeah, wondering the same thing Rain. He must have had an accomplice of sorts in Hawthorne don't you think?" Evan asked.

"My thoughts exactly. I have had months to rack my brain but have come up with no one. Izzy is the only one who knew him, but who knows if she knows more?"

"She was thoroughly investigated Rain. What Rolph didn't get out of her, you can bet Jack did,"

"I thought as much Evan. Good ole Jack; he's always got my girl's back, hasn't he Hon?"

I knew Jack would come up sooner or later. "Get on with it will you. I don't expect that Ada will be able to keep Pixie away much longer."

"Odd that not once did Black ever mention her. If he knew about Hawk, why wouldn't he know about Pixie? Just one more thing to wonder about I guess. Anyhow, boredom was starting to get the best of me and if something positive didn't happen I was going to lose what was left of my mind. Exercise consisted of me doing push-ups, jumping jacks, and tedious so-called jogging back and forth in the 15-foot cell."

"You were never much of an exercise fanatic anyhow, so good that you kept fit in the only way possible." I commended.

"Oh, for the want of a swimming pool…need I say more?"

"Rest easy Dad, the spa awaits."

"Best news I've heard all day. So, as I was saying, I needed some stimulation. I asked Lonnie for a few items that I would need to get back to my roots. Somehow Black discovered that I was designing. He arrived with a wagon loaded with everything any architect could ask for including an inclined board that would fit on the table. He told me he was running low on funds and wanted to know if I would like to enter into a partnership with him. I'd do the creative part and he'd do the marketing. I'm sure you know what my response was. He told me to think about it. I did for a few days and thought what the heck. Some of my best work is on display all over the valley that I'll probably never see or get credit for, but it was something to do. I was never privy as to what price he put on them, but he congratulated me every so often when one sold. It was sometime about six months later that he complained about not having enough mola to complete his new acquisition and maybe it was time he brought my little wife into the equation. He'd been holding on, but the last dog may have been hung, so what did he think she would pay for me. Before I could even object he turned around and left saying he'd let me know. It was the first time I hoped that Owen would have told you that he'd paid my ransom so you'd know not to fall for another fake exchange. Weeks went by and not a word about the threat and then he brought his sister down to meet me. I had heard loud female voices a few times before and had asked Lonnie who they were. He said I'd know soon enough.

"What did Leslie look like Daddy?"

"I'm not surprised that you know her name as I am sure Rolph ran a full dossier on Black's family. She was tall, short dark hair, plain and muscular. She had several ugly tats and a voice like a bullhorn."

"Not anything like Jorja then? Was she the voice you heard in the car?"

"No Rose, there was no resemblance to her sister at all, and no, it definitely was not the same voice I'd heard the night I was abducted. You can breathe now Vienna."

"I'll breathe when I hear the end of this. Why did he bring her to meet you?"

"I wasn't sure at the time, but I came to think differently later. She hadn't had any contact with Jorja for almost twenty-five years so wanted to know what I knew about her. I told her that I couldn't help her and why did she think I knew anything about her sister. I was a little surprised by her answer."

"How dumb do I look to you? Just because I don't have a college education doesn't mean I don't know things. Did you think you could keep your sordid affair with her a secret? Do you think we didn't know about you? I don't know what happened between the two of you but we never heard from her again after you deserted her. We didn't know whether she was dead or alive and then a few years back I get a letter from some prison down east regarding her shocking death. It took awhile but Blackie was able to find out who was in charge of her estate and you know damn well it was you, so don't you dare tell me that you had no connections to her after 1980!"

"Why was it surprising Daddy?"

"According to Jorja, she was an only child, so I had no reason to believe otherwise. My response to her was that I had nothing to say except that I wished I had never met her sister and that the conversation was over. She left with a mouthful of the most indecent expletives I have ever heard."

He looked at me as if he was waiting for a reaction. When I didn't blink an eyelash he continued.

"Two days later she showed up again. This time she had another woman with her. I knew who she was because Lonnie had given me the heads-up. Her name was Sonya Boyce. She had the same physique as Leslie. They were a couple, partners, or whatever. I gathered that she was the dominant one in the relationship as she was the one asking the questions now. She was not as curt as her mate. After she introduced herself she set right in to asking the same questions that I hadn't answered the day before. You understand that I had nowhere to go except the bathroom, but I would still have heard everything unless I turned the water on full blast and maybe not even then, so I sat down and put on a happy face. And, that's when and where I'm convinced I made a mistake."

Rainey looked at me but didn't say anything. Evan asked him what he meant.

"Only Vienna can answer that."

"I'm sure I can't, but why do you think I can?"

"Once they realised that their line of questioning and accusations was getting them nowhere they found another way to irk me. Sonya said she had a daughter that attended the same college as my twin girls. I told her that she had me mixed up with someone else because I did not have twin daughters. She asked me if Patricia and Novia were not my daughters. I guess I lost my cool hearing her mentioning Novia and I voiced rather loudly that Patricia Ann was not my daughter."

"Oh Rainey." I moaned.

"I didn't think anything of it at the time and I'm pretty sure they didn't react at all."

"I don't understand why denying that she wasn't your daughter would factor anything Dad."

"Did you miss the *twin part thing*, and that I called her Patricia *Ann*?"

"No, but… oh, my God, they look alike don't they… Novia and Patricia?"

"Well Rosalyn, seeing I have never seen Patricia I can't answer that. The thing is that I denied that she was my daughter. I used her full given name indicating that I knew her. I know it doesn't sound like much, but it was something that I believe was investigated by Black or whomever is the mastermind behind my abduction."

"Do you think that kidnapping you may have been a way for him to avenge Jorja's death?"

"No Rose, I do not. I honestly believe that she meant nothing to him, but I believe that he and Leslie may be in cahoots."

"So you believe that Black didn't act alone?"

"I do Evan. The man is cunning, but short on brains. Now why I believe something came of this blunder was what happened a few weeks later. He informed me that Vienna's English fortunes were safe for the time being as he'd come into a surprising windfall. It was enough to keep the royal mission afoot for the time being. Tell me if I am jumping to conclusions because I have no facts to base my suspicions on, but this is what I have come to believe. Black somehow discovered that Patricia

Ann is his niece and has connived his way into her trust fund. That's where you come in Vienna…are you still contributing to it every month?"

"As far as I know I am, but I don't keep track of it as that's Uncle John's job."

"We have to call him and make sure all is on the up and up, and Rose, I also think that Black and associates are behind the attempted takeover of McAllister Enterprises."

We all reacted to that declaration, especially Rosalyn. Rainey asked her if they could put that conversation on hold until the thing with the trust fund was taken care of because Patricia may very well be in danger. He asked me to make the call to Uncle John. Rosy volunteered.

"Let me call Grey as Uncle John only comes into the office once a week. I will tell him that we need to review Mom's personal financial portfolio as there may be a problem with it, but you need to fill him in on the details Dad. Are you all right with that? I know you need to keep a low profile but he's family so your whereabouts is safe. Mom, are you in accordance?"

Rainey said it wasn't a problem for him, but maybe it was for me.

"I have no objections and if your father has suspicions regarding the trust fund then I respect that his instincts are correct. If the results are found to be in order then no harm will have been done and he can rest his fears."

Rainey thanked me, but I had more to add. "After you found out that I had started the fund you never once asked what the size of it was so I will tell you now. It is only two thousand a month. She could not access it until she was twenty. You have only come to suspect that Blackie hacked into her account six months ago so twelve thousand doesn't sound like an amount to me that would satisfy him, so I have my doubts that he did."

"When did you start paying into it Hon?"

"I never thought about it until I got the letter from her the summer of 2003 when we were here, but I think it was shortly after Jorja's death or when you received the letter where she had named you as her executor, so around 1985."

"I remember that letter all too well. Patricia was adamant about not accepting the gift. She believed you may have had a hand in her mother's demise, or that perhaps you were her mother but didn't want her so the money was to ease your conscience. We had decided that we'd contact her when we got home that summer and set her straight but we didn't, did we?"

"No, because you disappeared just a few days later. Everything that has ever gone wrong with us is because of Jorja and somehow she was able to send her brother to destroy us. She'll never be done with us!" I blubbered.

Rainey tried to assure me that this was the last of her, but I knew better. Evan made his way over to me, pulled me up and said, "Let's take a break and go for a little walk."

We settled in the divan under the stairs where we'd met so many times before on our midnight rendezvous.

"This isn't how I visioned this day going Evan. It's supposed to be a day of celebration, but once again that witch has found a way to dirty it."

"You have to let it go Vienna. She's long dead and buried."

"If I'd had a say she would have been hung and burned on the stake because she was one witch who deserved it!"

"That's my girl, get it all out and then go back and tell your husband you love him."

"How can I? I can't get this bloody ring of Hawk's off, and Rainey thinks I cheated on him."

Evan tried but the ring would not budge. He asked me when I had put it on.

"A day or so ago. I honestly don't know why, I just did."

We went across the hall to the powder room and he soaped it up, but to no avail. He said he'd take a hacksaw to it later.

"You've prayed for this miracle for two years so quit making assumptions about his feelings. For all he knew Black could have just been handing him a line of bull about you and Hawk to add to his misery. You need to hear him out no matter how difficult it is. He's reliving the hell he was in with humor a great deal of the time for our benefit you know. At this point in time we have absolutely no idea how this is going to affect him in the days ahead, but I know you'll be the one who will pull him through the nightmares."

"You are always the voice of reason aren't you? You're going to miss me if I go back to Hawthorne, and for your information it was two years, two months, two days, and twelve hours and…"

He laughed and put his arm around me. "This might very well be the last walk we have down this corridor together for a long time so let's make it a good one. You're bloody right saying I'm going to miss you, but we've got Rain back so I'll live with knowing you're happy again."

I didn't apologise for my outburst as I took my place beside my husband but asked what we had missed. I was glad the ring was on my right hand as Rainy placed his hand on my left one.

"Nothing, but I'm glad you're back. I know how difficult this is for you Honey, but in a way it's therapeutic for me to talk about the whole ordeal. I only have one more thing to say about the trust fund and that is something for you all to ponder. Suppose if Patricia held true to her word and never touched the fund? Suppose if it just sat there for almost twenty years and gained interest… it could be worth two million by now. That would surely keep Black happy for a time don't you think? Time to make the call Red."

She agreed and went down the hall leaving us to discuss the possibility of Rainey's query. We all agreed that it was a definite possibility. Rosy returned and passed the phone to him saying that Grey knew everything. Rainey turned the conference button on so we could all hear. Grey's astonishment of hearing his voice was emotional. He promised that he'd only relay the news to Jannie, John, and Ash. Rainey thanked him for that and said that I'd be calling Jannie later. The remainder of the call was all business. Grey said he'd have all the answers we needed within the hour and that he'd have the conversation with Rainey regarding his suspicions regarding the attempted take-over of McAllister Enterprises. I prayed silently for a happy conclusion.

"There is just one more thing I'll touch on before the reveal of how I bought my way out of jail."

"That sounds intriguing Rain." Johnny remarked.

"It was just dumb luck John. Black's visits were down to once a month which suited me just fine for as far as I was concerned no news of back home was good news." He put his hand on my knee and gave it a squeeze. "Sometime in May he showed up with a woman and said she was an early birthday present so happy birthday. There was no denying what she was as her tight red dress and stilettos along with overdone make-up said it all."

"She was a call girl wasn't she?" Amma blurted out.

Johnny gave her a disagreeable look.

"Amma's right John. Call her a hooker, sex worker, harlot, or scarlet woman as that is what she was. I'm ashamed that I judged her as such before I knew what her story was. I'm not saying I insulted her to her face, but the accusations that I spewed at Black didn't leave much to the imagination. He laughed and said I'd regret the offer one day as it was only a one-time thing. I never thought I'd see the likes of her again, but I was wrong. Three days later Lonnie informed me that I was on my own for the weekend again. I was used to it, but he usually would bring me extra food fixings before he left, but he didn't that afternoon. It was along about four that afternoon when the aroma of roast beef wafted down to me. I supposed that for some reason Lonnie hadn't left after all. I waited thinking he'd be bringing me a hot meal. At five I heard the footsteps on the stairs. A figure that wasn't Lonnie's came around the corner. It was definitely a woman. Her first words were a little unsettling." Rainey squeezed my leg again.

"I know I'm the last person that you want to see Mr. Quinn so I will apologise up front for the intrusion, but I assure you I am only here to deliver your meals and nothing else."

She slid the window open and set the tray down and turned to leave. I asked her if we had met before because I didn't recognise her. She said she had been here three days ago. I almost choked.

"Are you saying you're the woman Black brought for me as a so-called gift?"

"The same Mr. Quinn."

"I see no resemblance whatsoever. Can you look at me please?"

She lifted her head, and there she was, the woman who was no longer in disguise as a harlot. I apologised for my insensitive remarks the other day.

"Think nothing of it Mr. Quinn as I am exactly the person you believed me to be. I hope you enjoy your dinner."

"I know I will as the smell is tantalizing." I asked her if she could stay and keep me company while I ate.

She said she had a peach cobbler in the oven so perhaps when she delivered it and coffee later that we could have a few words. She said she understood that I liked my coffee black."

I sat back. Every muscle in my body was tightening. I felt as if I was going to burst. He was holding me again. I wanted to pound on him. He was telling me to relax because whatever I was thinking didn't happen and I needed to let him finish. All I could see was him with Jorja and now he was going to have coffee and Lord knows what else with another whore. Then he kissed me full on the lips. I hadn't been kissed like that for over two years.

He said, "I love you."

I asked him if she smelled like cherry blossoms.

He burst out laughing. "I was never that close to her but she was always baking, so nutmeg I guess."

"Nutmeg makes you sneeze."

"Exactly. Now breathe and sit down and let me tell you all at this table a very sad story. Her name is Gemma. That first night I asked her if she could get me out of jail. She said she was sorry but no. She was not trusted with a key and even if she was she could never use it because she would lose her family which consisted of son Alec who was twelve, and her husband Roger who was ill. He had a debilitating disease that kept him from leading a normal life. He had been employed by some big company as a processing manager. It fell by the way as the illness took over his body. The company was sympathetic and kept him on doing menial tasks from home by computer. However, the income was no longer substantial enough to pay for his medications which were not covered by health or government assistance. The only solution was for her to find employment herself. Before she had met Roger she had worked for an escort service for five years to help with her schooling. Sounds familiar doesn't it? Anyhow, long story short, she was unable to find work anywhere at her chosen field, which was broadcasting, so she took a job at a restaurant as a waitress. This diner just happened to be Black Smith's habitat. It wasn't long before their conversations became personal and he edged his way into her family life. Hey, but he had the solution. Roger could work for him, and he did and took on the role as Black's financial manager. I know what you're all thinking and it might have some bearing on this trust fund thing, but it will take some doing to find out. Gemma was never privy to the details of her husband's dealings with Black, but the medications he needed to live somewhat of a normal life were now available to him at no cost. She became part of the deal and she feared if she didn't co-operate the consequences would be dire to her family. She played hostess and information gatherer to his guests at shindigs he threw, most were aboard a yacht. She said they were all platonic and it was always a different boat so she didn't think that Blackie could possibly own them all. To gain her confidences I had no choice but to believe her. Not that it mattered to me one way or the other. I viewed her as my way out. She was a good listener, but I like to think that I was a better interrogator. However, none of the information got me any closer to gaining my freedom. That was all on Lonnie. Before I get on with that undertaking I will say that Gemma and I became friends. She became my jailer, so to say, every other weekend as Lonnie took more and more time off. She was a much better cook than him and a decent challenger at crib and scrabble. Let me make this perfectly clear Vienna … there was nothing more than just chit-chat and games."

"Yes, you are very adept at playing games aren't you?" I mocked.

"Well, the game I played with Lonnie got me rescued so let's see what you have to say about that. The reason he wasn't putting the hours in anymore was because he had a problem, actually two problems, his lady Cindy, and his mistress, gambling. I knew he bet on the horses and would make a sport's bet now and then, but Cindy had introduced him to Keno at a restaurant one night. It was just for fun she had said, but it led him to a casino and a whole new kind of gaming. He was losing a lot more then he was winning, but he couldn't stop, he was hooked. Cindy set up a few ground rules. I'm sure you can guess what one of them was, but it didn't phase him until she threatened to have him banned from all the casinos. I don't know if it she could legally do that but Lonnie believed she could. He was in one rotten mood in late October. He practically threw my breakfast at me and stormed off cursing out loud. That went on all day. I just let him rant and never interceded until he stated that he may as well kill himself and then that would show her. I told him that suicide wouldn't solve his problems because he'd be dead and would never know how his death affected her. "Yeah, you're right; she's the one who has to go." was his response. It took a while but he finally starting talking about his dilemma. I told him there was a way around it as he could gamble on-line and she would never have to know. He didn't have a computer. I asked if he had a mobile phone. He did but it was programmed to only call Blackie and a few other people, so that was out. I suggested he buy a new one. He thought about it but decided he'd rather have a computer as the screen was bigger but he wouldn't know how to program it anyhow so he was screwed. I said that I could help, and so it began. Apparently. kidnapping wasn't Black's only vice; he was heavenly invested in the black market and had a warehouse on the property which was full of electronics, and computers was one of them. I guess Lonnie had a key to it because he arrived the next morning with a brand-new laptop. I even had to instruct him on how to turn it on so it was uphill from there. I managed to talk him through all the steps to get on-line. It wasn't easy as he was on one side of the cell and I was on the other. I needed the address before I could even think of sending out an SOS, so I asked him what it was. His answer was weird to say the least. "You know the Eagles song where they sing about being in the desert on a horse with no name, well, this is a street with no name." I said it had to have a name. He said he had just told me. I asked him what streets he took to get here. He asked why I wanted to know. I said I was just curious. I only needed to know what street intersected with the one the compound was on. After a few minutes of his detailed route from his apartment in New Westminster he got to Industrial Drive. I knew where that was, but what street did it connect with. His answer was no name again. I was computer and Lonnie weary so I missed the irony of it. We left it there for the day as he was off to go to the bank and get a new account solely in his name for on-line gambling. He was very excited and called Gemma to sub for him for the night. For what reason he didn't just leave me alone I don't know. I was glad Gemma was one of his allowed callers because she cleared up the street name for me. I felt very foolish over the reveal. She laughed when I told her his silly story about the street not having a name. She said it did. It was NoName."

We all had a chuckle with him. I heard footsteps on the kitchen stairs. Pixie would be here any second. I stood up and looked down at my husband. "You had all the information you needed then didn't you and you somehow managed to get the SOS off to Mason. I'm so sorry that it took so long to get to that moment, but you figured it out and you are here and I'm so very happy that you are."

Pixie ran straight into my arms. I picked her up and covered her with kisses making her laugh as usual. I excused myself from the table saying I needed to spend some time with my angel. Rainey stood up, gave Pixie's head a little tap and thanked me for sitting through the whole grueling rendition of his ordeal. I said there was no need to thank me as it was my ordeal also. Everyone had been relatively silent through most of his recapping of his captivity, but now the table was abuzz with admirations, sentiments, and questions. The last thing I heard as I made my way down the hall was Johnny asking Rainey how he had managed to book an international flight without a passport. I had been wondering that myself so stopped to hear the answer. He had been escorted through security by several RCMP officers and an Air Marshall who accompanied him on the flight. No questions had been asked.

Twenty minutes later Rainey knocked lightly on the open door of the family room. He said that he was off for a walk but he had one last phone call to make first. I wondered who he was calling so said we'd join him in the parlor as soon as I had cleaned all the silly putty off our hands.

He was walking towards the French doors talking to someone when we arrived.

"Looking forward to seeing you and Sissy. I'm off to get some air, so see you in a few days. Here's Vienna." He passed me the phone asking me in a whisper if everything was still status quo between Jack and me.

I gave him a dirty look, turned the alarm off the doors, took the phone from him and walked away. I didn't really want to talk to Jack, but I didn't seem to have much choice. I sighed. "Hi Jack."

"God, you must be over the moon Vienna! I can't imagine the elation. Tell me he's okay… I mean I'm sure he's emotionally traumatised, but physically…"

I interrupted. "He's physically unscathed Jack. I can't speak for his emotional being as it is all so overwhelming, but he seems to be in control of his feelings. We're letting him take the lead of just how much he wants to share. He hasn't shed any tears if that's any indication." I turned back to the glass doors and watched Rainey as he stood at the knoll looking down at the manor and the barns. I guess he gave a whistle because the three dogs bounded up the hill and ran circles around him. I watched, listening to Jack with one ear until the four of them disappeared up the rose gardens path.

"A lot has transpired in these past two years so we don't want to throw everything at him all at once."

"Everything will all fall into place Vienna because if there is one thing I am sure in this topsy-turvy world its's that you two belong together and your love will see you through anything. He doesn't need to know everything you know."

"There is nothing I can't tell him Jack, and just in case you believe that I have been unfaithful, I will tell you that I haven' been, so that is not an issue, but there other things. Two years is a long time."

"I seem to remember someone else who went missing for two years…"

"You have to admit that the circumstances were completely different, but as you say love will persevere hopefully. See you in a couple of days."

"We love you Vienna."

"Love you too."

I reset the alarm and returned to the kitchen with somewhat of a heavy heart. I plopped down in Duffy's chair holding Pixie tightly. Rosy asked where Rainey was.

"He went for a walk."

"Alone?"

"I wasn't invited." I shrugged. "I think he wanted to be alone." I said twisting the ring that seemed to have found a permanent place on my finger.

"It must be so very overwhelming for him, don't you think?" Amma said watching me twist the ring." What are you going to do?"

"I think we all know what she is going to do. My question is why are you still here Vienna?" Evan questioned.

"Do you think I should go find him? What about Pixie?"

Rosie came and took her out of my arms. "Put a coat on because it's cold Mom."

"And, for God's sake, put on a decent pair of shoes!" Evan ordered.

Promises of a Faded Rose

I stopped at the potting shed and filled two pails with peat briquettes and lugged them up to the sitting area overlooking the ponds. I deposited them in the three receptacles, threw in fire starters, lit them, and watched as they flared up. I walked over to the edge of the embankment and watched as Rainey threw fodder to the waterfowl. A few minutes passed before he turned and looked up. He didn't wave but called the dogs and started up the hill. I sat down on one of the benches and waited for him. The dogs ran to greet me. He asked me what their names were as he had forgotten.

I pointed to the golden retriever. "That's Barley, the Lab is Buckwheat, and the lady is Sage."

"Yeah, I remember now. I suppose I should try and send them home." He called them over and pointed down towards the stables. "Home; off you go, home."

They took off running. I was glad he remembered the command.

"This is nice." He said pointing to the fire pots. "Kind of smells like smoky bacon. I don't think I remember the smudge smelling like that."

"Every batch of peat is different. I think it's all in the way and where it was dried."

He walked over to a rose bush and picked a somewhat frozen rose. "I guess this is the last rose of summer." He came over to me and attached it behind one of the combs in my hair. "Is this the last rose I will ever pick for you Vienna?"

I placed my hand over his." I hope it won't be. I know you have questions for me..."

"Just one." He pointed to the ring on my finger. "Are you in love with him?" He sat down on a bench next to me but averted making eye contact or touching me.

"There are many faces of love Rainey. There is the love I have for our children which fills me with pride and I bask in the joy it brings me every day. There is the love I have for my sisters and my mother, my nieces and your parents. Then there is the love I have for Lara and Amma. Their friendship has sustained me through many a trying time. I have an endearing love for Jimmy and Ruth and Yates as they have been in my life forever just as you have been, and then there is Izzy and Meggie. I can't even begin to imagine my life without Jack or Johnny. That remark you made referring to my relationship with Jack was rude and it chilled me to the bone. I will be perfectly honest with you as I have nothing to hide. Ava and Lili were constantly hovering over me. Zander and Rusty were gone most of the day with Nash. We had sent Novia and Samie back to college so I had no one to distract me except JT. Izzy would come in the afternoon and rescue me for an hour or so. Dinner was always at our house. I did not help in the preparations because I would rather be catching up with the boys about their day. Nash and I would retreat into your office after dinner and talk expenditures almost every evening. I don't think we were fooling anyone as there wasn't much to discuss, but no one questioned us. It was Nash's way of giving me a break from everyone's mollycoddling. I looked forward to my time with him as he was just Nash. Now, I will answer your question about Jack's and my relationship as you seem to think there is more to it than just friendship and it isn't the first time is it? He and Sissy were with us from the get-go as were many others like Jimmy and Ruth. After a few weeks of this and the ransom attempt had failed I insisted everyone resume their lives. Jack reopened his shop and Sissy worked the front as always. She had enrolled in a night course at the school so after dinner weekdays she was off to that and Jack would come to see me. I looked forward to his visits more than anyone else's. He let me be me. Our escapes to the back porch were not enough for me and I wanted to see more of him so I contemplated moving to the Palace. I convinced myself that would give me the freedom I needed from Ava and Lili also. I needed Jack just like I did when you had set me free those many years ago. I hadn't quite gone over the edge yet and I came to my senses realising that **no one**, not even Jack was ever going to replace you, plus my sister was in that ugly picture I had painted myself into. I told Jack that he had to quit worrying about me and that he had to quit coming up every night. I hoped I would be able to keep my distance, and then fate intervened when I had the dream. I saw you with her and I knew you were gone from me forever. I picked up the phone and called Evan. I did not come to Avanloch because it had been my home for so many years, or because Rosalyn was here. I came because Evan was here, and he was the only one who could save me."

My name was on Rainey's lips. There was a sadness in his eyes that I had never seen before. I held up my hand. "I'm not finished yet. You may have your say after I am done if you wish, but you need to hear me out. Now I come to Nash and Evan, my sons-in-law. They are so much more than that and I love them as they love me…unconditionally. As I said I came here because Evan is here. He scolds me, he makes me laugh and cry, he listens and he lets me be me as does Johnny. The three of us have a pact, and you will hear all about our escapades, as Amma calls them, that we touched on earlier. I will not apologise for my feelings for Jack or believing that he was what I needed so you can live with it, or not. I do not know your plans for the future or if they include me, so it is a moot point at this time. Let's see, have I left anyone out? Oh yes, Hawk. You asked me if I was in love with him. I am not. He has been good to me and is a very caring man. He wants to make a home for me and Pixie, but I would never leave my family here to be with him. What

I feel for him is not love, and you are the only man in the world I would ever leave Avanloch for."

A tear slid down his face. He moved to the end of the bench, took my hands, and said my name.

I wasn't ready for him to talk yet. "The love I have for you is passionate, tender, and wild, and all consuming. I have loved you since I was sixteen and through all the years we were separated, and even when I didn't know who I was, I loved you. The last twenty-one years with you was a dream that came true. We had our ups and downs, but love always pulled us through, but this…these last two years have been a hell I never thought I'd get through, but then a little, blue-eyed Pixie came into my life and gave me the strength to go on. I'm a package deal Rainey. If you still want me, and I'm not sure you do because you have been rather nonchalant towards me. You didn't even kiss me or say that you missed me upstairs and maybe you don't love me anymore, and you think I have been unfaithful to you, but I wasn't. If you decide to give us another chance I'm just saying that wherever I go, Pixie comes too. I might be done now…oh, one more thing, this ring means nothing to me. I can't get it off because my hands are swollen and it won't budge, Evan tried soaping it, but that didn't work. He's going to take a hacksaw to it tonight."

There it was…the crooked little smile that made my heart flutter. "Well, we can't have that now, can we? Let me see what I can do to relax your hand. First, as usual I will say that I am sorry. I'm sorry that I didn't kiss you upstairs. I wanted to more than you can imagine. I should have ignored the crowd downstairs and my doubts that maybe you didn't want me anymore."

"That is the stupidest thing I have ever heard it my life!"

"Why is it any more ridiculous than you thinking that I don't love or want you anymore?"

"It just is."

"And, that is another reason why I love you. I am going to try and address all the things you said but not until I tell you that I love you more right now than the day I was taken away. It doesn't seem possible but it is.

That last night we had together was a renewed hope and promise for our forever commitment to each other but then the bubble burst and I was thrust into oblivion. When I woke up, cold and confused and found out that it was Labor Day, I knew that it was the last bad luck nightmare I'd ever have. There would be no more you, no family, no more freedom, no more anything and then to add fuel to the fire a few days later I thought I had paid my own ransom so I was destitute also. But what did it matter because I was a dead man anyway. I kept those feelings of despair out of the conversation because I didn't want to upset everyone, especially you, but it is because of you that I snapped out of that despondency. It was your love that made me fight for survival. I'm sorry it took me so long to achieve that goal, but I'm here and I have something for you. Let's get this thing off your hand because I want to place this one on your heart hand, that is if you will consent to be my wife again and someday I'll replace it with a real one when I get a job." He snickered, "As if anyone is going to hire a 65-year-old has been."

"Well, you're my old man, always have been and always will be and if you want a job I'll give you one and it's the hardest job in the world, catering to my every wish and desire."

"I think I signed up for that twenty-five years ago so how about another twenty-five? Will you take my name again and do me the honor of becoming my wife once more Vienna LaFontaine?"

"I am still your wife Rainey, but yes, I would dearly love to renew our vows and wear this one-of-a-kind ring. Where did it come from?"

"It's just one of a dozen or so that I tried to hone out of a little bolt of lead. Lonnie supplied me with the material and believe it or not *the piece de resistance,* the file. It's crude but I think I've got all the jagged edges filed down, but it's just a gesture until I can get the real thing."

"I already have the real things but I will let you buy me another one to go with them and I will want it as soon as we get home. Do you understand?"

"I'm not sure I do."

"In all honesty do you believe that Owen didn't inform me of the ransom note and do you really think I would trust that he could come up with the two million?"

"No, I do not, but the way it was set up made Black believe that he left me penniless. Of course he thought he could get more from you anytime he wanted so it was all just a scam wasn't it? Anyhow, thank you my darling. Having you and my family means everything to be, but now there is an added bonus…that little girl waiting down there for you. It will be my greatest pleasure to raise another daughter with you. Just like all the others it was love at first sight. Now let's table everything and plan our wedding but first I want to hold you and kiss you and tell you once more how much I love and need you."

It had been two years, two months, two days and a million nights since I had been kissed like that so I didn't mind if we ever went back to the castle but I had one more question. "I know we have to get moving but I have one more thing to ask and I'm afraid I'm going to rock the boat. I hope you will answer honestly."

"You can be sure I will, so rock away Sweetheart. I've been waiting two years to be rocked by you."

"You said that Black brought Gemma to you as a gift, but you didn't elaborate very much on the subject except to say that she became a special friend. Perhaps you wouldn't say how special that association was in front of Rosalyn and the rest so I am asking you outright if there was a time or times, when your cell was open for visits? Perhaps she was trusted with the key?"

"You've got it all wrong Honey as I was the one who had the key. You see, I loved being in captivity away from you and my family, so when I wanted a little lovin I'd open the door for her and when I was done with her I'd send her out and lock myself in again. Does that answer your question sufficiently?"

"**That** is definitely the stupidest answer you have ever given me!"

"Was it any stupider than your question?"

"You know that I hate that word, I just wanted to know if she did indeed become a "gem" to you."

"It's good to know that you are still the same, the same Vienna who doesn't trust me. Anyhow I think I'll invite her to our wedding and maybe that sexy little waitress from the Falls Restaurant, and oh yeah the notary republic, what was her name…"

He suddenly looked confused. I asked him what was wrong.

"I don't know. It was like a memory or something. It flashed before my eyes and it was gone before I could catch it."

"I know just how bewildering that is as it happened to me a lot in Spain when I was masquerading as Katerina but knew I was someone else. I do trust you Rainey; it's them that I don't trust."

"I'll be perfectly honest with you. Not a night went by that I didn't want a warm body lying next to me on my prison bed, but…" He paused and pulled something out of his shirt pocket. "this is her and every night I took her to bed and talked to her and then I hung her up on the wall so I wouldn't trample her."

It was our wedding picture. He had circled me. Words were lost to me, but tears weren't. I managed to ask him if he had been allowed to bring it with him. He said it was what Black had left for him that first Christmas morning and added that it was the best present he'd ever had and gave him renewed hope that Black would free him shortly. He laughed crudely at that.

"Now, have we heard the last of this?"

"We haven't, but it's good for now, and I'm sure you have more questions for me too."

"Time will tell. Now when were you planning on telling me what's wrong with your leg? I think it's a lot more than a little misstep on the stairs, and I will apologise for rushing you."

"It isn't my ankle or my leg; it's my hip."

"Have you had a fall?"

"I think that a few more bone chips may have come dislodged as it is the same type of pain I had twenty years ago. I had an appointment for an ultrasound on Friday."

"What do you mean "had"? Why didn't you mention this before, and do Rosy and Evan know?

"Evan knows and we have already discussed it and I cancelled the appointment. I've lived with it for several months again so it's no big deal and I'll be in good hands in Bridge Falls so that's why."

"Okay then, it will be the first thing we take care of when we get home."

"After the wedding."

Everyone was still sitting where we had left them. Pixie was sitting on the table as usual. She reached for me. I hugged her and asked if she had a hug for Rainey. She said "Wainey Daddy."

Rainey was shocked. He looked at Evan. "I thought she called you and Johnny Daddy?"

"Nope, I'm DaDa, John is Joho, or something along that line." Evan laughed. "The only one who calls you Daddy is Rose and I suppose Vienna does too. Here have a look." He passed Rosy's phone to him which opened to a smiling picture of himself. "Every time Rose shows Pixie your photo she calls you Daddy so Pixie already knows what you look like. You can talk with them later but right now Grey's waiting for your call. I got the feeling that it isn't good news."

Rainey gave Pixie a hug and a kiss, took the phone from Evan and reminded me that I had a phone call to make also. He dialed Grey's number as he walked down the hallway.

"Who do you have to call Mom? Everything's good with you and Dad isn't it?"

"It is Dear." I answered showing off my new ring. "Rainey made it and he wants us to renew our vows when we get back to Hawthorne. He says he will replace it with a *real* one when he gets a job. I told him that he wasn't penniless so he could afford a new one but I didn't really need one as I kind of liked the ones I already had. Anyhow, we decided to have the wedding right away because we want you and Evan to be there so you have the job of phoning Ava and asking her to work her magic and make a wedding happen."

"Oh Mommy, I'm so happy I could cry." Rosy tried hard not to, but didn't succeed.

"Well now that you've got everyone teary-eyed let me have a look at that ring." Johnny said amusedly.

I took it off and gave it to him saying that Rainey would explain how he made it. "Here, will you see that this one gets back to the owner please." I asked as I took it out of my pocket. "Now I guess that I had better go and call him and tell him that Rainey is home. Does anyone know where my phone is?"

Amma had it in her hand even before I had finished the sentence. She brought it over to me still crying. "I am so very happy for you my dearest friend and I am going to miss you something dreadfully. I would so love to be at your wedding and if I didn't have to run this here castle I would be the first passenger on that plane for sure."

"Well Amma, good try but as the saying goes "when hell freezes over." We all know that to be true in this case. But, if you are really serious I think we can find someone to run this joint for a few days, but you'll have to take a different plane because I won't see you jumping out of mine." Evan kidded.

We were all still laughing when Rainey returned. His face said it all. He sat down beside me. "The account you set up for Patricia Anne is empty. Actually, that account doesn't exist anymore." He consulted a notepad. "On July 31st the monies were all transferred to another bank thus closing out the one you'd set up."

"Was Patricia the one that did that?"

"Yup; according to the bank manager she was. He also remembers that an older gentleman was with her. It is all on file under the name of Patricia Anne Elliot. The transaction was witnessed by several people as it isn't everyday that a large sum of money is transferred without reason."

"Surely signatures were compared." Rosy stated.

"Apparently, everything was on the up and up."

Evan asked if photos were taken and how much was in the account.

"Grey never mentioned anything about photographs and I never though to ask, but I'm thinking that it isn't a common thing to do. There was two million, seven hundred thousand, five hundred and fifty-nine dollars in the account."

Evan whistled. "We're assuming this so called gentleman who accompanied her was Black right?"

"Right and I'm assuming that it was his sister's daughter who played the role of Patricia. Now the question is, where do we go from here?" Rainey's eyes were questioning me.

"You know exactly where we go Rainey. We need to find Patricia and bring her into our fold. I doubt she even knows that Black is her uncle or what he has done, but he may see her as some bargaining chip if he believes you to be her father. I don't know if Novia and she are close enough friends that they have exchanged phone numbers but there is only one way to find out." I said. Liliana answered on the first ring.

"I guess I don't have to let the answering machine get your call anymore do I Mama?"

"No, you don't Lili. Is Novy with you?"

"Yes, thankfully she is Do you want to talk to her?"

"Yes, please." I waited anxiously for what seemed like half an hour before Novy finally answered. She apologised saying she was in the pool. I relayed how happy I was that she was safe and sound at home, but it was winter so what was she doing in the pool and wasn't there snow? She asked me to give her a moment so she could dry off a little. I whispered to Rainey that it would cost a fortune to heat an outdoor pool at this time of year. He shrugged his shoulders and said that I had a fortune so… After a few more minutes Novy was back. I asked her if she was aware that this was a long distance call. Rainey gave me the evil eye. She apologised and I said we'd talk when I got home but right now there was something important that had to be done. I asked if by any chance she might have her friend Patricia Anne's phone number. She said she did and asked why I wanted to know. I passed the phone to Rainey. "Your father will explain."

He patted Pixie on the head and started his pacing back and fort down the hallway again talking calmly to Novy. "What's this about the pool…" was all we heard before his voice became too faint to understand.

Pixie wanted down. I thought she needed the exercise so told Evan to let her go. She ran after Rainey giggling all the way. He picked her up and they disappeared into the Harem room. Rosy and I looked at each other and agreed that there was nothing in that room that we cared about. Ten minutes later they reappeared. Pixie was in Rainey's arms and was holding something. It appeared to be a tube of some sort. He told her to give it to me. I unrolled it. Unbelievably, it was the eighteenth century photo of Avanloch Castle, minus the picture frame, that had gone missing over twenty years ago. I think we were all shocked beyond belief. I asked Rainey where he had found it. He said he didn't; Pixie did.

"Dad, that room has been used and cleaned hundreds of time and no one has ever found that photo, so where was it? You must have seen where she found it?" Rosy insisted.

"I didn't really. She was admiring the Grandfather clock and I guess I took my eyes off her while I was writing Patricia's number down and when I looked up she was holding the photo. I guess Grandfather had another secret." Rainey said grinning.

"That's impossible!" I exclaimed. Everyone agreed and followed me down to the gaudy room I hated.

Rainey was still holding Pixie. He put her down and told her to tell Mommy where she found the picture. I wasn't sure that she understood because she didn't move. Rosy had the photo and gave it to Pixie and told her to put it away just like she did her toys. She put it down n front of the clock. Rosy asked her if she found it on the floor. She shook her head no and touched the clock door and said, "In".

Evan tried opening the door. Of course it didn't budge. I asked him if he knew if any of those clock experts he'd hired to try and get the clock running again had ever opened the door.

"I think I would have remembered that and I supervised all the undertaking, so no. What about you Rain, did you notice if the door was open?"

"I'm pretty sure it wasn't. What say we make a visit to the other side?"

"I'm with you Rain. Let's take the stairs as it'll be faster than moving the sideboard." Johnny suggested.

"Give us a holler when you get there. It'll just be a waste effort I'm thinking."

"Nothing ventured, nothing explained Evan." I answered watching Amma wander around with Pixie.

A few minutes later Johnny called out that they were at the backside of the clock. We waited.

"Well, what?" Evan yelled.

"Nothing Boss, there's nothing here, but the door is hanging by its hinges."

"What do you mean?" I called out.

"Just that."

Rosy said she'd put Pixie down for a nap as Rainey and I needed some time to ourselves. The conversation regarding the Grandfather clock was going to go on for a while between Evan and Johnny. I had added my two bits worth saying that I had walked down that hall to the clock half a dozen times since the new stairs had been installed and the back of the clock had always been intact and you can bet that I tried my best to get it to let me in, but to no avail. I left them with a new theory to ponder.

"Suppose if this anonymity has nothing to do with the photo? The gilded picture frame s still missing so suppose it is the answer. Maybe we overlooked its purpose and that it's the key to unlocking some hidden information regarding the castle?"

"What information would that be Milady?" Evan asked.

"I haven't a clue and I'll be out of here in two days do it's your riddle to decipher. Just one thought though…it was a very large and thick frame if memory serves me correctly. Large enough to hold and conceal something important, like say the original plans to this citadel. Hey, it may even mention the subterranean room." I supposed nonsensically.

"You're imagination is on overdrive and just like twenty five years ago you're going to leave us with another mystery aren't you?" Johnny questioned.

"I'm thinking you'll put it all together just like you did with *the key*." I winked and took my husband's hand. Johnny reminded me that I had a phone call to make.

Rainey kissed me at the bedroom door and went to have a shower. I went into my parlor. Hawk answered on the forth ring and said I had caught him at a bad time and could I give him ten minutes. I said, "No, there is no time left. I will not be seeing you this weekend or ever again. Rainey is here and I am going home to Hawthorne with him. I hope you find someone who is worthy of you. Goodbye Hawk." He had tried interrupting me asking why and saying that I couldn't mean it, but I never answered him. I said it like it was and that was it. I changed into a pretty nightgown, climbed into bed and waited for my husband,

He came out wearing nothing but a towel. "I don't suppose that I left a shirt and pants behind last summer did I?"

"Well, it would have been three summers ago and yes, you did, but you won't be needing them right now." I threw back the covers.

"No, I guess I won't." He said taking me in his arms. "I've been waiting all day to hold you like this."

"Well, I've been waiting two years, two months, two days and seven hundred and fifty two lonely, lonely nights, so let's not waste anymore time my sweet."

Bits and Pieces

I kissed her and sat on the edge of the bed. She ran her hand down my back and asked if I was all right. I said I was more than all right. I pulled my chinos on and went into the bathroom. She was getting dressed when I returned. "I always liked that color on you." I said and asked her to join me on the settee. I took her hand and said that I felt like a hypocrite because she had been so honest about her relationship with Hawk and I had lied about what happened with Gemma.

She lashed out at me immediately. "So, that silly remark you made about you having the key to your cell was true only it wasn't you who had the key but it was her and she used it." She stood up and looked down at me and said with disgust. "How many times Rainey. How many times?"

"She did not have a key."

"So it was sex through the bars." She laughed vulgarly. "That must have been a little uncomfortable but so rewarding and right up your alley of lecherous fornication. Was she as good as Jorja or better? I don't expect an answer, but poor you having to settle with normal lovemaking with me all these years."

"You're jumping to conclusions Vienna without hearing me out. Nothing like that happened. I'm not saying that it may have been a possibility but I was not that degraded or desperate. My love for you was too strong for me to even think about such a thing. The confession is that we did kiss through the bars, but just **once**. It was after I had sent the SOS to Mason. It was just a kiss goodbye. That's all, just a goodbye and thankyou. Can you live with that? I have told you a thousand times that I have never and never will cheat on you. I admit there were many days when I thought I'd never get out of Black's prison and that I'd never have a woman's arms around me again … those arms were always yours Vienna."

"If I am going to believe that you never had sex or only kissed her once then I am just as gullible as you are when you believe that I never kissed or slept with Hawk. I will let you bask in the joy that befell you when we made love because I am sure in your mind you were visioning me as Gemma."

"I can't win with you can I; one little thankyou kiss and I'm the adulterous. I'm just supposed to ignore the fact that you had an affair for two years; is that right?"

"I did not have an affair!" She stated vehemently.

"Not sexually, I know that, but are you telling me that you never kissed him?"

"I never kissed him!"

"And, he never kissed you?"

"I didn't say that."

"Okay then, but what about Jack?"

She was out the door before I could even get up. She was nowhere to be seen in the hallway. She must be in Miss Mary's room. I chuckled to myself as I passed the foyer. "Well, at least I know you're not in Avaleena's room." Nor was she in any other room on the second floor so I took the back stairs into the kitchen. It was quiet. There didn't appear to be anyone anywhere. I moseyed on down the corridor and found Evan in the family room relaxing in the recliner. I asked him if he was sleeping.

"Just resting my eyes Rain. What are you and Vienna up to?"

"Five hours into the best day of my life and I've already upset her. I was honest with her but she put her own morbid conception on what happened and ran off. I have no idea where she is. Does this sound at all familiar Evan?"

"Yup, and it's nothing less than I expected."

"What do you mean?"

"I can read her like a book Rain. I saw the way she reacted when you were talking about this Gemma. I was pretty sure that her name would come up again. Am I right, or was it you doubting her denial of her relationship with Hawk? You know he wasn't the only one…"

"The only one what?"

"He wasn't her only admirer. Come on, surely you have thought about it. Here was this beautiful woman without her man so maybe, just maybe they would have a chance with her now as surely she'd be lonesome and looking for some comfort."

"Anyone I might know."

"Chandler Tait, Detective Janzen, Willie Wallace…"

"Chandler, you have to be kidding, she hates him and who the hell is this Willie Wallace?" ?

"We'll get into all of that later, but right now we need to find your wife. Follow me Buddy."

"So, a new hiding place?"

"Not really. She's never run away from any of us. Let's take the grand staircase."

"Sure, but I've already scanned all the rooms."

"All that you know about maybe."

"What are you saying Evan? Why are you stopping here?"

He laughed. "You're in for a surprise Buddy, so hold onto your hat."

I watched as he went to the bookcase in the little foyer and voila it opened. "What the hell…you built a new staircase…why? I thought we all decided it was a good idea to tear the old one down." I followed him down the stairs. "Good job if I do say so. What the hell is that? Why do I hear a generator running?"

"It's only turned on when someone is in there and I'm supposing that someone is your wife."

"In where exactly?"

"Into what we are calling "Rainey's Roost" which we found due to her curiosity and determination."

I passed under an arch that was over an opening in a brick wall into an empty room except for a pulley device that was holding up a large stone block. Evan waited for me as I checked out the apparatus. I joined him at the top of a well trodden narrow granite stairway. It was well lit up. The wooden handrail appeared to be newly built and was attached to a nearly invisible buttress. The steps were each a good foot high. I counted them. There were 13, Vienna's favorite number. I wondered what my wife would be doing down here and then I stepped onto the last step. I don't think I had ever been more surprised or amazed in my life.

"Vienna, Rainey's here Honey."

"What took you so long?" She asked sarcastically.

She stood up from a stone bench. She had a ledger in one hand and a magnifying glass and pen in the other. She had a dozen bangles around her neck. The largest was a turquoise pendant of Nefertiti. Egyptian cats dangled from her ears and gold bracelets from her arms. She had a large ring in her hand and reached for my left hand.

"Me thinks you need to wear Horus as he is the God of Kingship and protection. I fear it is you who needs the protecting. Do you want a tour or what?"

I guessed I was forgiven. Evan said he'd give us some privacy. I looked around at the treasures. She was in close proximity to several terrifying weapons. I walked over to her and asked if she planned on using any of them.

"Not today, but then the day is still young." She answered taking the jewels off and placing them in a large already overflowing basket. There's no time for a full tour and inventory right now but I'd like you to see these drawings so you can have a gander while I catalogue a new find. Do these figures on this tablet look familiar to you?"

"Yes, of course. The main stairway is filled with the same characters. but I am a little confused as to why there is all this Egyptian jewelry and artifacts here."

"As are we. Here take this walking stick."

I didn't know why I needed a walking stick. It had the head of Horus on it. I followed her remarking on some of the artifacts. She didn't contribute anything about any of them but directed me to a wall of artworks. She sat down on a bench and started talking.

"This is what's going to happen after we leave here. Colleen and Beth will be home anytime now so you are going to greet them and you and I will continue to act as if everything is copacetic between us. Tomorrow someone will take you on a guided tour of this room and you can investigate to your heart's content. It won't be me or Evan though as he is flying me to Waverly where I have an appointment with someone. We will go to Hawthorne and get remarried because Ava and Lara will have gone to a lot of trouble for us. Then we will secretly get divorced and you will be free of me once and for all and go back to the coast and do whatever you want with your "friend" Gemma. You may want to go back to work for your company but that has nothing to do with me. You may chose to return to Hawthorne and your family once in awhile, but I won't be there. Pixie and I will be back here where we belong. Now we should go as time is wasting away. I'll let you lead the way up the stairs and I'll meet you in the foyer as I have to close up here."

I didn't question her as to what that might entail. I stopped just before the first step at a huge wooden door. I asked if this led to outside. Surprisingly, she answered me.

"Probably, but the guys haven't been able to open it completely yet as there is a bank of trees on the other side. They have started to cut them down but have decided that it's going to be a lot more work than they originally thought so will take up the task again in the spring. There won't be anything on the other side but trees anyway so it's of no importance that I can see."

I proceeded up the stairs and left her to do her thing. I sat down halfway up the new stairway and waited for her. She didn't seemed surprised to see me there and sat down when I asked her to.

"I listened to your plans for our future and I didn't much care for them so this is what is really going to happen. I trust that whomever you are seeing tomorrow is someone who is important to you so I will not interfere. I can't even imagine all that's happened here since I've been gone. I am happy that you went on with your life, but I'm back and I am pretty sure that you still love me. So, we will go to our home in Hawthorne and get married as planned. There will be no divorce and I will not be going back to Vancouver. I will not take up with Quinn Enterprises again and I will not be seeing Gemma. I may phone her from home to see if she has any insights as to what is going on. She may have been arrested for all I know and I would be sorry for that but I have no other interest in her. She was a friend when I needed one and I never thought of her in any other way. You were the one I held onto every night and the one I will be holding for the rest of my life. So say in three or four months we will come back to Scotland to our family here and then we'll come up with some sort of schedule that will keep us all happy, say six months here, then six months there or…"

She was up and pushing me back against the step. She straddled me and kissed me over and over just like she had an hour or so ago. I did not resist. When I got my breath back I remarked that I was getting too old to play these silly games with her anymore and couldn't we just be like a normal couple.

She laughed. "Yes, right after Atlantis rises from the sea. Come on, the girls are probably home."

She pulled me up and kissed me again. "Do you love me Rainey?"

"Whatever gave you that crazy idea?" I teased.

"Well you used to tell me everyday a few dozen times so just checking as it's only been half a dozen times today."

"The day is still young as you so reminded me."

We reached the foyer. She stopped at a portrait I had not seen before. It was of a beautiful young woman with golden hair and light brown eyes. No one in the McAllister family was fair haired so I wondered who she was to have gained a special spot close to Vienna's bedroom. Marianna

Gibson was the name that graced the painting. I asked who the beauty was.

"Beautiful isn't she? She is Pixie's mother. She visits now and then."

That was disturbing as I knew that Pixie's mother was deceased. I let that go and asked who painted it as it had no signature. The answer was more disturbing.

"Her name is Margareet. It is her hobby and she has painted all her girls."

"Marianna's mother?"

"No, my aunt Evelyn is Mari's mother. Mari was one of Margareet's ladies at the Blue Parrot."

"What's the Blue Parrot, and who is this woman you called aunt and what do you mean by *ladies*?"

"Well Margareet is a Madame. It was kind of her to send me the portrait don't you think?"

I was shocked to say the least. Before I could comment my wife astounded me once more.

"Did you notice how I was repelled when you first mentioned Gemma? Well it was an act because that's the way a lady should act but as you know very well, I am no lady. You probably noticed that no one else reacted and that's because we were all there at the Blue Parrot, well not Mary or Amma but they knew. Come along Dear, the girls are probably home."

"Hold on for a second. Pixie's mother was a call girl and you have been to the brothel where she works and you're telling me that all this negativity regarding Gemma's once profession has all been a façade?"

"Just trying to stimulate you Darling, and maybe you're the one jumping to conclusions about what Mari did at the Blue Parrot. She's my niece you know."

"Your niece? I'm either in some crazy fantasy of yours that could only take place here at Avanloch, or else you are dead serious and I don't know which I prefer at the moment."

"I will tell you the whole story later on and many, many more. It's a long trip home so there will be lots of time to fill you in on all of Avanloch's mysteries. Come along now as the girls are surely home by now."

She took my hand and led me down the hieroglyphic stairway. She stopped at the first landing. "There are 44 steps here but there were only 22 on the old stairs that were behind the bookcase so how do you explain that? Evan says it's because of age and different widths and kind of woods."

Funny she would bring this up now. I was sure we'd had the discussion several times before. I answered anyway. "Evan's right and the marble and carpet on these steps raises the height and then there are the landings so that accounts for the difference."

"I guess so but I still think it's an oddity just like it's an oddity that you told me there was an exit in the back of the mausoleum when there isn't."

"When did I tell you that?" I asked curiously.

"Twenty some odd years ago."

"And you're just asking me about it now?"

"I had a lot of reminiscing to do while you were gone so that just popped up."

She stopped again on the second landing. I asked her if she would like an answer.

"No, I've been there with you as you know so it is no consequence that you lied to me about it. The person I am seeing tomorrow is Willie Wallace. He is a young man that I am sponsoring. It was a one in a million chances that we met at a new restaurant in Waverly a year ago last June. Do you remember our Irish house maidens Caron and Jeanette? It's their restaurant. Anyhow, Will had a proposition for me and I accepted and last year Uncle Walt's murder was solved. You may come with Evan and me if you like."

"I like, but I'm going to need a little more information. You've filled my head with so many bits and pieces of things that have happened since I've been gone and then you leave me in limbo because you never finish the story."

"I'm sorry Rainey. I guess I just want to tell you everything all at once that I don't even realise that I am just confusing you with not completing anything. I'm still so overwhelmed that you are here…"

Tears were running down her face like a waterfall. I held her as tight as I could. "I'm overwhelmed too Sweetheart and I'm afraid that I might break you because I just want to hold you like this for the rest of our lives. Here, let me wipe away your tears before you start me crying."

She smiled a little. "You never cry."

"Tell my bed in the jailcell that. Now, don't we have granddaughters to make cry?"

I walked into the kitchen two minutes after Vienna had. Mary was at the end of the table where she always sat. Evan was next to her flanked by Rosy and Amma. Johnny was at the head of the table. Colleen, Beth, Ada and Vienna were on the other side. Pixie was sitting on the table in front of Mary and Evan playing cards. I walked in and said, "What's going on in here?"

It was exactly as we had expected…complete exhilaration. I didn't mind at all. After the hugging and the crying the questions began. First how long had I been here, why didn't Evan come and get them from school, how did I escape and so on and so on. After half an hour or so Beth asked a question.

"Ana, now that Papa is home will you wear the bracelets again?"

"I wish I could Honey but I believe that Black found them and took them when he kidnapped your Pappy because they went missing at the same time."

Beth seemed puzzled and said that was impossible. Rosy asked her why she would say such a thing.

"Well, they couldn't have disappeared then because Ana forgot to take them with her that summer."

"I'm not sure what you are saying Beth?"

"Neither am I Mom. Beth, I think you are confused. If Ana says they are missing I think she knows what she is saying."

Beth got up and said she wasn't confused and ran out of the kitchen. We could hear her running up the back stairs. Rosy apologised for her daughter's behavior. Beth returned and laid the Infinity Bracelets in front of her grandmother. We all gasped.

Vienna picked them up and held them to her heart and then spoke to them as if they weren't inanimate objects. "I've missed you because you were a love connection to the man who gave them to me but he is with me now so I want to share you with everyone I love if it is okay with him." She looked at me with a tear in her eye. "This is what I propose Rainey. I will keep one as together they are too heavy for me and then I would like to have the jewels removed and made into rings or pendants for everyone in our family. What do you think?"

"I think it's wonderful idea." I hugged her and asked what everyone else thought. Of course they all thought it was an amazing act. I undid the bracelet I knew she would keep and passed the other two to the girls and told them to pick out the gem they wanted. Vienna said to pick out two as there were more than plenty to go around. She asked Mary if she would like a necklace made with one.

"Thankyou, but no. I would like to place one on Duffy's resting place if that is all right with you and maybe you could save one for mine."

Vienna hugged her. "Then they will be diamonds as that is what you and he have made all the days that I have lived here with you."

"Way to make everyone cry Milady." Johnny said emotionally.

"And you Johnny and Evan will have rings made from the Lapis Lazuli as it is the stone of friendship and comradery."

"On that note I think I'll take this little tyke for a run down the hall." Evan babbled lifting Pixie down.

The rest of us continued examining and discussing the bracelets. Fifteen minutes later Vienna said she had better go and see what was keeping Evan and Pixie. Another ten or fifteen minutes passed and she didn't return so I excused myself and went to find them. I found them in the small reception room. Evan had his arm around Vienna who had her head on his chest. Pixie was playing with a puzzle on the floor.

"So I guess I have been wrong for all these years thinking that it was O'Shea who was going to run off with my wife and all along it has been you Govern, is that right?"

"Yup; we've been carrying on right under your nose. How do you feel about that Quinn?"

"I'm just relieved that it's you Evan as I know she's been safe with you."

He laughed. "It's been a chore I'll tell you that. Johnny and I have had our hands full but I can speak on his behalf that we are going to miss her more than you can imagine."

"I don't have to imagine as I know what you mean. I was feeling guilty about taking her and Pixie away from you and everyone else so I've come up with a plan and I'm pretty sure Vienna approves."

She got up and came over to me and embraced me. "I do and I think you will too Evan."

"What is everyone doing down here?" Rosalyn asked coming in the door.

Vienna took her hand. "You're just in time to hear Rainey's plan for us."

Chapter 19

Family and Friends

We boarded the plane at noon Friday the 4th of November. Because of the eight hour time difference we would arrive in Bridge Falls late afternoon. Evan took his place next to the co- pilot Dale Vernon who had arrived in Waverly the night before. He had chosen Dale from half a dozen candidates as the pilot because he had kin just across the border in Washington so had somewhere to spend the week.

It wasn't but a few minutes after takeoff that Rainey said it was time to fill him in on the events of the last two years and be sure not to leave anything out. Pixie was seated between us so she was the first and most important story to tell. It was a long flight but by the end of it I'm sure he had a vivid picture of the years he had missed. Rosalyn and the girls did their part, so to speak adding a little humor and drama into the sequence of events.

We arrived in Bridge Falls in late afternoon thanks to Evan's expert planning and the eight hour difference in time. It was pretty much bedlam from then on. Rainey's cousin Lara, and husband Coop were in the carpool to take us to Hawthorne. She was my best friend and reason why I had met Rainey. We cried as we embraced while Rainey was being mauled by Ava and Liliana. Nash had bypassed them and the rest of us encircled him in a group hug. He and I would have our one on one later.

Eventually Ava and Lili came over to embrace me. I knew they were still upset that I had chosen Avanloch over my home here but it wasn't about me, it was Rainey's day. I rode with Lara and Coop as did Evan and the girls. Rosy was with Nash, her sisters and Rainey. I had wondered where Novia and Zander were but there they were as we entered the gate and stopped right behind Nash's car. They were side by side with Rainey's parents, Paul and Patricia. He was out of the car in a flash. Tears were shed by all, especially Novia when Rainey picked her up and swung her around. She had lived under the presumption that he loved her sisters more then he did her. That was not true of course. I hoped she knew that now. She clung to me as Rainey and Zander had their moment. My sister broke free from Jack who had been holding her back and ran to us. Emotions were taking their toil when Jack embraced me. He shook hands with Rainey who insisted they were closer than that and hugged him brotherly. Then there was Rainey's best friend Jimmy and his wife Ruth and Yates and Izzy and everyone else we knew. Even our favorite cop Lou Rolph was there.

"You old bugger!" Rainey said shaking his hand. "Don't tell me you're still on the job"

"Thanks to you I am and I will be until I see that rotten bastard Black behind bars."

"I'm with you there. I'll catch up with you later as there is much to talk about."

"It's good to see you still kicking Quinn. It's a celebration so just enjoy it and your freedom and your family and your beautiful wife. It's lovely to see you Mrs. Quinn."

I laughed a little. "Oh I think we know each other well enough for first names don't you Sergeant?"

"That we do. Don't let this man out of your sight ever again."

"That's the plan but right now I have to track down our youngest daughter."

Rainey smiled and said she was safe with Ava. He kissed me and joined the party.

A huge tent, much like the Halloween one at Avanloch, had been set up, no doubt Nash's and Zander's doing. There were chairs and tables inside and food and drinks galore. Lara handed me a cup of coffee and I mingled with the guests for awhile and then stepped back out of the limelight, so to speak. This was Rainey's night, not mine. I hoped all the tears had been shed and now family and friends could get on with the celebration of his return. There was one person I hadn't met yet so sought her out. She was standing in the back with Novia. Yes, there definitely was a resemblance.

"Mom, I was just going to bring Paticia Anne over to meet you."

I held out my hand to Patricia. "And, I have been waiting to meet her."

She clasped my hand. "I never thought I would see the day that I would meet you so that I could apologise for the horrible things I accused you of…"

I stopped her. "No, no, none of that. You said what might have been true and it was up to me to fix the misconception. I am sorry that it has taken so long. If you don't mind Novy, I'd like Patricia to come with me to the house so we can have a chit chat alone away from all this. Will you pry Pixie out of Ava's arms and join us at the house in twenty minutes or so? Would that be all right with you both?"

Patricia said she would like that and Novy said she'd rescue Pixie from Ava. I laughed and told her not to say anything to her dad. I had been fighting the pain in my hip for some time now and hoped I'd hidden it sufficiently from my husband, but Patricia Anne noticed my hesitation as we exited the back door of the tent and started up the incline. She asked if she could take my arm. I accepted gratefully.

The house looked exactly the same as it had when I had left it two years ago. I turned the kettle on, took two mugs down and placed an assortment of teas and a jar of honey next to them. I told Patricia that I needed to sit on something soft and asked her to join me in the living room. She offered to wait for the kettle to boil. A few minutes later she came in with the tea. She said she had been told that I didn't like tea so she had added a lot of honey to mine. I thanked her and wondered what else she knew about me. This wasn't about me though. It was about her mother. I asked her to sit in a comfy chair across from me.

"I know you have a thousand questions for me. Hopefully, I will answer most of them without you having to ask and I will be as honest and gentle as I can be as it will not all be pleasant. I first heard the name Jorja before Rainey and I were married. We had not been together for twenty years. It's another story regarding our estrangement which has nothing to do with your mother. He said his relationship with her was very tainted. He met her in the autumn of 1981 at a nightclub where she worked. She was an exotic dancer." Patricia did not flinch. "They did have a physical relationship for six weeks. Rainey thought they were exclusive but one evening he found her with another man and that was the end of that. He had no further contact with her. I met her in September of 1984 when she came to the door of our home in Bridge Falls. She came to see Rainey because she said that he needed to know that he had a daughter. Her name was Patricia Anne. She was three years old. Rainey was very angry and denied the parentage. I convinced him to take a paternity test. He objected to it at first but relented. It came back negative. We never heard from her again until December. It was four days before Christmas when she came to the front door and insisted that Zander and I go with her. She had a very large knife."

Patricia was in tears at that revelation. I reached over and took her hands in mine. "I believe your mother really did love Rainey and you will come to love him also as he is a one-of-a-kind man, husband, and father. You have already been a recipient of his kindness and compassion. The minute he discovered that the account I had set up for you had been hacked he knew he had to protect you. He believed it was your uncle Blackie Elliot, the same man who had abducted him was now going to use you as a pawn and that your life may very well be at risk. He will explained it all in detail in the days to come."

The tears were still falling but she seemed to be in complete control. "I do not want him or need him to focus on me Vienna. I know he has been through hell at the hands of my so-called uncle, an uncle that I never knew existed, so he needs to heal himself and just concentrate of you and his family. Mason explained a lot to me so I am not totally in the dark. I was told that I was adopted when I was ten or twelve. My mother's name was Jorja Elliot and she had died on February 14th, 1985. My father was unknown and I had no living relatives. I have always celebrated my birthday on June second. I believe that may have been the day the Crammers adopted me. I have since found out that the actual date of my birth is February twentieth. My adoptive father passed away two years ago and my adoptive mother has dementia and doesn't know who I am anymore, and now I am here with a most loving family that I wished were mine too."

My heart was breaking for this child of my sworn enemy and I was about to have a complete meltdown when I heard the kitchen door open and the patter of little feet running towards me.

"We're here Mom. Ava came to help put Pixie to bed."

"Good. Just give me a minute with her as I see she can barely keep her eyes open." I kissed her and handed her back to Ava telling her just to lie Pixie on my bed and to cover her as I'd just be a few minutes.

I asked Novia where they were all sleeping. She said at Ava's and Colleen and Beth were already there with Calla. I told her that she and Patricia Anne should join them and make sure they didn't stay up all night as it was a big day tomorrow. I had a last word for Patricia.

"Sometimes wishes do come true so sleep on it and we'll see what tomorrow brings."

She squeezed my hands and said she would but she wouldn't be able to sleep until she knew the answer to a question. I told her to go ahead and ask it.

"How did you manage to save yourself and Zander from Jorja?"

I smiled. "A story for another day, but let's just say she tried to kill me and I tried to kill her but neither of us succeeded. That's all you need to know right now. Off you go girls; good night and sleep content."

I whispered out loud. "Well, that didn't solve the riddle did it?"

Ava had returned. "What did you say Mom?"

"The riddle…the riddle of why the three of them are so alike…what's happening…what am I seeing…oh, I know…I know. Call your father… and Evan, yes, I need Evan." I sat back and closed my eyes. I heard Ava ask me what was wrong and I was scaring her and I saw myself and Sissy sitting on a sofa with my mother who was holding baby Addy. I could hear my mother talking and yet I could hear Ava telling Sammie to get Pappy and Uncle Evan because Ana was having some sort of spell. I tuned her out and concentrated on what my mother was saying.

"I am going to tell you girls a story and you will put it away and we will never speak of it again. I am so happy that I have you three girls, but I should have four. Vienna, you had a twin sister, but she did not live. I believe she died of suffocation as the nuns did not want me to deliver before the doctor arrived so they stuffed me with towels. She came first and was taken from me immediately. After you were born I went into some sort of shock and was unaware of what had happened. I never even got to see her as the nuns said it was best. Your father agreed and the Catholic church handled the burial. I named her Eden."

"Vienna, open your eyes Sweetheart…"

"Oh Rainey, you're here!" I exclaimed.

"Of course I am. You asked for me didn't you, and Evan? What's happened Honey? Ava says you went into some sort of trance."

"It's me Rainey, it's me, I'm the connection to the girls. It was never you because you had no blood line to Genevieve, but I do and Jorja is the missing link. She's my sister don't you see?"

"Mom, that's preposterous and impossible!" Ava stormed.

"Just a minute Ava, let's hear her out. What would make you think such a bizarre thing Honey?"

"My mother told me. She said her name was Eden."

"When were you talking to Lily?"

"Just now…well actually I wasn't talking to her, she was telling us a story. It was a true one and we would never speak of it again."

"Who was with you?"

"Sissy and Addy."

"Can you tell us the story Hon?"

"I'm not supposed to but I will. I had a twin sister but she was still born. Lily never got to see her because the nuns took the baby away and told her that it was best not to see her and they looked after her burial."

"So, for some reason you remembered this story from when you were young just now, is that right?"

"Yes Rainey. I would have been seven as Addy was just a baby. I saw me sitting with them and then I saw Novia and Genevieve and Patricia Anne and I knew it was me. I'm the common thread that binds us all together and the only way that can be possible is if Jorja is related to me. I haven't gone out of my mind as I am sure you are all thinking, but what if somehow the baby Lily named Eden lived? Suppose if one of the nuns or nurses breathed life into her and kept her as their own or sold her? Neither Lily nor Dad ever saw her, so what happened to her? I'll tell you what…somehow she became Jorja. I told you didn't I Evan that she was never going to leave me alone. Well, here she is back again and her daughter is my niece."

Rainey got up off the floor where he had been kneeling in front of me holding my hands. He pulled me up and took me in his arms. "Ava's right Honey, this is inconceivable. There is no way in hell that Jorja could be your sister. Let's sit down and talk about what brought this on. It has been a long day and you're probably exhausted. I understand that you've had a little talk with Patricia Anne so talking about her mother has brought back a lot of unpleasant memories and was stressful, but why you had this so-called memory is baffling but I can assure you that Jorja is not your sister."

"Of course she isn't! She was way younger then you Mom anyhow, and that would mean that Black would be your brother. Can you imagine the horror?"

"Actually Ava, your father never said how old she was, did you Rainey and what if she was adopted?"

"I never saw a birth certificate or anything. I thought she may have told me she was thirtyish, but she could have been older. To my remembrance, she never mentioned any family."

"Yes because her age isn't what interested you was it?"

"You don't have to hit beneath the belt Vienna."

"Why not, you think I made the whole sister thing up so it's all fair game."

"You are a good storyteller Hon, but no, I don't believe even you could make up such a nonsensical story. No doubt you remember a conversation with Lily, but somehow it got distorted and came out as such. I also told you I didn't want to play games anymore, remember?"

I ignored him. "Do you believe me Evan?"

"I have never doubted anything you have ever did or said Vienna. Last year is a testament to that. I do agree with Rain that you are probably overtired as are the rest of us, but there just might be some validity to your story so the first thing you need to do in the morning is to call Lily."

"You can't be serious Evan!" Ava exclaimed curtly. "Mom, you have to put this away as just a bad dream."

"I can't and I won't. Evan's right and I'll call Lily and all of you will be my witness as she won't like it but she will confirm that it's true. I will not tell her of my suspicions until I have proof and I will have after Patricia and I have done a DNA test and know the results. Now we are done with this for the night so get back to celebrating please."

Rainey kissed me and said that yes that's exactly what we were going to do. Ava was not appeased but said she'd stand by me whatever. Then she asked us if there was someone that she had missed that should be added to tomorrow's guest list. I said I didn't but her father might have a few. She asked him who.

He grinned. "Your mother's being facetious. There isn't any additions on my account."

"Who were you thinking of Mom?"

"Well, Gemma comes to mind first, but she may be in jail so…then there is your dad's favorite little sexy waitress Shari, and oh yeah, his lustful notary, Ms. something or other." I answered light-heartily.

"Who is this Gemma? But speaking of Pamela Clark, she called here and asked for me. No one was home so she left me a message. Lili told me about it."

"What did she want?" Rainey asked nonchalantly.

"She wanted to know if there was any word of your whereabouts yet as she was reviewing all your assets, investments and insurance policies and said that they all needed updating. If you weren't available then perhaps I could go over them with her. I never got around to calling her back and then you were rescued so I forgot about it until now."

"When was this exactly Ada?"

"It was just before we knew you were alive so November first I guess."

Rainey suddenly seemed interested. "Is there any chance that the recording was saved?"

"We were advised to never erase anything Dad, so it should be here. Let me check. Yes, here it is?"

Halfway through the recording Rainey told Ada to shut it off as he'd heard enough. He looked at me and Evan and spoke grievously. "I'm the reason for the attempted takeover of McAllister Enterprises. I'm the reason for all of Rosalyn's woes."

"You can't be Rainey. Why would you suddenly assume that you are?" I pleaded.

"Do you remember me telling Rosy that I might have some insight into the problems at McAllister? Well, it was just conjecture then but now it's a harsh reality. I recognise the voice on the phone. It's the getaway van driver's voice and the same voice I heard on the stairs at the compound. It's Pamela Clark's and she's Black's partner and the brains behind everything and I gave her all the information they needed for the takeover and my abduction. She knew I had escaped when she made that phone call. She was just testing you to see if I was home."

"How could that be Rainey? She was just your notary, not your analyst." I said hopefully.

"Yeah, well apparently I have a big mouth and I'm too gullible. She knew all about Quinn Enterprises and my investments, the biggest one being McAllister Enterprises. She knew because I told her everything."

It was my turn to comfort. "You can't take all the blame Rainey. You didn't know you were dealing with an immoral woman. You're not gullible but maybe over trusting. You didn't care one iota for Black but you befriended him because of Izzy. We are going to take this revelation one step and one day at a time and we are going to do it together with everyone who has been at our beck and call for two years; understand?"

The frown on his face became the crooked grin. "I have to correct you my dear; it has been two years, two months, four days and an infinitude amount of grief, but we will be the victors. Besides this, there is your assumption about Jorja which we have to address immediately. The part I may have played in the takeover of McAllister is mine alone to address. Red may never forgive me I fear."

Evan laughed. "Oh ye of little faith. Rose would have given up the whole damn company if it would have brought you home. You are the Dad that she never had and in her eyes you could do no wrong, I know the same goes for you too Ava, and you know what … I kind of think of you as a father figure myself even if you are only fifteen years older. Don't you worry about our Rosebud. She'll be putty in my hands."

"Thanks for the encouragement Son. I've only got a couple of years on you Ev so brother fits the bond better don't you think?"

"Right you are Bro. Now, you need to get down to the tent and tell Rolph and Jake everything. They'll want to put a tail on Pamela immediately. Ava and I will stay with Vienna."

"This isn't the way I wanted to start our new marriage and life Honey." Rainey said taking me in his arms. "I knew I wasn't done with Black yet and that it might take some time to get any answers but I didn't think it would start happening so fast and then there is this peculiarity with the likeness of Novy, Genevieve and Patricia that are I agree disturbing. It is just a way out there supposition, but how would you really feel if Patricia Anne is somehow related to you?"

"Well Rain, I genuinely like her and I am going to make her wish come true."

"Which is what?"

"To be a part of such a loving family as we are. One way or the other, it will be so."

"I love you Vienna LaFontaine and tomorrow I'm going to make you mine again."

"I've always been yours Rainey, right from the day I met you on June 11th, 1960, so forty five years later nothing has changed. We have been up and we have been down, but we are still together and always will be come what way. Our story is not over yet."

"It is not, and tomorrow will just be another page in our never-ending story."